Pulled

A WALKER SECURITY NOVEL

UNDER

New York Times Bestselling Author

LISA RENEE JONES

ISBN-13: 978-1682303924

Playlist

Back in Black by AC/DC

Light It Up by Luke Bryan

Impossible by James Arthur

What Lovers Do by Maroon 5

You Really Got Me by Van Halen

Look What You Made Me Do by Taylor Swift

Can I Be Him by James Arthur

Unforgettable by Thomas Rhett

Losing Sleep by Chris Young

Chapter One

ASHER

Leather. Tattoos. Wine. Whiskey. Music. Women.

I left a world filled with those things ten years ago, and did so tattooed, fucked in the head, and with a vow to never return. And yet here I am, behind the bar of one of New York City's dive bars, AC/DC's *Back in Black* blasting through the speakers, handing a dude with long hair, tats, and more eyeliner on than the blonde chick with him, a beer. He grabs the bottle, tips me a whole two-fucking-dollars, and leaves. His chick however, does not. She lingers a few beats, casts me a glance with her bedroom eyes, the kind filled with an invitation that says: Get me naked in the back room right now. As far as I'm concerned, any chick banging a dude with eyeliner isn't getting a piece of this.

I motion her onward. She glowers and turns away, attaching her arm to that of eyeliner dude's, leaving me with only one question: How *the fuck* a chick who gets off on *that* guy, gets off on me? I mean yeah, sure, I'm inked, and my blond hair is on the long side, but those are holdovers from deep cover special ops. And the only damn make-up I wear is the kind I've kissed off some hot chick's mouth right before I kiss her everywhere beyond as well.

I toss the money into the tip jar for whatever poor soul that ain't me who needs two bucks to help them survive New York City. I'm not that guy, literally or figuratively, nor am I a victim or a fool, all of which I can thank the hard lessons this shitty lifestyle taught me. Though at the moment it's not quite as shitty, considering one of the staff's female members is dancing on top of the bar a little to my right, in shorts that barely cover her fine ass. But then, a fine ass is not why I'm here, any more than the music. I'm here to give a mother and father the justice they deserve over a daughter gone too soon, along with three other look-a-like young women, all dead after visiting bars like this. All dead after doing some cocktail of a drug that no one else seems to be dying from.

My motivation to give the parents peace, and catch what might be a serial killer, is the only reason I let my boss talk me into this hellhole in the first place. I scan the dimly lit area, surveying the bars left and right that frame the warehouse-style room, both with neon blue skulls over the top that match the one behind me. In between them are double doors that lead to the stage and seating, which are shut now, set to open soon.

Two young guys stop in front of the bar, snickering as they order drinks with dirty names, amused in a way I hope like hell I was never amused by such things. I pour the mixtures and slide glasses in front of them. "Two buttery nipples," I say, leaning forward, to shout over the music, and add, "Come back when you have the real thing and the drinks are on me."

They curse at me and this time I don't even get two dollars for a tip. In a highly appropriate moment, the music shifts to Def Leppard's "Pour Some Sugar on Me," and *now* I actually am amused. I bark out laughter, while my gaze catches on the entryway to the lower level of the two-level building, and my target, the guy my team at Walker Security believes is *the* guy we're after, walks in the door. "Ju-Ju," he calls himself, a nickname for drug dealer in his mind, and in mine: stupid fucking idiot, and perhaps, a killer. In which case, I'd like to nickname him "Dead," but the law says I'll just have to call him "Arrested," instead. In times like these, I miss those Navy SEAL days, when I dealt with shitheads like him in jungles, deserts, and dark caves, and was even ordered to do so.

Ju-Ju gives me a two-finger wave, his one-tat sleeve accented with black jeans and a white T-shirt not so unlike what I'm wearing. I chose my get-up to blend with the crowd and I'd bet my new BMW that the same applies to him. He's stupid, but he's not dumb, and anyone who doesn't understand that stupid is a mentality, and dumb is just plain dumb, is lucky. They haven't met someone like Ju-Ju. I have, too many times.

I pour him what I already know to be his usual: whiskey Sour, a short pour, and plenty of lemon. It would be a simple drink if not for the high-end whiskey he favors, combined with the short pour that tells me he needs a level head and he won't waste an expensive whiskey. That level head he maintains is about that stupid business of selling drugs. He motions to the women with him to sit down on a love seat, and heads in my direction.

I serve a customer, and by the time I'm done, he's standing in front of me, slapping a hundred on the bar. "For you," he says, shoving the bill in my direction before sipping his drink, and doing so a little too properly to match his spiky black hair and tattooed-up neck. This isn't where he's from. It's where he burrows.

I grab the bill and shove it into the tip jar. He frowns. "That's for you."

"Community tip jar," I say.

"No one else is on duty."

3

"New guy is starting tonight."

He leans closer. "Let's talk after the bar closes. Meet me."

"Sorry, man. Unless you get a whole lot prettier, which is doubtful, you aren't my type."

He laughs. "You're a funny man. I'm going help you make some cash. Take a break before the club closes. We'll talk." He motions behind me. "Bring something the girls will like." He slides another hundred on the bar. "The extra is a gift, not a tip. Keep it." He walks away.

Bingo.

I'm in.

And the father of Lily Waters might just get the justice the police haven't delivered. The man deserves that justice, and then some. His kid was eighteen and on her way to Yale when she died, poisoned on a night friends say she just wanted to watch a band play at a similar club. Which was the same story for every girl now dead and buried, all with the same drug in their systems, laced with poison. A drug that I've determined that only Ju-Ju sells, and since he's favoring this club now, I'm favoring this club now.

Aiming to satisfy his women where I doubt he can, I make two chocolate martinis in between filling three orders before I deliver the drinks to Ju-Ju and his "girls." I don't look at them. I barely look at him. I'm hard to get like that. I turn away from them, which is when I find Riley, the grumpy old ex-rocker who runs this place, standing behind my bar with some new dancer chick next to him. She's brunette, with long hair, a slender frame, and big breasts. I'm guessing I'll round the bar to find short shorts, and an ass that will make me stand at attention. Hey. I deserve it. I've just broken through with Ju-Ju.

4

I close the distance between me and them, and join the duo on the other side of the counter. As soon as I'm there, I'm filling an order. The minute it's done, Riley points to the woman. "Train Sierra. I got shit to do." He leaves me with the woman, who is not wearing short shorts, but faded, snug jeans that are almost as cock-worthy, despite the absence of naked skin.

I'm about to question her uniform choice when the music cuts out, a sign that the crowd is about to be allowed into the auditorium, where a dance floor is set up on weekend nights. A big portion of the bar traffic will soon move there, at least temporarily, offering a breather and a chance to monitor Ju-Ju with more ease. The dancer currently on top of the bar jumps down and heads in that direction, where she will take the stage with several others, or so I'm told, and entertain the crowd before the band starts playing. I give the new woman a once over, and decide she really is ten shades of hotness, and fuck me, *my* kind of hotness, which is why I happily dole out my advice and "training."

"You'll get better tips with your ass hanging out," I say.

"Then you'd better go change and hop the hell on top of the bar," she says, her voice a raspy, southern sexiness that has my cock saluting. "The music is bound to start again soon," she adds, "and I can't wait for the show—the one you'll be putting on—while I watch."

My lips curve. "My shows are private."

"So are mine."

I arch a brow. "Isn't that going to make it hard for you to do your job?"

"You seem to be doing just fine without your ass hanging out."

"Some asses just look good no matter what they're covered in," I comment dryly.

Now she arches a brow. "Are you saying mine doesn't?"

"Turn around and I'll give you my expert opinion."

"Never."

"Challenge accepted," I say, surprising myself by how damn much I mean those words. I want this woman, and since I don't do relationships, it doesn't even matter that she's of this world. I won't be part of it for long.

"You enjoy defeat," she replies. "I get it. Some people are like that."

"Hey!" someone shouts as a rush of people swarm the bar. "Over here!"

"Yeah, hey!"

"Over here!"

"Hang tight, sweetheart," I say to my *new trainee*, who I might just school in more than her wardrobe. "We really do need to address the fact that you're wearing too many clothes." I rotate to the bar to be bombarded with another half-dozen demands, which tell me the side bars are closed to push traffic. It's a strategy meant to keep people near the dance floor where they stay thirsty and drink more. A rush of even more customers has me looking left to discover that the new dancer chick is filling orders, and is clearly not the new dancer chick, but my new bartender.

She's also now standing next to me, reaching across me to jab an olive with a toothpick, pausing to look at me. "I can handle this rush if you want to climb on top and perform." Anger lights her eyes, and hey, I get it. She's pissed at my assumption that she's the entertainment. I deserve her wrath, but holy fuck, bring it on and let me kiss it all better. "Private shows only, remember?"

"Chicken," she laughs, but doesn't wait for a reply as she moves down the bar and drops that olive in a martini she hands to a woman.

I reluctantly give my attention to my next customer instead of her, plowing through three orders before a familiar, pretty brunette, a look-a-like to the four victims, steps in front of me. "White Russian," she says, playing the undercover role of patron for the third night in a row, when she's really one of Walker's own, and a badass ex-FBI agent to boot. "Make it weak like you," she adds.

"You're starting to tell lame jokes like Blake," I say. Blake being both her husband and one of the founding brothers of Walker Security. "Poor you and me," I add.

"If I sounded like Blake," she replies, "I'd say make it *fucking* weak like you."

"That's more like it," I say, considering Blake is one fuck-happy motherfucker, pouring her drink sans the booze.

I slide her drink across the bar. She tosses down cash and picks up the glass, testing the pure cream for flavor before smacking her lips together. "Nothing like a virgin Russian to get a girl hot," she murmurs, before amending with, "a *fucking* virgin Russian. Let's hope it's our lucky night." And with that, she turns away and heads in Ju-Ju's general direction, hoping tonight is the night that she gets his attention rather than some other sweet young thing that can't protect herself.

Keeping an eye on her and Ju-Ju, I fill another order while she sits down at a table alone and crosses her bare legs, exposed in a short skirt. Almost instantly, several men circle her and holy hell, I don't know how Blake stays sane in these situations. He's outside in a van watching, torturing himself right this very minute, which is a good thing since a rush of people encase the bar waiting for service.

I glance left to check on Sierra and find some big bald dude reaching over the bar and grabbing her hair. "Fuck," I murmur, launching myself that direction as Sierra proves she's not an easy victim by slamming a steel mixing pitcher against the jerk's head. He cocks his arm to punch her and I am there in time to catch his hand. "Let her go," I demand, but my grip has already delivered the desired effect. He releases her hair, and at the same moment Big Bruno, the bouncer who favors this side of the bar, grabs him from behind, pulling him away from us. My hands go to Sierra's shoulders, turning her to face me. "You okay?"

Her chin is on her chest. "Yes," she breathes out. "Yes. Fine." But she doesn't look at me.

"Sierra—"

"I'm fine," she insists, but when her gaze lifts for just a moment, there is vulnerability in her pale blue stare, a hint of a past trauma that she quickly blinks away while firming her chin and adding, "Thank you for grabbing that bastard. I mean that. Sincerely. *However*, you're still the asshole who assumed I was a dancer because I have boobs and a better ass than you." And with that bravado clearly meant to hide the vulnerability she dared to show me, she steps firmly backward and twists out of my reach. Sierra immediately attends to another customer but I watch her, ignoring the shouts in my direction, trying to figure out why I can't look away from her. I mean, yeah, sure. She has secret, heavy baggage of some sort, but then, so do most people. The difference between them and her is that I usually don't ask questions unless the person has become my duty. It's safer that way.

Obviously, she's not my duty, but I have this gut feeling that despite her obvious ability to protect herself, she'd be better off if she were. I ignored a feeling like this once and someone died. Since I learned my lesson, I don't ignore feelings like this. *Ever.* Which means that Sierra just inherited her own personal protector. I have a feeling I might be taking a lashing when she finds out. But my gut also tells me that I'm going to enjoy the hell out of it.

LISA RENEE JONES

Chapter Two

ASHER

Houston, we have a problem.

Fuckhead Ju-Ju has eyes on Sierra and watches her all damn night while I watch him and keep her close, *"accidentally"* creating opportunities to join her in her personal space. She steps toward me to grab a bottle of booze, and I move in her direction. The minute we gently collide, I have an excuse to touch her. I catch her arm and turn her into me, making sure we look all kinds of intimate. Making sure Ju-Ju thinks she's mine, when she's not. *Yet.*

"Sorry, sweetheart. You okay?"

"My name is Sierra," she says, but she doesn't push my hand away.

"Sierra," I say. "Are you okay?"

"I'm fine, but since you're holding yourself up with my arm, are you? How delicate are you?"

I laugh. Fuck. When was the last time a woman put me in my place and made me laugh? Right. Never. "Sweetheart, as long as it's you I'm bumping into, I'm on top of the fucking world."

"Sierra. Not sweetheart."

"If we're ever naked together, I'll call you Sierra, and make damn sure you know I'm with you, just you, and one hundred percent me. Until that time, you're sweetheart. That's just how it is."

I turn away and help my customer. She does the same. We get a small break and she yells, "Hey, you!"

I frown and look her direction. "You talking to me?"

"Yes. Because you're 'hey you' until otherwise notified." She walks toward me and stops a wide lean from touching me. "Until we're naked, at which time I'll call you Asher and let you know I'm with you, and just you, one hundred percent. And since that's not going to happen, because amongst other things, 'sweetheart' irritates me so damn much, you stay 'hey you' for as long as I endure this hellhole." She whirls around and gives me her back and a sweet view of her heart-shaped ass. Apparently, 'sweetheart' hits a nerve. 'Hey you' works for me, as long as she's talking to me and not Ju-Ju or really, any other fucking guy, because yeah. I want her. I want her in a bad way.

I pour a shot for the hot chick next in line, while she offers up a view of her breasts hanging out of a low-cut shirt. They're impressive enough to get the guy right next to her to gawking, but these college kids in this bar don't get me off. I like a grown ass woman like Sierra, and apparently, Ju-Ju agrees, considering he's staring at her with a heightened fierceness. The blonde moves on and I turn to Sierra at the same moment that she catches Ju-Ju staring at her. Discomfort radiates off her, and she turns away and walks to the back bar. *Good move, sweetheart*, I think, but Ju-Ju doesn't like it. He's now challenged. He gets up and heads in her direction.

I walk to the back of the bar and join Sierra. "The creep coming your way is trouble. I am too, for him, not you. Stay close to me and don't smash me in the head with a cup or bottle."

"Are you going to make me want to smash you in the head with something?"

"Perhaps, but in the process, I'm going to either back him off by being nice to you, or break a bottle over his head for you."

"Men like him prey on weakness, which means let me handle him myself. Back off."

"He's not that drunk asshole who grabbed you earlier. He's a drug dealer and that's the nicest thing anyone can say about him."

"Asher, man," Ju-Ju says, stepping to the bar. "Who's the babe?"

Sierra turns away from me and walks straight to Ju-Ju. "He doesn't like when you call him babe and it might blow your cover with those girls if you do it that loudly. What do you want to drink?"

I laugh. I can't help myself and I don't try either. I bark it right out and just go with it. I follow that purposeful cackle by joining the two of them and leaning an arm on the bar, arching a brow at Ju-Ju. "Something you want to tell me? Because, man, if you're gay, that's cool and all. I support gay rights and to each their own. But for the record, I don't do cock. I'm a straight tits and ass man."

"Then you and I should talk tits and ass later tonight because I can show you plenty." He glances at Sierra. "Bring her. I like my women hard to get."

"I don't share," I say. "And you'd be smart to remember that."

He smirks. "Sounds like we need to talk quid pro quo. You keep her and I get you." He looks at Sierra and slides a hundred on the bar like he did to me. "There's a whole lot more where that came from," he promises and turns away.

She looks at me. "I am not touching that. I'm not even picking it up and putting it in the tip jar."

"Good decision," I say, snatching it up and placing it in the jar before I step to her, close without touching her, when all I'd like to do is tunnel my hands in her hair and kiss the fuck out of her. "You're tough. I like that."

"What the hell was that? He'll trade me for you?"

"I got this, sweetheart. Don't worry."

She studies me for several intense beats. "I need this job," she says, and there is a hint of desperation to her voice.

"And you have it," I say. And she has me, even if she doesn't want me.

Yet.

I've already decided that I'm going to do my damn best to make her want me. What I'm not going to let her know is just how badly Ju-Ju's attention means she needs me.

Chapter Three

Sierra

Once upon a time, a young girl dreamed of her very own Prince Charming. He would be handsome and debonair in every way. He would sweep her off her feet, and they'd live happily ever after. As she got older, that same girl—me in fact—had career goals and dreams, but she still believed in love. She still believed her Prince Charming would support her dreams and goals while she supported his. They could have it all. And so, it happened. My prince arrived and life was good, until it wasn't. Until it was bad. So very bad.

Flash forward to now, and I'm standing in the break room of a bar, waiting for tip money I need just to eat, while Asher talks to the boss about my performance. In other words, did I pass the one-night trial I begged for earlier today? This is my reality, which I would never have believed possible just last year, or even nine months ago when I ran to stay alive. But this is as real as it gets, and that fact punches at me pretty much every moment of every day. I could blame Cinderella for all this. I could analyze the psychological reasons that being raised by a single mother made me take the story too literally. But I'm not a stupid person and I have no excuse for looking at life through Cinderella-colored glasses.

I'm the one who took the fairy tale too far. I'm good at taking things too far. I want to be perfect and I dive in and grab what is in front of me, and sometimes it backfires. Boy, did it backfire this time or I wouldn't be here now. I wanted to be the perfect everything. I press my hand to my forehead. "Perfectly stupid," I murmur, tunneling my fingers through my hair.

"I hope you're not talking about me."

At the sound of Asher's voice, I whirl around to find him leaning on the doorway, and the bright lights do nothing to disprove his rock star, bad boy hotness. I fold my arms in front of me. "I would never call anyone stupid."

"But you just did," he says, his eyes, which I now know to be a bright grass-green, are fixed on me too intently for comfort. "I heard you say—"

"Why were you listening?" I ask, my fisted hands settling on my hips.

"It's my experience that when someone speaks, they want to be heard."

"I was talking to myself. I wanted me to hear."

"Did you?"

"Yes," I say, silently adding, *too late.* I heard the warnings in my head too late.

He arches a brow, those full lips of his, lips that I shouldn't notice, hinting at a smile. "Do you always talk to yourself?"

"Yes, actually," I say. "I do. Can we move on?"

"Yes, but for the record, no one is perfect, sweetheart. Take it from the guy who not only made an ass of himself when he met you, but also spent too many years of his life trying to be perfect and failing."

"Is that why you're here?" I ask before I can stop myself.

"You think being here makes you a failure?"

He's here. If say yes, I've called him a failure, and I have no idea what his history is any more than he does mine.

16

"No," I say. "Being without a job is a failure. Do I get to keep this one?"

"Yes. You do."

Relief washes over me. "Thank you. When do I come back?"

"Tomorrow night."

"And tonight's tips? How much did we make?" I manage to sound quite matter-of-fact when I don't feel matter-of-fact at all.

His eyes narrow ever so slightly, intelligence in their depths, and I have the feeling that he sees my desperation. He doesn't push though. He simply pushes off the doorframe and, reaching behind him, produces an envelope, the colorful tattoo sleeves covering both of his arms on display, random images creating a collage: a jaguar, a ship anchor, an ace card, just to notice a few. I don't care for tattoos. I don't care for this place, and he's a part of this place but, the art is beautiful, he's beautiful, and I'm in an ugly mess that—

"You gonna take it or are you just going to stare at it, sweetheart?"

My gaze jerks to his, and he arches a brow. "What?"

"You're staring at the envelope like you think it will bite."

We both know he's not talking about the envelope any more than I was looking at the envelope, but I go with it. "Because you're holding it like bait for a fish and I'm the fish. I don't like that and for the record—I might bite."

He moves to close the distance between us, with this loose-legged swagger that I have no doubt is meant to mask cool calculation. I've given him the excuse he wanted to step within a lean of me. Too close, so close that scent of his reminds me of a winter wonderland of spice. It's an assessment I'd come to hours ago, in one of the many up close and personal moments I'd shared with him tonight. The most personal moments I've shared with anyone in nine months.

"It's all yours," he says, handing it to me.

I reach for it, careful not to touch him. I already know the jolt that delivers. "How much cash?"

"A grand even."

My eyes go wide, chin lifting to search his face. "A grand. We made two grand tonight?"

He studies me for several beats, seeming to weigh his reply before he says, "You made a grand."

It's an odd way of replying, but I let it go. Maybe he took more than fifty percent, but I'm not going to complain. I need this money. I unzip my purse at my hip and stick the envelope inside, because pulling up my shirt to get to my money belt isn't exactly opportune right now. "I'll see you tomorrow night," I say, stepping around him, and hurrying toward the door.

"This isn't your kind of place," he says.

I pause for a moment at the doorway without turning, a million replies fighting for my tongue in my head, but I settle on a simple reply. "It is now."

With that, I turn into the narrow hallway and walk the short distance to the exit, and push the bar to open the steel door, stepping into a dark alleyway, compliments of a burned-out light. I don't need to be seen with lights on anyway. I don't need to be memorable. I hurry forward, and I've barely taken two steps when the feeling of being watched washes over me. I speed up to a near-run, thinking of the thieves who might wait for a bartender or waitress to get off work to steal their tips. Thinking of that creep Ju-Ju. Thinking of the death threat I believe to be real or I wouldn't have run.

I reach into my purse and remove my bottle of mace. I place my finger on the button, and round a corner, but it's dark and empty except for me, some random trash blowing around, and the footsteps behind me. What if they found me? What if he found me? I can't die. I don't want to die. I dart around another corner and flatten myself inside a wide archway to a building entrance. Those footsteps follow, stop in front of me, and a huge man faces me. I spray the mace.

"Holy fuck, Sierra."

Oh God. I've just sprayed Asher.

LISA RENEE JONES

Chapter Four

Sierra

Asher rotates and flattens himself against the wall next to me. Instinctively, I follow, stepping in front of him. His eyes are shut, and even in the shadows of the dimly lit, deserted street, I can see the pain etched in his face. "Asher, I'm so sorry. I didn't know it was you. I was alone and—"

"Stay away from the fumes," he orders, his voice a deep rasp, and his eyes are watering to the point that it looks like he's crying, when he's not. "They fan outward," he adds.

"I'm fine," I say, not sure how he's worried about me right now.

"You're not fine."

I have the mace in my hand and I hastily shove it back into my purse and zip it. "What can I do?" I ask looking left and right, down rows of concrete, old buildings shuttered for the night or just plain vacant, but there is no one in this area this time of night. "There's no one to help," I say. "I don't know what to do. How do I help?"

"You don't," he says, huffing out a breath and blinking several times before he gives up opening his eyes. "It—will—pass."

"How do you know? What if—?"

"I *know*." He squats down, pressing his hands on his knees, lowering his chin to his chest. "It's passing."

I squat, but I'm already too off-balance as it is, clearly or I wouldn't have sprayed him, and I just give in and settle on my knees. "Asher—"

"It's passing," he breathes out again, but as he sucks air in, it's with a horrid wheezing sound.

"It's not passing," I say urgently. "You can't breathe."

"Give me a few minutes," he says gruffly, lifting his head and actually opening his eyes. "It doesn't affect me like other people."

I blanch. "What? How would you know that? Do you make a habit of sneaking up on women and getting maced?" The accusation is out before I can stop it, that part of me just trying to survive going on defense. I regret it instantly, but it's too late. He reacts before I can retract my words.

"Jesus, Sierra. I was going to walk you the fuck home." He stands up and leans on the wall, his head resting against the hard surface.

"I'm sorry," I say, scrambling to my feet, fighting the urge to touch him, when his clothes are contaminated and I shouldn't be touching him anyway. "I'm jumpy on these streets back here and we just met. But you don't deserve that and I shouldn't have said it."

His phone rings, and somehow he actually reaches into his pocket and pulls it out, but when he looks at the screen, he makes a frustrated sound. He lifts his head and looks at me, the whites of his eyes burned red. "My vision is shit right now," he says, holding it out to me, the glow of a streetlight illuminating the pain in his handsome face. "Who is it?" he asked.

I glance at the caller ID. "It says... 'Dickhead'.'"

He apparently likes whoever Dickhead is, or feels obligated to talk to this person, because he answers the call immediately. "Blake," he bites out. "You're on speaker."

"Why do you sound like you have a stick up your ass?" Blake asks. "And why the fuck am I on speaker?"

"Before you say anything else," Asher warns. "Sierra, from the bar, is with me."

"Make me understand," Blake says. "Why am I on speaker with Sierra from the bar?"

"I got maced," Asher says, his voice gravelly. "I don't want the residue on my phone."

"*Fuck.*" Blake curses dramatically. "What happened? Who the hell maced you?"

"Me," I say. "But I didn't know it was him."

Blake is silent two beats and then barks out laughter. "Holy fuck. Way to be a smooth operator, Ash. Holy fucking hell. How bad is it?"

"Tear gas," Ash replies as if that answers the question, his voice not as gravely now.

"Ah well, hell, man," Blake says, "You're good, right? Luke told me your boys were hit with that shit in training so many times it's now like drinking a cheap shot of tequila. It burns hard and fast, and then you beg for more." I can't help it. I have to ask. "Who is Luke and what training?" I ask, but I'm ignored.

Asher responds with a pained laugh as he lowers his chin to his chest again. "Yeah, man. I'm smelling daisies right now and doing it without a water supply."

"You gotta find some water to at least rinse your eyes," Blake says, bypassing my question for admittedly, and obviously, more important matters. "I can't get a car and clothes to you for at least thirty minutes."

"I'm not going in a public place with the residue all over me," Asher says. "Send a pick up. I'll ride in the back and I'll wait right here."

"Where is here?" Blake asks.

23

"I live in this shithole of a neighborhood," I interject despite the many reasons I shouldn't do what I'm about to do, but I have to help. I did this to Asher.

Asher lifts his chin and looks at me, a chill in his stare that wasn't there before my accusation despite my spraying him with mace. There is also surprise, and thankfully far less pain than even minutes ago. "I'm two blocks away," I say, doubling down on my offer, and my apology.

"Problem solved," Blake says for him. "I need your address, Sierra."

"I have to buzz you up when you get there," I say before dictating the street and apartment number.

"Got it," Blake says. "I'll make sure you get clothes, Ash. Sierra. He's more valuable than you know. Try not to kill him before I get there, will ya?" He doesn't wait for a reply. He disconnects.

And I immediately try to make peace. "Asher—"

"You sure you want me in your apartment?" he asks, speaking almost normally now. "I might be a stalker who makes a habit of attacking women on the street."

"I'm sorry," I say again. "I'm very edgy for reasons that have nothing to do with you."

"I'm standing right here, sweetheart. I'm pretty sure it has at least something to do with me."

"It really doesn't," I say. "But like I said, I'm—"

"Don't apologize again," he says firmly. "But when the time is right. Say my name, Sierra, like I just did yours. Now more than ever, I'm going to want to know you really do know it's me you're with."

I cut my gaze, afraid this man who is a stranger will see more than anyone has in years now that I'm honest with myself. Afraid that comment already infers that he does. Afraid of the intimacy he infers, as much as I crave it, when

I cannot. It's wrong. It's unfair to him. It's dangerous to him. Because I still have a Prince Charming who I now know is really The Beast.

"Sierra," he says, a prod in his voice that I can't seem to resist. I look at him and he adds, "What happened tonight is done, but we aren't."

"There is no *we*."

"*We* work together. And in answer to your earlier question about the gas. I'm an ex-Navy SEAL. I've done extensive gas training and Luke is Blake's brother, who I served with in the SEALs."

"Oh," I say, surprised and embarrassed. "You were—but—you—you're—"

"Tatted up and have long hair?" he asks.

"Yes, actually."

"A blond pretty boy American screams military overseas. It would have been a death wish."

"I see."

"I don't. My eyes are fucked right now. My vision is waning in and out. And for the record, I'm capable of functioning with this stuff in my eyes and on my skin. That doesn't mean I enjoy it." He pushes off the wall and looks down at me. "Either take me to your place or I have to find a place I won't contaminate to rinse off."

"I'm not letting you go someplace else," I say. "Can you walk?"

"I can walk. I can fight if I have to. Apparently, I can survive armed assassins, but not a five-foot-four brunette named Sierra with mace." His lips curve. "But that's okay. Next time it might not be me."

"I really am sorry."

"You don't need to keep saying that. Just take me to water."

"Right." I turn and start walking and he's quickly by my side. The streets are deserted except for a homeless man lying on a step in front of a small church. The wind is non-existent, the night a warm September evening, and I don't know New York City enough to know when that will change. I just know that I don't have a coat which is on my list of must-buys with the cash in my purse. We walk the full two blocks and I don't speak and Asher doesn't speak, but I am aware of this man in ways I'm not sure I've ever felt with anyone, even my Prince Charming once upon a fake fairy tale. But then, I'm different now than when I met him and everything with Asher has been up close and personal from the moment I met him tonight. I'm not sure how I correlate those two things. Actually, I do. He's overwhelmed me in too many ways to count, mostly good. Obviously, I've overwhelmed him now, too. I sprayed the man with mace. I know how to leave a lasting impression.

"We're here," I say, halting our progress in front of the ancient concrete building that cost me a small fortune, despite it being a rat trap, quite literally. "And I hate to break the news to you," I add, "but we have to walk up four flights of stairs." I punch in the code to the door that buzzes open, and turn to face him. "My place is pretty bad. I just moved here and—"

"I don't care about your apartment, Sierra," he promises, and I notice that he's using my name still, not some generic endearment. "Let's go inside," he adds.

I nod and turn to open the door, he catches it and holds it. I walk inside and turn to him again. "The stairs and your eyes—"

"I've navigated much worse than stairs in much worse conditions."

"Because you're a Navy SEAL," I say, telling myself that means The Beast can't hurt him, but that's a lie I want to believe.

"Ex-SEAL," he says, a distinction that seems important to him, and it is to me too. He can't be plucked from a mission and killed by one of the many powerful people in the government that owe The Beast favors. It's a ridiculous way to comfort myself for obvious reasons. The Beast could still come after him and for nothing more than looking in my direction.

Inhaling on that thought, I turn away from Asher and cross the small foyer to the narrow, steep staircase where I begin the treacherous climb that kills me daily, but I'm not thinking about the pain. I'm thinking about Asher behind me. About how good it feels to be with one of the good guys for once, which is how I read Asher. But then what do I know? I haven't exactly proven my assessment of character to be stellar, which would be a problem if I still had a future as a clinical psychologist, but I don't. That career choice, and my internship with a world renowned clinical psychologist, and mentor, crashed and burned nine months ago when I'd been forced to start my city and state hopping to finally land here.

I shove that thought away, as we reach my floor and the tiny hallway I share with only one other tenant. Pausing at my door, Asher joins me, and I unzip my purse and grab my key, quickly sticking it in the lock. Asher steps to the landing with me, so close I can feel the warmth of his body encase mine. "Wait to go inside, Sierra."

I leave the key in the lock and turn to face him. "Afraid I'll spray you with mace again once I have you trapped inside?" I ask, using the witty remark to hide the fact that his nearness, and the way he's towering over me while smelling all deliciously earthy, jolts me.

"You've already maced me," he says. "Find another way to torture me that we can both enjoy. If you need ideas, I'll offer a free tutorial on another occasion. But right now, my clothes are contaminated and yours most likely are as well. Tear gas has a way of finding places to settle and can become a problem later. You need to take off your clothes, bag them, and shower. Stand in the bathtub when you undress and bag your clothes there. And I mean everything. You can wash your clothes, but trash your purse."

"It's my only purse."

"Replace it," he says.

That costs money, I think, but I bite my tongue. "Is this really necessary?"

"The way that gas affected me," he says. "That was about twenty percent of what most people will feel."

"That was obviously a yes. I need to replace the purse. You need to shower first. You're the one with burning eyes and skin."

"Unless you want me walking around in a towel, I have to wait for clothes."

"Oh."

His lips curve and I have no idea why I'm so obsessed with this man's mouth.

"Is that a yes or no?" he asks.

My gaze jerks to his. "What was the question?"

"Me in a towel."

"I'll give you my pink robe. You have to shower first, though you sure aren't acting like you need instant relief."

"I'm good at hiding pain, sweetheart, and this isn't as much about me right now as it is ensuring I don't expose anyone else."

"Is that a yes on the robe?" I ask.

"As much as I like pink," he replies, "I'd rather see it on you. And since chemical contamination will really screw up any mood we get going, I'm forced to move on, right when I'd rather not. Do you have plastic bags?"

"Yes. I do. Under the kitchen sink."

"Good. Go to the sink. Wash your hands and arms thoroughly. You don't want your fresh clothes to end up contaminated. Then get the bags and pick out new clothes with as little contact with anything else as possible. Whatever we touch, we'll wipe down."

"I had no idea this was such a big deal."

"Most people don't. We should go inside."

Right. His eyes. They're red and I should be rushing him to water. Still, when I turn and grab the knob, I can't seem to make myself open the door and invite the questions I know will follow. Asher knows, too. He is suddenly a little closer, when he was already close, his hand on the door above me. "Nothing in that apartment matters to me," he says.

He's wrong. It will matter. I feel it, but I can't change what's to come at this point. I open the door and enter what is quite literally my hole-in-the-wall efficiency where the kitchen and the rest of the place are one room. A bathroom and a closet that is barely a closet are the only attachments. The door shuts behind me, the lock turning into place, both of which tells me that Asher now consumes the small space because he's that big and it's that little.

I'm also alone with the only man I've been alone with since leaving The Beast nine months ago. I'm alone with the only man I actually might like for far longer and how fitting to my dilemma that we're covered in toxic chemicals.

Because I'm toxic and I'm not going to give Asher a chance to try to play hero and get hurt.

Chapter Five

Sierra

There was no avoiding this moment.

I brace myself to endure Asher's reaction to my tiny living quarters, and then turn around to find him focused to his left where my entire apartment exists, his jaw set hard. I scan the room, taking in what he sees: a twin-sized bed with plain rose-colored sheets and one pillow, a classroom-size student desk and chair, a small fan, a suitcase in the corner because it won't fit in my midget closet. No photos, art, or personal anything.

He turns to face me and just that quick he's erased the small space between us, he's close again, so very close, but he doesn't touch me and I hate how much I want him to touch me. "Do you know how many questions I want to ask you right now?" he asks.

"Don't ask them," I say.

He stares at me for a few incredibly long beats, his jaw tight, his expression unreadable. "Go wash up, Sierra," he orders.

I don't like orders. I took them from The Beast to protect my mother. When I left him, I swore I wouldn't take them from another man or anyone for that matter. However, in this case, Asher's just trying to do what *I've* ordered *him* to do: Don't ask those questions he wants to ask. So I comply with this particular command willingly. I walk to the sink

31

and turn on the water, pumping soap into my palm and working it into bubbles. "All the way to your sleeves," he says from behind me, his breath warm on my neck, sending shivers down my spine.

I glance over my shoulder, and he's practically on top of me. "Do you have to hover?"

"Yes. I can't sit down. I can't lean on anything and there isn't exactly a lot of space."

"None that creates a need for you to stand this close."

"Correct," he says.

"And yet you're still standing this close."

"Also correct. Where did you work before the bar?"

"Another bar," I say, happy to have a question I can answer honestly. I flip off the water and surprisingly, he actually takes that as a cue to back up. I open the cabinet below the sink and pull out the box of garbage bags. When I turn around, I'm sandwiched between him and the counter, and he still smells too good for my sanity. I pull two bags from the box and then shove it at him. "The sink's all yours."

He takes the box but doesn't move, those piercing green eyes of his fixed on my face. "Do you know how many questions I want to ask you right now?"

"Didn't we just have this conversation?"

"Yes."

"Repeating it works for you about as well as your suggestion that I take some clothes off and dance on the bar tonight. Not at all."

"How long have you lived here?"

"I'm not going to tell you that. I'm not going to talk about me with you at all." Aware that he won't touch me until he showers, I step around him, easily escaping to my closet. Pulling open the sliding wooden door, I grab a T-shirt and a pair of black Victoria's Secret PINK sweats, the only pair I managed to haul across the country. I don't look at Asher, but I feel him staring at me. I feel him every second I'm in his presence, in every nerve and pore of my existence, and I don't know how that is even possible.

I walk into the tiny bathroom, shut the door, and stare at the tiny shower, that doesn't actually have a bathtub, and wonder how Asher is even going to move around in here. He knocks on the door and I jump. "Undress in the shower and bag your clothes. And wash your hair."

"Yes. Okay. Got it. There's bottled water in the fridge and I have milk and cereal." I cringe. Milk and cereal? Am I trying to seduce him or just point out that I have nothing but milk and cereal in the house? Whatever the case, I need to get done in here and let him get cleaned up. I hurry forward and follow his instructions. First things first, I clean out my purse, and stick my cash and the other few contents in the small medicine chest. I then toss my purse in the shower, and step inside with it. Once I've stripped, I bag everything that might be contaminated, with the realization that I'll have to have my boots cleaned. I'm not replacing them. Once the water is flowing warm, I lean under the spray wondering what Asher is doing out there. He said he can't sit down. Is he just standing there in the center of the kitchen?

That question has me reaching for the cheap Suave shampoo in the corner, and stepping up my pace. In five minutes, I'm drying off. In another few, I've dressed in my sweats, and I don't bother drying my hair or doing more than washing what's left of my make-up away. I'm a mess who will likely scare Asher away and that should make me happy. Yet, it doesn't, and I can't analyze why right now. I swallow a knot of about ten million emotions, grab my phone from the edge of the sink, and stick it in my pocket, before opening the door and exiting the bathroom.

33

I step into the kitchen to find Asher waiting on me, facing me, and my lips part at the sight of him gloriously naked from the waist up. My heart pounds and somehow my gaze lands on his abs, and I decide suits are great and all, but I have a new appreciation for his low-slung jeans and the hard work Asher must put in to sport such impressively ripped abs. With good intentions of actually looking at his face, my gaze roams upward, and I'm now fixated on his broad shoulders, every muscle, of which there are many, colorfully etched with ink that travels all the way down to his wrists. The artwork like an open invitation to explore his body and study it. Kiss it. Lick it? Not that I'll ever be licking this man.

I can't be with him. I can't be with anyone.

That hard, cold reality, jolts me and my eyes lift, colliding with his. "Hi," I say, because I can't come up anything more brilliant. I've been gaping at the man's body.

He laughs. "Hi. I had to take my shirt off. My skin—"

"Is beautiful," I say appalled that the words come out of my mouth. "Your ink, I mean, and I don't even like ink."

"But you like mine."

What am I doing? "I'm not going to reply to that," I say, not sure what I'm doing with this man. "The shower is all yours."

He steps closer, mischief in those green eyes of his that are just as beautiful as his body and his ink. "Next time you're naked and this close to me, I'm going to have to show my appreciation. Consider yourself warned." He steps around me.

"Next time?" I say, whirling around to face him, to try and undo the wrong message I know I've sent him. "Do you plan on making me mace you again? Because that's the only way this happens again."

He pauses at the door and gives me a sideways look. "Whatever it takes to make sure there's a next time, works for me." And with that, he enters the bathroom and I press my hands to my face. I need to make him go away and it sucks so badly.

I rotate and put the bathroom behind me, staring at the room that I've come to call home, and it is home. It's freedom, or some version of freedom while the massive house I'd shared with Prince Charming in Denver had been a prison. If I can make a thousand dollars a night like I did tonight a few times a week, I can fix this place up and save the money I need to get a fake passport. Though I have no idea where to go or how to do that, I know it's going to cost a chunk of change. The shower comes on and I walk to the bed and sit down. Grabbing my pillow, I reach inside my pillowcase and pull out the travel book inside, reading the cover for the millionth time: A Guide to Terre-de-Haut, Guadeloupe Islands, a small island in the Caribbean that requires a ferry to and from. The last place The Beast will look for me.

There's a knock on the front door and I jolt, stuffing the book back inside my pillow. My heart starts to race and adrenaline surges through me. I stand up and fold my arms in front of me. No one can get up here without me buzzing them in. Has The Beast found me? My God. I pant out a breath. Has he found me again?

"Sierra!"

At the sound of Asher's muffled voice I rush across the room and stop outside the door. "Yes?!" I call out. "I'm here."

"Open the door," he shouts.

There's another round of knocking at the front door, and I don't hesitate. I go in the opposite direction. I open the bathroom door.

Asher pokes his head around the shower curtain, all kinds of satisfaction on his handsome face. "I meant the front door, but if you'd rather join me—"

"Asher!" I snap, my knees trembling. "Stop. Please. No flirting right now. I don't know who that is knocking. I haven't buzzed anyone up." I try to cover what must seem like irrational fear. "This is a hellhole neighborhood, remember?"

"It's okay, Sierra. It's only my friend."

"*You aren't hearing me,*" I say, trying to sound calm but my heart is about to jump out of my chest. "I haven't buzzed anyone up."

"Easy, sweetheart," he says, attempting to calm me.

"You don't understand."

"But I want to. Very much, but right now, you can relax. My friend sent me a text. He followed someone into the building when they got buzzed inside."

"You're sure it's him?"

"Yes." His phone buzzes on the counter. "That's probably him again. I can come and—"

"No. No, if you're sure it's him, it's fine." But I'm not sure, so I need a weapon. I open the medicine chest. My hand comes down on the mace and I shut the cabinet door.

"Oh fuck," Asher murmurs, evidentially aware of what I'm holding and not pleased with my plan. I turn away from him right as he turns off the shower and yanks the curtain open. I don't even think about looking at him, not now. I just need to know who's at the door. I need to know that I haven't been found.

36

Chapter Six

Sierra

The knocking begins again.

I exit the bathroom and walk to the door but I'm not opening it yet. I push to my toes to look through the peep hole, which turns out to be an impossible task since it's too high for me. I exhale and consider calling out, but if it's The Beast, he'll know it's me before I spray him.

"I got it, sweetheart."

At the sound of Asher's voice, I turn to find him walking toward me, in nothing but a towel that looks much bigger when wrapped around me, water droplets on his naked chest, his hair wet. He moves past me to the door, and I instinctively back up, holding up the spray, ready to defend him as he flips the lock. He opens the door to reveal our visitor, a tall, dark stranger, that I quickly assess. He's good looking, in his thirties, dressed in faded jeans, the name 'Walker,' printed in white on his black T-shirt. His dark hair is thick and neatly trimmed and he has no apparent tattoos. He's also holding a small duffle bag that has the same Walker logo printed on the side.

Asher takes the bag and eyes me, his gaze flicking to the mace. "Don't mace him. Invite him in. He's one of the good guys."

The man, who I assume to be Blake, looks at me and arches a brow. I lower my weapon. "Come in." I stick the mace in my pocket. "There's a chair and a bed. Take your pick."

"Chair it is," the man says, crossing the room while Asher closes the space between me and him, to stand in front of me. "You okay, sweetheart?"

"You're in a towel," I say.

"Glad you noticed," he replies. "If you hadn't, I'd be upset."

"I can't talk to you when you're in a towel."

"I can take it off," he offers.

"*Asher*. Stop. Please."

He lowers his voice. "Whatever just happened, Sierra, know this: I got you."

I suck in air with the impact of that promise, and I have a moment where I actually want to just fall into this man. Literally. But I can't. He's in the moment, and this problem is forever for me. And yet somehow I have fallen into him. My hand is on his chest, nestled in the center of blond, springy hair. I try to pull it back.

He covers it with his, holding it over his heart which seems to be racing. Why is his heart racing? He doesn't even know the danger he's in with me. "Sierra," he says, willing me to look at him but I do not.

"Please go get dressed," I whisper.

"That is generally not what a man wants a woman to say to him. But under the circumstances, I forgive you." His hand falls away from mine, and when he turns and walks back toward the bathroom, my palm is damp from his skin and warm from his touch.

He shuts the bathroom door and only then do I remember his friend. I whirl around to find him sitting in the chair by my desk, looking like a giant in a room made for a child, he's that big.

38

He's at the foot of the bed, so I walk to the side, and sit down, angling toward him. "I'm Sierra," I say and looking for a way to take attention off myself, I blurt. "Are you Blake, otherwise known as Dickhead?"

"No," he says holding his hands up stop sign fashion. "I'm not Dickhead, though my wife occasionally might disagree but I pay the price when she does, believe me. I'm Luke. The middle brother of the three."

"Meaning, you, Blake and Asher?"

"Asher and I are SEAL brothers," he says. "Blake and Royce are my blood brothers."

"You and Blake are nothing alike," I say, my interest in sibling personality variations part of my used-to-be-studies. "Actually, from what I can tell, Asher and Blake are more alike than you and Blake."

"That becomes obvious rather quickly," he agrees. "Royce and I are the more reserved of the Walker clan. Asher and Blake are not. And nothing if not colorful right out of the gate."

"Colorful," I say. "Yes. They are both quite colorful." We laugh easily and he doesn't even seem to notice my pathetic living situation. I like him. I like that he is someone Asher calls brother and friend. "How long were you in the Navy with Asher?"

"I think it's best if I let Asher reveal his own history, but for what my opinion is worth, since you don't know me. He's a good man. I owe him my life about three times over."

"I believe I owe you mine four times over."

At the sound of Asher's voice, I rotate to find him walking towards us, now dressed in a snug black T-shirt, and a pair of black jeans, tucked inside biker-style boots. His hair that isn't nearly as long as I thought, damp and loose to his shoulders.

"We're even then," Luke says. "Because I'd bet that hundred bucks you owe me that you saved me from getting maced at the door when I got here."

"Oh no," I say quickly. "Don't let Asher off that easily. I would not have maced you."

"But you maced me?" Asher challenges, leaning an elbow on the mockery of a short bar, dividing the kitchen from the living area.

"You got up close and personal," I remind, "*in the dark* without announcing yourself and you know you did."

"Are you saying I deserved it?" he asks.

"I am," Luke interjects. "She was alone after dark." He looks at me. "You were right to spray first and ask questions later."

"Especially in this neighborhood," I say, because he's too nice to say it.

"In any neighborhood," Luke corrects me.

His phone buzzes and he pulls it from his pocket, glances at his messages, and then at Asher. "The wife needs me and Blake says he has a situation." He stands. "I'll meet you on the street. Do you want me to take your bagged clothes?"

Asher motions behind him. "By the shower in the bathroom."

Luke walks that direction and by the time I stand up, Asher is in front of me. "Hi," he says, this time.

"Hi," I say, finding myself blush at the silly, innocent exchange.

"I deserved it?"

"You kinda did," I tease.

"Next time I'll leave with you."

I meant to object, but suddenly he's looking down at my bare feet, and just as suddenly, I'm glad that I splurged on a five dollar bottle of pink polish way back when. "Why are you looking at my feet?"

"I didn't want to step on them" he says, easing closer, the heat of his body radiating into mine.

"You looked too long."

"How long is too long, Sierra?" he asks, and I don't think we're talking about feet anymore, but he doesn't give me time to reply anyway. "I like you like this," he adds.

"A wet mess with bare feet?" I ask. "I'm wet and—please tell me I didn't say that."

His lips twitch, eyes filling with mischief. "I won't go every place I could go with that comment. I'll just say this." He lowers his voice, to a gravely seduction. "You're *beautiful.*"

My breath hitches with the almost spontaneous way he says those words. I don't know what I'm doing with this man but it's happening too fast. "Asher, I can't—"

"Nice to meet you, Sierra," Luke calls out heading to the door, reminding me that he's even here.

I wave at him. "Nice to meet you, Luke."

The door opens and shuts, and Luke is gone. Asher and I are alone, the room somehow even smaller than normal. The energy between us, around us, charged. "I'm going to have to go," he says.

"Right. Of course." And I can't help but wonder where a man goes at two in the morning. I shouldn't be wondering. He needs to leave. He has to leave.

"The Walker brothers own a security company," he says, seeming to read my mind. "I have a job with Blake tonight, or I wouldn't leave."

"You don't have to tell me that."

"No," he agrees, "and the crazy thing is that if you were any other woman, I wouldn't."

"I don't know what that means."

"Neither do I, but I want to find out. Do you have your phone?"

"Yes. In my pocket."

"Put my number in it," he orders. I open my mouth to argue and he doesn't give me the chance. "You're living alone in a big, dangerous city. Be smart and have a resource if you need help. No strings attached, Sierra. If you end up hating me, I'll still be here if you need me and so will my people. That's who we are."

I believe him and regardless of how my judgment failed me in the past, it's also kept me alive these past nine months. I pull my phone from my pocket and set up his number in the contacts. "Thank you," I say, when I slide it back into my pocket.

He retrieves his phone from his pocket. "Are you going to give me your number?" I open my mouth to speak, and again, when I would object, he heads me off. "You maced me, sweetheart. Surely I earned your number and yes, I'm pressuring you, because I have to go."

The man offered me his unconditional help after I maced him. He also came to my rescue in the bar when that idiot attacked me. "Yes," I say, and I give him my number. He punches it into his phone and sticks it in his pocket. "Thank you, Asher," I say because it has to be said. I might need help. I might really call him and his people.

His eyes warm again, and magically it seems, once again, I warm with them. "Sorry, sweetheart," he says, "but I have to do this." His hand settles at my hip, and one of mine instinctively goes to his arm. In that short distraction, his other hand has slipped under my hair, cupping my neck, and he's lowered his mouth a breath from mine. I tremble with the promise of what's to come, and he feels it, too. "God, woman," he murmurs and in the next moment his mouth slants over mine and he's kissing me, his tongue stroking mine. I try to resist, but it's impossible. I kiss him back. I melt into the hard lines of his body, and when he pulls back, his forehead against mine, I breathe with him.

"I *have* to go or I won't be able to leave," he says, releasing me and walking to the door. "Lock up behind me."

He pulls it open and exits, and I dart across the room and flip the locks, my hand flattening on the wooden surface. He's still here. I sense it and seconds tick by before he says, "Good night, Sierra."

"Good night Asher," I reply, and I swear, I feel him smile. And I smile the first smile I've smiled in a very long time.

Chapter Seven

ASHER

I head down the stairs, leaving Sierra in that shithole of an apartment she's living in and it's killing me. This woman affects me, and I have no explanation for just how much. Maybe it's simply that she's in trouble, and saving people is what I do. Maybe it's that I like to solve puzzles and those blue eyes filled with secrets make her a puzzle. Not to mention she's fucking gorgeous, smart, and tastes like sweet honey, and please fuck me.

I round the corner on that thought to find Luke waiting on me at the bottom level, still inside Sierra's building, which tells me his wife isn't waiting on him and there's a bigger problem than he hinted at inside.

"What's happening?" I ask, joining him.

"When Sierra left the bar, Ju-Ju followed her."

"No," I say, rejecting that idea at every level. "I followed her. I didn't see Ju-Ju."

"He was on the opposite side of the street. Kyle distracted him and tried to buy from him."

"Kyle?" I ask. "Please tell me he changed out of that fancy suit he's been wearing for the bodyguard job he's on."

"Unfortunately, no," he says. "We were short manpower and he had to act in the moment. Needless to say, Ju-Ju got spooked and took off but that's why we need you. Ju-Ju landed at an after hours bar, and Kara is already there. But we obviously can't send Kyle in with her after he spooked Ju-Ju. Blake went in."

"Seriously? She's his wife. He won't be able to be in the same room as Kara and let her get pawed on like she will in that club."

"Which is why we need you in there. And this gives you another chance to have that one-on-one with Ju-Ju."

"Ju-Ju has eyes on Sierra, and me in that bar without her tells him she's really single. And we both know he targets single women."

"Tell him you were meeting someone to do some business," Luke says. "And that you keep your woman out of your business."

"No," I say rejecting that idea. "Aside from the Sierra situation, my gut says this is not the right time. Kyle spooked him tonight. If I show up where he's at, I look like I'm chasing him, and he might make me, too. He needs to come to me. He needs to think I'm hard to get. He already believes that I'm the eyes and ears he needs to help him sell more product, and stay off police radar."

"Okay," Luke says. "Valid points. But we're going to fight about this with Blake."

"Because he wants Kara out of there and I do, too. She's another one who's going to look like she's chasing him. She needs to stick with me at the bar. Pull them both out of there."

His phone rings and he snags it from his pocket and glances at the number. "Ju-Ju just left the bar with a woman, and if she's doing the juice he's selling, she's doing him first. We called in Jacob for duty. He's following the woman. Kyle is following Ju-Ju. Blake wants us to meet him at the office."

I nod and Luke heads for the door ahead of me while I reluctantly follow. What I really want right now is to go back upstairs, kiss Sierra again, and then strip her naked in every possible way. For her protection, of course, Ju-Ju needs to know she's mine.

It's three in the morning by the time Luke and I walk into the strategy room of the Walker Security offices. Blake and Kara are already sitting on one side of the conference table, a couple dozen clocks with worldwide times on the wall behind them. Rick Savage, a newer recruit who just came off an overseas gig, is with them, sitting at the end cap.

"Can you get Savage a doorman job?" Blake asks as Luke and I claim the seats across from him and Kara.

"No," I say. "I don't work with fuckheads." I also don't mince words. The dude's six-foot-five inches of musclehead ex-Beret that rubs me ten shades of wrong. He's also the only member of the many Walker employees across the country that I just plain fucking hate.

The room is silent and for a reason. Everyone knows I worked with him on his first assignment and it didn't go well. Savage breaks the quiet with a laugh. "Don't be scared. I won't hurt little Asher."

I cut him a look. "A man I knew and trusted died because of you," I say. "Because you went when I said hold, and he followed to protect you."

"It didn't go down the way you remember it," Savage bites out. "And you think I don't have nightmares about him dying? I do."

"I'm sure you're sucking your thumb in the fetal position," I say, glancing at the rest of the room and moving

47

on. "I'm on Ju-Ju's radar. I'm close to getting into his inner circle."

"If the guy even has an inner circle," Luke says, ignoring my exchange with Savage. "In a full week of watching him, we haven't seen him with one person on repeat."

"Serial killers are loners," Kara says. "We all know this."

"Yes. He is a serial killer," Blake says. "One who likes young, pretty brunettes. That's you, Kara. It's time to get you off this case."

"I can put Ju-Ju down," she says. "Those young college girls can't."

"What's the word from Kyle?" Luke asks. "Have we confirmed the woman he left with tonight is safe?"

"She was blonde," Kara says. "She doesn't fit the profile."

"Translation," Blake says. "Ju-Ju fucked her in his car and then sent her packing, but Jacob followed her. We now know who she is and where she lives."

"I'm going to try to make friends with her," Kara says. "Maybe she knows more about him than we do."

"I need inside," Savage says. "I'll hear things at the door and I'll rough up a few dudes if I have to. I'll make 'em talk."

"You're a little too obvious Savage," I say. "Stroke it, don't pull it."

"You're so fucking funny, Ash," he says. "So funny that I don't want to stroke it or pull it. I want to punch it—that 'it' being your face."

I wink. "I do like it rough, Savage. Didn't know that, did you?"

"Let's talk about Sierra," Blake bites out, and he suddenly has my full attention.

"What the fuck about Sierra?"

"Obviously she's got Ju-Ju's attention. You got close enough to her to assess her character. Can we hire her to try to get close to Ju-Ju?"

"Go fuck yourself, Blake," I say. "We aren't using an innocent to bait a damn serial killer."

"She's already on his radar," he says. "And she's living in a shithole. We'll pay her and pay her well and get her the hell out of that place."

"As far as Ju-Ju is concerned, she's my woman," I say. "And if he doesn't know that now, he will."

"I'm going to put on the brakes right there," Luke says calmly, always the mediator, his focus on Blake. "You asking Ash to have Sierra do this, is like you asking me to have Julie do this. It won't happen."

"He just met her," Blake argues.

"Irrelevant," Luke states. "Think back to what you felt, thought, and wanted when you met Kara."

"I wanted to fuck her and kill her," he says, glancing at me. "Is there a comparison here I'm missing?"

"You thought I was one of the bad guys," Kara says. "But there was still a connection between us."

"She matters to him," Luke says.

"She's the flavor of the month," Blake counters. "He wants to fuck her and it's not like I'm trying to fuck her over. I want to change her life and save lives while we do it."

"No," I say. "You will *not* use Sierra. I'll get Ju-Ju."

"And what if you don't?" he challenges.

"Sierra is already running from something," Luke says. "She's scared. She's on edge. She will read like trouble to anyone who is looking for trouble, which means Ju-Ju."

"Running?" Kara asks. "From what?"

"I don't know," I say. "But when Luke made it to the door without her buzzing him up, she flipped out."

"Yeah, she did," Luke agrees. "She was locked and loaded with that bottle of mace. Add to that the fact that she's living in complete poverty without one single personal item in her apartment. She's running."

I point at Blake. "Don't bring up the money. I'm gonna help her. She isn't in a position to help us."

"Then you can't let her know you're undercover," Savage says. "She'll blink at the wrong time."

"I'm completely fucking aware of that," I say, "thank you very much."

"Run her prints," Blake says. "Find out what's coming at her before it comes at us, too. That's what I did with Kara."

"That was different," Kara argues. "I was working for a drug lord, and you didn't know I was undercover. You thought I was a criminal."

"I hate to tell you this, sweetheart," Blake says. "But Sierra is reading like one, too."

"Sierra's not a criminal," I snap.

"The guy who wants to fuck a woman is not the guy who needs to decide if she's a criminal or not," Savage says. "Take it from the guy who swore another woman wasn't a criminal."

"You're about to get a scar to match the one you already have," I promise, eying the huge mark down his right cheek. "And if you think being bigger than me matters, think again. I like a big target."

Luke laughs and everyone looks at him. "Sorry," he says, holding up his hands. "Poorly timed laughter, I know, but Savage just gave me a walk down memory lane."

"Germany," I say, which is a reference to a bar fight.

Luke cuts me a look. "He was a big dude."

And together, we say, "Just not big enough," which is what we say every time we tell the story we won't be telling today.

"Back on point," Blake says. "You can't even trust the weatherman. If it were me, Ash, I'd run her prints."

"What's big to a civilian is usually small to us," Kara says. "If you run her prints and she finds out, she'll never trust you again. Think about it before you do it."

"Don't think too long," Blake say. "Your gut will tell the story."

"Not always," Savage says. "And man, put aside you anger. I fell for a woman. She was a spy and she tried to kill me. I never saw it coming."

Blake stands up. "Let's get some rest."

He and Kara head out of the room, with Savage following them, and for Blake and Kara, sleep is nearby. The Walker Brothers own the building and apartments above the office. I don't know where Savage lives and I don't care. I'm just glad he's gone.

Luke isn't, though. He hangs back with me, waiting for the room to clear. "Blake's not all wrong," he says when we're alone. "Sierra's in trouble and she's afraid. You're smart enough to make a list of the possible reasons. You need to decide if you can deal with those things before you get pulled under with her." He stands up and walks out of the room.

Thirty minutes later, I'm at my building, three blocks from the Walker Security property. I enter my industrial-style apartment on the fifteenth floor of the high rise, and arm the security system. Two years after putting a million dollars down on the place, compliments of a contract job in a hellish jungle overseas, I still feel a sense of home every time I enter this place. It might not compare to the luxury I grew up with, but it's mine. All fucking mine. Not a penny of it paid for with my father's money. But Sierra has nothing that is hers and she's living in barely livable circumstances.

I cross the room, heading toward the open kitchen, and while my floors are a mahogany and gray mix of wood, Sierra's floor is ugly, old laminate. My walls are a mix of brick and windows. Hers are white chipped paint. I toss my keys on the wooden island that matches the floors and walk up to the stainless-steel fridge and grab a bottle of water before making my way to the black steel stairwell and the second level. My bedroom is at the top to the right, and as I enter I'm struck by the fact that this room is bigger than the entire place Sierra is living in now.

I sit down on the edge of the four-poster, gray-finished bed, and set the water on the nightstand, emptying my pockets next to it. I waste no time afterward, stripping down and climbing into the bed, but I stare into the darkness, sleep nowhere in sight, Sierra in her shit bed on my mind. Luke's words play in my head: *Blake's not all wrong. Sierra's in trouble and she's afraid. You're smart enough to make a list of the possible reasons. You need to decide if you can deal with those things before you get pulled under with her.*

He's right. She's in trouble, but no one deals with trouble better than Walker Security. We're going to help her. *I'm* going to help her. Aside from that, I can't walk away from this woman. I've never said that about a woman before. Something about this one gets to me. I want to get to know her.

I grab my phone and pull up her number and I don't even consider the fact that she might be asleep as I type: *You okay, sweetheart?*

She replies almost instantly: *What's my name?*

I smile and type: *You okay, Sierra?*

She replies with: *Yes. Are you?*

Better if you were here, I reply.

Stop, she replies.

Stop is not a word I like and it's also a word a man has to take seriously when spoken by a woman. I dial her number. She answers on the first ring. "Asher."

"Holy fuck, I like it when you say my name all breathless like that."

"Stop," she repeats.

"Is that what you really want?"

"We just met. How can you be this insistent that you want to know me at all?"

"Your answer is all in that kiss. We have chemistry, sweetheart. I know it. You know it."

"Stop," she says again.

"You keep saying that. I need you to tell me if that's what you really want."

"Asher, damn it,"

"Answer, Sierra," I order softly.

"You *have* to stop."

"I'll stop when you tell me that's what you want and that's not what I'm hearing and that's damn sure not what I felt when I kissed you tonight."

"Go to bed, Asher. It's four in the morning." She hangs up.

But that's okay. *She's* okay. And the message in that call was clear. She doesn't want me to stop, but she thinks she should. I don't know why, but I'll do as Kara instructed:

Earn her trust and find out what she's running from. For tonight, I settle for typing her one last message: *Goodnight, Sierra.*

I stare at the screen, waiting for her reply and waiting and waiting, willing her to answer. Finally, she replies with: *Goodnight, Asher.*

I smile and set my phone down on the nightstand. "Pull me under, baby," I murmur. "I can't wait."

Chapter Eight

ASHER

Four hours of sleep does me just fine and I wake at nine to the alarm I'd set right before bed. By ten, I've showered, downed two cups of coffee, and a bowl of cereal. By ten-fifteen, I'm out the door, a leather bag with a computer inside on my shoulder. I don't bother with my car, which is parked in the Walker garage. I bought the BMW just because I wanted my father to know I could buy the damn thing. I haven't seen him since driving in the city is hell, and I'm pissed at myself for being this fucking old, and still motivated to show him up.

I take the subway and by eleven, I've hit up a hardware store, a liquor store, and grabbed a bag of my favorite sweets. By eleven-fifteen, I'm at Sierra's apartment, hoping she's awake when I buzz her call button. She doesn't answer. I buzz it again. Fuck. I pull my phone from my pocket and dial her number. "Hello," she says.

"Where are you?"

"Standing right behind you."

I drop the phone from my ear and turn around to find Sierra, the sunlight catching auburn in her brown hair, and amber in her blue eyes. "You're up," I say.

"I went grocery shopping," she says. "Why are you here?"

LISA RENEE JONES

"I went shopping too. Invite me up and I'll show you what I bought."

"Asher—"

"Keep saying my name, sweetheart, but don't finish that sentence the wrong way. I brought gifts."

"I don't need gifts."

"Actually, you do need these. They're practical."

"Practical." She laughs. "Now I have to know how you define the word practical."

"Then invite me up. Both of our arms are tired."

"Okay, but just—"

"No limits. They aren't practical."

She shakes her head and laughs. "Fine. You win." She walks to the panel, punching in the code: 1877. She looks over at me. "You memorized it, didn't you?"

"Yes. I did. Now you don't have to tell me."

"How gentlemanly of you to save me the trouble," she says, reaching for the door.

"I'm glad you think so," I say, catching the door and giving her room to enter first. She starts up the stairs and I happily follow behind her, with a perfect view of her cute heart-shaped ass in snug black jeans. "Are you looking at my ass?" she asks one flight up.

"Yes. I am. Don't tell me to stop. I can't. It's right in front of me."

She stops walking at the first level and motions me ahead. "You go first."

I smile. "That's just evil," I say, but I do as ordered, and one flight up, I say, "Are you looking at my ass?"

"Yes," she says. "I am. Don't tell me to stop. I can't. It's right in front of me."

I laugh, and in morning light, I'm still fucking crazy about this woman. I want to know her story, and I want *her*

56

to tell me, not her fingerprints. And I believe I can get us there. I reach the top level and step back to allow her to join me, and she sets her bags down to dig out her key. It's all I can do not to reach forward and pull her to me, but the bags in my hands offer willpower. She pops open the door and grabs her bags. I follow her inside and she heads to the kitchen.

"Can you lock the door?" she asks over her shoulder, that locked door obviously important to her.

"No, actually," I say, setting my bags down on the floor. "Because I'm going to change your lock out and install a chain and deadbolt."

She turns to look at me. "That's expensive," she says. "I don't have that kind of money."

"It's a gift," I say.

"I can't take that."

"It's already paid for," I say. "And you need it."

"How much?"

"I got this, Sierra."

She folds her arms in front of her. "I don't want you to spend money on me."

I cross the room to stand in front of her but I don't touch her despite the fact that I really fucking want to touch her. "I told you. I do work for Walker Security. They pay me well. I want to do this for you."

"Why do you bartend then?"

"That's a complicated story I'll tell you another time."

"I understand." She grabs a jug of milk and puts it in the fridge, effectively giving me her back, but not before I note the discomfort and disappointment in her face. She feels shut down which isn't wrong. I did shut her down because Savage was right. If she knows I'm undercover, she'll act differently at the bar, and blink at the wrong time. Damn it. Fuck. Damn it.

"I'm going to get started," I murmur, walking away from her rather than pulling her close and explaining everything. I cross to the door and grab the leather bag I left on the floor, squatting down and pulling out the MacBook inside. I set it on the desk which is what amounts to a hop away, and turn on Amazon Prime Music to a country channel.

She leans on the counter, facing me. "I didn't take you for a country boy," she says, as Luke Bryan's Light It Up fills the air.

"I'm a clusterfuck of contradictions, sweetheart," I say, standing up, my bag in hand as I walk back to the kitchen. "I love country and I was in a rock band for several years." I have no idea why I just admitted that to her. I don't talk about that part of my life, and I quickly pull out a six pack of beer and the cookies. "I brought snacks."

She laughs. "Beer and cookies? That's a crazy combination."

I unscrew the top on a beer and hand it to her before grabbing one for myself. "I told you. I'm a clusterfuck of contradictions. Try the cookies. Best black and whites in the city. And I know my black and whites."

"Are you from New York?"

"Born and raised right here in the city. What about you?"

"No," she says. "I'm not from here."

"Where?"

She hesitates but gives me a little morsel. "Colorado. Don't ask why I'm here."

"Where in Colorado?"

"Denver," she says.

"How old are you?"

"Twenty-eight for a little longer. My birthday is next month. October 22nd. How old are you?"

"Thirty-three. My birthday is next month as well. The 21st."

She smiles. "Really?"

"Yes. Really."

"You get older sooner than me."

"I've learned that any time you actually live long enough to get older, is a good day, and so I'll happily get older."

"Yes. Yes, I do believe I appreciate that statement."

I don't ask why. She barely told me where she's from and I want to draw her out, not push her back. "Then we'll celebrate together."

"Yes. That would be nice."

"Yes," I repeat. "It would be—nice."

She laughs. "Nice is not a word that works for you. You can barely even say it."

"I'll practice." I walk across the room and kneel by my leather bag.

"Please don't," she says, crossing to sit on the side of the bed, her beer in her hand. "Nice doesn't fit you."

"You might be surprised how well nice can fit me," I say, pulling out a variety of tools. "A lot of things about me might surprise you."

"When were you in a band?" she asks, sipping her beer.

I test the electronic screw gun and hesitate. "Before the SEALs."

"And the real story?"

"I don't talk about the real story."

"I understand."

I rotate and lean an elbow on the door facing her. "A little too well."

"Is that a problem for you?"

"Yes. It is."

"And yet you don't talk about you?"

"I'm not the one running," I say.

"If you won't talk about it, you're running from it."

"Says who?"

She gives a choked humorless laugh and looks away a moment before looking at me again. "Not me. I know nothing. I've proven that the past nine months."

"What happened nine months ago?"

"Nothing. Everything. Except..."

"Except what?"

She downs a big swallow of her beer. "You seem different." She sets the bottle down by her bed and lays back on the mattress.

I don't ask her what different means. There had been a soft rasp to her voice and a softening to her eyes that tells me different is good. And I'll take that.

I start working on the lock, and by the time I have a deadbolt installed, she hasn't moved. I walk over to her and sure enough, she's breathing deeply. I look around for a blanket to pull over her and there isn't one. I try the closet, and my gut clenches when I realize just how little she owns. There sure isn't a blanket. I cross to the bed again and stare down at her, watching her sleep. She's peaceful and that tells me a story. She's exhausted emotionally and physically. She's always on edge, but with me here, she feels safe, whether she consciously knows it or not. That's the biggest fucking compliment she can give me, and she doesn't even know she offered it up. That's progress. That's trust. Quid pro quo. Which means I can't keep giving her standard answers. I have to give to get.

I walk back to the door and add a chain to the top above the deadbolt. Next comes a camera that I program into the

MacBook. Everything else I have with me, I need to show her how to use. I walk over to the bed and sit down next to her. She doesn't move. I lay back and she rolls over and curls to my side. She's asleep, but she instinctively came to me. And I'm not sure any woman has ever done anything that rocked my world. She trusts me. At least in her sleep. I just have to convince her she can trust me when she's awake.

And what the fuck happened nine months ago?

Chapter Nine

ASHER

I don't sleep. I lay there holding Sierra for more than an hour, and I don't think about anything but her. Her smell: floral with a hint of vanilla. Her hair: soft on my cheek, light brown with streaks of red. Her fear: right fucking everywhere. I shut her down about the bar for her protection. I shut her down about my past for her protection. I'm going to have to open the fuck up if I want her to do the same and that's new territory for me. Everything with this woman is new territory for me. I'm just diving into about my fiftieth analysis of why that might be when she shifts next to me. I think she might roll away, but instead, she snuggles closer, and I smile. Oh yeah, I smile. This woman, up close to me, makes me one happy motherfucker.

She inhales deeply and flexes her fingers on my chest before her head lifts and she looks at me.

"Oh God. Did we—were we—?"

I laugh. "No, sweetheart. When we fuck, and we will, you'll know. I make you that promise."

She sits up and runs her hands through her hair. "That can't happen."

"And yet it will. You know it. I know it."

"No, it won't. How did we end up here? I was so knocked out I don't even remember."

"You laid down and were out in about thirty seconds," I say lifting up on my elbows. "I decided to lay down with you and you curled up next to me."

"Oh. Sorry. I—"

"Why would you be sorry? I'm not." I sit up and face her, brushing my knuckles down her cheek. "I'm not sorry at all."

She catches my hand and holds onto it, but I'm pretty sure she meant to set it aside. "My life is a mess, Asher. I can't pull you into it."

"I'm really good at cleaning up messes."

"You barely know me. I barely know you."

"I get it. You don't trust me yet."

"And you trust me?" she challenges.

"Actually, I do. I have a knack for reading people."

"Be careful," she warns. "Sometimes you think you have a knack and then you're proven wrong."

"Are you saying you'll prove me wrong?"

"I'm saying there are things about me you might not like."

"Try me."

"No. I'm not going to do that."

"Not yet," I say. "But you're right. You did just meet me. For now, I'll take a leap of faith and take my chances on you. Maybe then you'll take your chances on me." I lift our hands and kiss hers. "I have a few more of those practical gifts for you."

I stand up and walk across the room to grab the bags I left there and set them on the bed. "The locks are really fancy," she says, noticing my work.

"They're top of the line for a reason," I say. "But a bad guy good at being bad can get past them, which is why we have back-up. Before we get to those things, though, I put the keys to the locks on the kitchen counter, and no, I did not keep one for myself. Because I installed the lock does not give me a right to a key. Only you can do that."

She studies me for several beats. "I appreciate that."

"Whoever the asshole is that made you think you had to thank me for that needs an ass whooping. I'll be happy to deliver it. Just say the word."

"I wish it were that easy."

"It's easier than you think. You'll find that out when you decide to trust me." I move on before she withdraws and pull out a new canister of mace. "This is real pepper spray."

"And it's better than the tear gas?"

"Yes. People like me who've been exposed to tear gas can become immune. Some people simply have a natural partial immunity. And if the person is drunk or high, it might not affect them at all."

"I had no idea. So, it's basically worthless."

"Not worthless, but not your best option. With a pepper spray, immunity is not going to happen. I've known a few guys who can survive it better than others, but they still feel it. But—"

"There's always a 'but,' isn't there?"

"Most of the time. The problem with all these sprays is that you can spray yourself instead of the enemy or with the enemy."

She laughs. "You're such a soldier with the enemy talk."

"That I am," I say, motioning her to her feet and to the small open area near the front door. "You need to know how to handle any weapon you choose or it can be turned around and used on you."

"The mace is pretty simple. Just aim and spray."

I grab an empty canister and hand it to her, sticking the good one on the kitchen counter. "That's a fake you can practice with now and later. Let's see how easy it really is

because I wasn't trying to attack you when you sprayed me."
I charge her and press her against the wall, her soft body
against every really fucking hard part of mine. "You didn't
spray me, sweetheart."

"You surprised me."

"That's the point."

"Right. Of course."

"Spray me now," I say. "Before I kiss you."

She holds up the bottle and sprays the empty canister.
Air puffs in her face. "You would have just sprayed yourself."

"That was unfair."

"Criminals aren't fair."

"Right," she looks down. "You're right. They absolutely
are not."

Her reaction tells a story. She's not just running from a
man. She's running from a dangerous man. I release her.
"Let's cover some basics."

"Make sure I point it at them, not me."

"Let's talk about how to do that." I grab the filled
canister. "I put a raised arrow sticker on the button." I show
it to her and let her run her finger over it. "Can you tell which
way to shoot from that?"

"Yes. Yes, that's perfect."

"Good." I set it back down. "If you're really being
attacked, your adrenaline will be high, and mistakes
happen. If you fire wrong, you're the one on the ground and
incapable of stopping an attack. Where do you keep it?"

"In my purse."

"If someone grabs your purse, you'd never get to it. If it's
in your purse, the seconds it takes to find it could be one
second too many."

"I can't just walk around with it in my hand."

"In this neighborhood, you need it in your pocket," I say, "with your hand on it."

"It was the cheapest place I could find."

"I'm not judging you, Sierra," I say. "I'm just stating facts. Once you spray, run. That gets you out of the fumes and away from the enemy. Don't stop and look at them like you did me. And one final thing and it's important. If you spray into the wind, it could blow back at you, and never hit your attacker. That makes you the one on the ground and at the bad guy's mercy."

"That really happens?"

"Yes," I say. "It does."

"So I'm supposed to spray fast and run, but only if the wind is just right? That's impossible."

"Do you know how to shoot a gun?"

"No. I do not."

"I'm going to teach you. I'll take you to the shooting range tomorrow."

"Isn't that expensive?" she asks.

"I have Walker Security privileges."

"You don't have to do this."

"Yes, I do. I'm going to give you the tools to feel a little less fear. Practice with the mace." I don't warn her, I go at her again, and she puffs air in my face. "Good," I say, "but you didn't run."

"I can't in this place."

"Get away from the spray."

She nods. "Thank you. I really appreciate all of this."

"We're not done." I grab the computer off the desk and motion her to the bed, where we sit side by side, the MacBook on my lap.

"See the camera icon?"

"Yes. I see it."

"Click on it and you have two views. The exterior of the building and your front door."

"Oh my God. That's incredible. How did you do that?"

"I hacked a nearby camera for the front of the building and I installed a camera by your door and I put it in an obvious place. That way anyone who approaches knows they're being monitored."

"Thank you so much, but how do I see it? On my phone?"

"You keep the computer. And as a plus, it has Netflix. We'll have something to watch when you invite me to hang out."

"I can't keep the computer, Asher. That's not happening."

"It's my back-up. I never use it."

"No, Asher, I—"

"Be smart. Take the resources I've given you." I stand up and pull her to her feet. "Let me take you out to a nice dinner. I know a place where we can have a few drinks and then get a table."

"I can't do this."

"Drink? Eat?"

"Whatever this is. Date you or—"

"You don't want to date me?"

"It's not about you. You know that. I just don't date."

"Why?"

"I can't date."

"Are you sick or something?" I ask.

"No. I'm not sick or something. Are you?"

"Aside from the fact I was poked and prodded in the Navy, and tested up and down, I'll tell you what us SEALs say: If you love it and want to keep it, cover it up. I have a lot of love for the particular part of my body we're discussing."

She laughs. "The things you say."

"I am who I am."

"And who is that, Asher?"

"Find out. Go to dinner with me."

"I can't do that."

"Then we won't date. We'll hang out as friends."

"That kiss was..."

"Damn good."

"You can't kiss me again."

"You sure as hell can kiss me anytime you want."

"Friends don't kiss," she says.

"Friends with benefits do."

"Friends. No benefits."

"Okay. Just friends Nothing wrong with being friends first."

"Not first," she says. "Forever."

Yeah, no, I think, but what I say is, "How about that dinner?"

"I can't afford that dinner and you've spent too much money on me already."

"All right. Let's go find a decent pizza joint."

"I've been living on two-dollar slices of pizza. I want a salad. One of those places in nicer neighborhoods where they have all kinds of add-ins and you can pick. Do you know a good place?"

"I know every place in this city. Grab your purse."

"I don't have my purse. Apparently, Luke took my clothes too, by the way. I really need to try to get my boots and purse cleaned. How can I get them back from him?"

"I'll make sure you get them back and cleaned at a place that handles our toxic chemicals."

"How many toxic chemicals do you deal with?"

LISA RENEE JONES

"Walker is a national company. They handle about half the airport security across the country and private jobs all over the world."

"And you're bartending?"

"Didn't we just have this conversation?"

"Yes."

"Repeating it won't change my answer," I say, giving a spin to what she told me about her apartment.

She laughs. "I deserved that."

"Yes, you did. We'll find the things we can talk about and work up to the rest." I step to her, cup her face and kiss her forehead before looking down at her. "I want to kiss you."

"You just did."

"That wasn't a kiss." I slide my hand under her hair, around her neck. "One more for the road."

"No," she whispers.

"But you taste like honey and sunshine. I really need to taste that again."

"I taste like no."

"You taste like yes. You just keep saying no."

"Every man wants what they can't have."

"Now I know why you don't date."

"And why is that?" she asks.

I lower my mouth a breath from hers. "You picked the wrong men." I release her and step back and her lashes lower, her neck bobbing with a deep swallow.

I'm right. There is another man. And I'd bet my left arm that he threatened her and anyone she cares about. Maybe anyone who helped her escape. I'm going to meet this man. I'm going to hurt this man. And then I'm going to celebrate by kissing Sierra all the fucking time. As often as she'll let me.

Chapter Ten

ASHER

The minute we're on the street, my Spidey senses go off. Someone is watching us. I don't know who they are, or where they are, but they're here. Sierra feels it, too. Nerves are jumping off her but then, maybe she walks around like that. She's running. She's hiding. "I don't seem to know what to do with my hands without my purse," she says when we stop at a light on the way to the subway. "That's silly, right?"

I grab her hand and place it on my arm. "Why don't you leave it right here," I say. "If you don't have a problem with that."

"Actually, I don't," she says, apparently just as eager as I am to tell whoever is watching that she's not alone.

The light turns and we start walking and that sense of being watched intensifies. I grab her hand. "Come on." I take off running, and in her jeans and tennis shoes, she's pretty darn agile, which gives me incentive to keep moving. We turn a corner, and she never questions why I'm hurrying. Another corner and we are rushing down the subway stairs and it's not long before we dart into a train just before it closes, both laughing with the success and exertion.

"That felt good," she says as we sit down on two open side-by-side seats, our legs aligned. "I used to run all of the time."

"Used to?" I ask, taking the liberty to press my hand to her knee.

"Yeah," she says. "Used to."

"Weather permitting, I run in Battery Park in the mornings. You want to go with me tomorrow? We can go to the shooting range afterward."

"Yes," she says. "I'd like that, though I doubt seriously I can keep up with a SEAL—or ex-SEAL."

"You'll do just fine."

An elderly woman walks in our direction and we both push to our feet and move to a pole, standing face-to-face. "You're a gentleman," she observes, while my mind goes back to that sense of being followed I no longer feel.

"SEAL's honor," I say, leaning forward and pressing my cheek to hers. "Honor is the only reason I haven't kissed you about ten times over." I cup her face. "Because no is no with me, but I want you every second that I'm with you."

She shivers, and I know she's affected. I want her to be affected. I damn sure am. The car stops and an announcement is made for our stop. "That's us," I say, pulling back, and when her eyes meet mine, fuck, the connection punches me in the chest and I've never had any woman do that to me.

I take her hand and we exit the car, hurrying forward and up the stairs. Once we're topside, we're not only clear, we're only a few blocks from my apartment and the Walker offices. My spidey senses are calm and she breathes out, relief evident in the softening of her shoulders. I wrap my arm around her shoulders and pull her close. "I got you, sweetheart," I say, and when she settles her hand on my back, I smile again. She makes me smile, and the funny thing about that. I like it. I might even kill to keep it.

A few minutes later, we're in a little joint where you stand behind a glass and tell the person making your salad which of about thirty toppings you want. I watch as Sierra lights the fuck up over avocado and egg and I know she wasn't exaggerating about living off pizza slices. We get to the register and I'm not about to let her pay. I pull out my black Am Ex and hand it to the person behind the register. "For both of us," I tell the clerk and when I expect Sierra to object she doesn't.

She walks the fuck away. Fuck. Fuck. Fuck. I sign the slip and grab the bag of food and take off after Sierra.

Sierra

I'm shaken. I don't want to be shaken. I don't want to distrust Asher, but that black Am Ex not only gives me flashbacks of The Beast flaunting his, it makes me question Asher in what I hope is an illogical way. It *is* illogical. Asher has given me no reason to distrust him, which is why I walk down the stairs toward the lower level seating, not out the door. I just need a moment to think. I need a moment to breathe and assure myself that I'm not being the fool I was with The Beast. But I oddly breathe better with Asher. Before him, alone felt safer, better. I feel a connection to this man and I need to slow down. I probably need to pull away. But I don't want to. I want to kiss him. I want it to be *okay* that I kiss him.

I reach the last step and bring a dozen white tables with attached chairs into view and no other guests. I walk to a back table and rotate as Asher comes down the stairs, and he's so damn good looking, and sweet, and funny. He makes me laugh and sigh, and it's not logical that I'd still be alive if he was hired by Devin. The Beast. I need to call him by his name because he deserves to be named the bastard that he is. The bastard that would ensure I was dead right now if Asher worked for him. I just can't risk being a fool. I need to ask Asher questions. I need to hear his answers. And so, I wait for him, ready to scream, fight, and run. I've been there, done that back in Texas when one of Devin's goons came after me, but I want to stay with Asher like I've never wanted to stay with anyone in my life.

Asher stops in front of me and sets the bag of food on the table. "Talk to me, Sierra."

"Bartenders don't have black Am Ex cards."

"I told you. I work for Walker Security. Our clients pay and pay well."

"So the bartending job is a cover for a Walker job?"

"Yes. And I'm not saying more than that because I can't have you nervous at the bar. It could get us both killed."

I'm always nervous, I think. It's my life now. "Were you hired to follow me? To get to know me? To kiss me?"

He steps closer, and I don't even think about backing away. He shackles my hip, walking me into him and I have zero instinct to run, zero desire to run. "Sweetheart," he says, as my hands settle on the hard wall of his chest. "I kissed you because I wanted to kiss you. Because we want to kiss each other. Because this thing between us works far fucking better than anything I've ever known, and I want more. And to be clear: No. I do not work for whoever you're running from, but if you tell me who the fuck he is, I promise you that you won't have to run anymore."

My fingers curl over his shirt. "It's not that simple."

"I can make it that simple. Trust me."

74

"I need time," I say, wishing he *could* make this simple. Wishing Devin wasn't so damn powerful. "We just met."

"That's not a no. I'll take that."

"It's not a yes."

"Google Walker. We're well-known. We're well-respected. We don't play games with people in the way you accuse me of playing with you."

"You don't need to convince me I can trust you. I don't really think you're setting me up. It's just been a long road for me and I needed to look into your eyes and hear you say it."

"I think you need to come to the Walker offices and meet the team. See how powerful the operation is. How far we reach."

If they reach far, Devin knows someone they know. Devin could use them to get to me, and then destroy Asher, if not them. "You trust them completely," I say.

"Yes. I do."

And that's the problem. That's the reason I can't tell him everything. Not yet. Not until he'll hear me fully about that reach. So maybe not ever. "I was overreacting, Asher."

"Let me help you, Sierra."

"You are helping me just by being you. We're friends, right?"

"Yes. We're friends."

And before I let us be more, I have to tell him everything. But I can't do that if it means destroying him. "And friends buy friends salads, right?" I ask.

His lips hint at a smile and he motions to the table. "You want to eat?"

"Yeah, I want to eat."

"Then we're over my black Am Ex?"

My cheeks heat. "Yes. We're over your black Am Ex."

"Good."

He holds onto me a few beats longer, though, like he can't let go, and I like that. I really don't want him to let go, but he does. And I have to let go anyway. We sit down, and he starts to open the bag when I reach for his hand. "Thank you for lunch."

He kisses my hand and his lips are warm and I'm so cold, so often now. "Can friends do that?" he asks.

"Yes," I say, because I really need to kiss him when I can't. "They can."

"Where else can I kiss you?"

Everywhere please, I think, but I don't know how to make that right in my mind. I'm not free and I'll never be free and alive, so for now, I look away. I say nothing more than, "Let's eat."

We both pull the lids off our salads and I take a bite and I smile. "Is it silly that I'm really excited about salad?"

"I've know that feeling. After months in some foreign hellhole, small things, feel really damn good."

"You saw a lot of bad things."

"I did."

I know asking questions invites questions, but I can't help myself. "Why did you get out?"

"A bad mission. One that still gives me nightmares and made me question everyone who sent me there. I hit a wall. I had a job waiting with Walker anytime I wanted it and I took it."

"Did you know Luke before the SEALs?" she asks.

"No, but we bonded on the whole New Yorker thing."

"New York is like an entirely different planet," I say. "And I know it's your home, but it's crowded, dirty, and expensive."

"You're living in the slum. That makes a difference. You need to experience the real city and the people. And I know just the way."

"How is that?"

"I have a baby shower next weekend for Lauren, Royce's wife," he adds. "Go with me and help me survive the damn thing."

"Baby shower?" I ask. "*You* have a baby shower?"

"Holy hell yes."

"Isn't that usually for women?"

"This is the Walker clan. We do everything together. And that's the fucking truth, so help me God. They torture us over there, but I love them all. I need a gift. You have to help me."

They do everything together. They're close. He won't see the potential of anyone being dirty enough to help Devin. *Damn it*, I think, but I say, "Yes. Of course." And now I've committed to a baby shower, and a birthday celebration. Like I'm starting a real life here, when I just need the money to leave.

"Do you have siblings of your own?" I ask.

"No," he says. "Do you?"

"No."

"What about your parents?" he asks.

"My father died of a heart attack a few years back. My mother is a retired school teacher."

"Is she safe, Sierra?"

"I hope so. I took steps."

"I can find out."

I want to say yes. I *so* want to say yes, but that will open the door to him finding out who I am and who The Beast is as well. "We have a check-in time. I'll talk to her next month actually." I move on quickly. "What about your parents?"

LISA RENEE JONES

"My father is here and my mother died of an aneurysm when I was ten and she was too young."

"Are you close to your father?"

"No," he says. "I hate my father."

"Why?"

"Aside from the fact that he's a very wealthy man who uses his money against everyone?"

Like Devin, I think.

"I was young, but I remember him abusing, controlling and intimidating my mother," he adds.

Like Devin. I think again.

"What did you do in Denver, Sierra?"

"If I tell you—"

"I won't look beyond what you tell me. Give me that trust or we'll never get to know each other."

"I'm terrified to trust anyone."

"You already trust me."

"It's too soon to trust each other."

"And yet, instinctively we all trust and distrust people when we first meet them."

"And sometimes we're wrong."

"Is that what happened to you?" he asks.

I consider that. "No," I say. "I was just too stupid to see what was in front of me."

"I'm in front of you now. Choose to see me. Choose to let me see you."

I swallow hard and I don't let myself think too hard or I'll run. I've trained myself to run and with good reason. I've been inches from death two times in nine months. "I'm a year from my Ph.D. in Forensic Psychology. I'd already have it, but I had the opportunity to intern with one of the most sought after forensic psychologists in the country. That meant finishing slower, but having him on my resume and gaining the experience, which was vast, by working his cases with him."

"Then you're one of us?"

"What does that mean?"

"Walker protects people, and Luke oversees a wide range of airport security now, but at our core, we find the bad guys and we take them down. We consult with law enforcement across the country and even beyond."

"I don't catch bad guys," I say. "Or I didn't. I just helped people like you figure who they were and how they think."

"Are you good?"

"Yes. I am. I was." I move on. "Who were you before the Navy? You were in a rock band, right?"

"Yeah. I was."

"What role in the band?"

"I sang. That was my thing then." His lips thin. "I was rebelling against my father. I joined the band and traveled. He called me a druggy and a loser."

"Did you do drugs?"

"No. I'm too much of a control freak, but one of my friends did. He overdosed and died. It shook me, and I dropped out of the band."

"And went into the Navy?"

"No. I did my father's bidding and I went to Harvard."

"Harvard? That's very prestigious."

"My father's a very powerful man and I had exceptional grades. That and a large donation and I was in."

"But ended up a SEAL."

"I graduated with a business degree, and was set to work with my father afterward, but I knew if I did, I'd destroy him. I hate him that much."

"Because of your mother?"

"Among other things. While I was in college, I saw him do some pretty horrible things. My hate became my motivation. He didn't see it. He didn't know that I'd take the company from him. He didn't know that's why I excelled at Harvard."

"But you didn't destroy him. Why?"

"The day I graduated, he told me I was just like him. That I was going to destroy the world. It hit me hard. I was like him. I decided right then I needed to help save the world. Ironically, that coldness in me that is like him is why I can kill. What does the psychologist in you say about that?"

"Good. It kept you alive and now you're sitting here with me. How is your father so powerful? What does he do?"

"He's the CEO and founder of Max Electronics."

I blanch. "The *Max*? The new Apple of the world?"

"Yeah well, it's not new. He just did exactly what Apple did. Worked at it for years and then finally hit with a product that took off."

"You walked away from Max," I say, and it's not really a question but a statement.

"Yes."

"All that money."

"Yes."

"All that power."

"Yes. Is that a problem for you?"

I reach out and cover his hand with mine. "No. I like you even more now."

He studies me several moments, his expression unreadable. "Because the person you're running from has money and power?"

"Because I do. That's all. Because you're you. That's even better."

"I don't tell anyone that story, but I told you."

"Why?"

"Because I want you to get to the point where you tell me your story. Not today. Not even tomorrow. But it can't be a long wait, Sierra."

"And if I'm never ready?"

"You're already ready, but for good reasons, you have to be sure you can trust me. But you're going to have to tell me."

"And if you hate me?"

"Did you kill someone and do so willingly?"

"No."

"Did you commit a crime?"

"No."

"Are you being blamed for either of those things?"

"No."

"Then I won't hate you."

Until The Beast shows up.

Chapter Eleven

ASHER

Sierra and I step outside the lunch spot and into the crowd, and I slide my arm around her waist. She twists away and steps in front of me. "Friends, Asher." A man rams into her and shoves her into me.

I settle my hands on her waist and pull her to me, molding her body to mine. And damn, I really like her body against mine. "You okay?" I ask.

"Yes." Her hand flattens on my chest and she stares at it a moment before granting me a blue-eyed stare. "Yes, now I am, I think."

And I don't believe she's talking about the crowd or the shove. "You were saying something about friends?" I ask.

"Was I?"

"Yes. I believe you were."

She holds up her phone, dodging the topic without pulling away. "What subway do I take to get to this address?"

"What's at this address?"

"A store I need to go to."

I pull her around to my side and slide her hand to my arm, giving her the choice to hold onto me or not, but letting her know what I want. Her holding on to me the way I plan to hold onto her. "I'll take you there."

"You don't have to do that," she says, and she holds on. She doesn't let go.

I cover her hand with mine and turn us down another street. "I know," I say. "But I am."

She smiles up at me and I smile down at her, and in these small moments, it would be easy to forget that she's obviously running for her life and I'm hunting a serial killer that's killed five women that look just like her. But then the next moment comes, and we're walking down the street, my senses on alert, waiting for whoever was following us back near her place. And someone *was* following us.

"Do you have an actual car?" she asks when we step onto another subway car, standing at a pole together again, and I make damn sure our legs are touching. "Do people have cars here?"

"I do," I say. "Though I rarely drive the damn thing."

"Is there a garage at your apartment? I see cars stacked on top of each other at random lots."

"Those are common and it's a nightmare to get to your car with any urgency. I live three blocks from Walker Security. The offices have a large garage where I have parking privileges. I leave it there and if I ever need it, it's usually work related anyway."

"What do you drive?"

"Do you really want to know?" I ask.

"Of course," she says. "If it's a nice car, so what? Your success is a good thing, not a bad thing. It just didn't match bartending."

"It's a BMW."

"What color and make?"

"Black. M4. What did you drive in Denver?"

"A BMW. Also black. 3 series."

"You had money."

"A 3 isn't that fancy, but yes. I did."

"And now you have nothing," I observe.

84

"I have my freedom," she says, despite the fact that she's running, which tells me once again, this is a man she's running from. Someone like my father. Someone powerful that she doesn't yet know I can take on and beat. But she will and soon.

Our train arrives at the stop and we exit together, and I am quick to place her hand back on my arm, because yeah, I want to touch her. I want her to touch me. But I also want her to feel that she isn't alone. That she can walk the streets and not look over her shoulder, because I will hurt anyone who tries to hurt her.

We walk a few blocks and reach our destination, which turns out to be a thrift store. She smiles up at me. "Now you're going to wish you wouldn't have come along. You have to wait for me to shop."

"I'll go find the 'guy' chair I'm told exists in all stores," I say. "Or so the Walker brothers tell me."

She laughs and starts shopping while I hunt down that chair that I find in the corner. Sierra starts looking through racks of clothes, and fuck, it kills me not to just take her to a real store, but I watch her, I see the way her eyes light up as she picks her items. That thousand dollars in tip money made a difference for her. She can shop and pay her own way and she's basically told me she is running from a man with money who controlled her. Taking care of her is a slippery slope. Lord only knows I've watched the Walker men try to manage a balance with their women, and they didn't have the circumstances I'm experiencing with Sierra. And fuck, again. I'm thinking of her as my woman and I just met her. I'm also sitting in a chair in a store while a woman shops. I've never done this shit. I've never been willing, but I am now. I will do anything to be close to this woman and keep her safe.

She appears in front of me with two handled bags and a smile on her beautiful face. "I'm ready. Your torture is complete."

I stand up, thinking about that protection I just vowed. "I assume you didn't use your real social at the bar?"

Her smile fades. "I told them I'd work for tips only."

"Which was smart, but it also tells the dickhead manager of that place that you're hiding from something. It makes you vulnerable."

"I know that," she says. "But I had no choice."

I slide my hand under her hair. "You have me now."

"No," she says. "I don't. Don't say—"

I kiss her, God I kiss her right here in the back corner of a store between racks of clothes. I drink this woman in, and press my tongue to hers, with the slow, savoring of her taste that I have hungered for again, every moment, since I last kissed her. "You have me now," I repeat.

"That was unfair," she whispers breathlessly. "My hands are full."

"Feel free to drop the bags and touch me, sweetheart. I won't complain."

And she does. She drops the bags and her arms wrap around me and her mouth closes over mine, and I can taste her urgency, her fear that I am going to erase. She arches into me, and I can feel a dark seed of need and torment in her. A push and pull that is a warning before she shoves against my chest. "I can't do this," she whispers, her fingers curling around my shirt. "Don't you understand? We can't do this. He will *kill you.*"

"Whoever he is, whatever he said he'd do to you —"

"My husband. He's my husband and I can't ever change that."

I feel that announcement like a punch in the chest, but when she tries to pull away, I reject her withdrawal and I feel none of my own. I hold onto her, damn glad we've managed to remain alone in this corner of the store.

"He's not your husband. He's the man you're running from and I feel no guilt over kissing you. And you shouldn't, either. Tell me who he is and I'll make this go away."

"He *will* kill you."

"Ex-SEAL, sweetheart. I promise you that I've faced much nastier people than this man, and I am not afraid."

"He is far more powerful than you are dangerous."

"You underestimate me and Walker Security. You're smart. Be smart now and let me help."

"I am smart. That's how I've stayed alive for nine months. I'm also smart enough to keep your over-confident macho ass, who thinks he can save the world and me, alive, too. Which means we are no longer friends."

She tries to pull away. I kiss her again. She tries to resist, but in a hot minute she's melting into me, but fuck, she's kissing me like it's goodbye. "Stop doing that," she whispers when I pull back.

"We're not saying goodbye."

"I just did and I'm sorry. I never should have dragged you into my hell."

The store attendant clears her throat and I'm forced to release Sierra, who grabs her bags and starts walking. I'm on her heels in an instant and following her out of the store. The minute we're clear of the door, I take one of her bags and slide my arm around her waist. "He doesn't get to win."

"He always wins."

"Not this time."

We head down the subway steps, a rush of people suffocating us, but I don't let her go. I hold her close, and when we are finally in a subway car, at another pole facing each other, there is a crush of people around us, pushing against us. I cup her face and press my cheek to hers. Her hand presses to my chest. "I won't let him have you."

Her fingers curl around my shirt, holding onto me, not pushing me away, but she won't look at me. And that's fine. We need to handle this alone. Scream. Fight. Fuck. Whatever it takes. Yeah. Fuck. We need to fuck and just get past that wall. The wall she's put up between us because of this bastard I am going to destroy.

Finally, we reach our stop, and while we wait for the doors to open, she looks at me. There is that punch of connection between us and I see it register in her face. Neither of us were looking for this, but it's here, it's happening, and I'm damn sure not letting us walk away from it for some asshole who didn't deserve her. We exit the car and head toward the street and once we're there, we don't speak but there is a distinct crackle of tension between us, an explosion that is just waiting to erupt.

We reach her apartment when the sun is setting, and when Sierra punches in the code, my spidey senses go off right about the time there is a flash in my peripheral vision. I turn and find nothing, no one, except an old lady with a walker talking to an old man. I'd say that flash was my imagination, but I'm not one to see or feel things that don't exist. And those spidey senses of mine don't want to be ignored, but I've never been quite so ready to face an enemy and end them as I am the man in Sierra's life.

Chapter Twelve

ASHER

Sierra opens the door to her building and we enter the lower level foyer, which is basically a box leading to a stairwell. The door shuts behind me, sealing us inside, and I refocus any concern I have for what, or who, might have been outside following us, to who, or what, might be inside waiting on us and for good reasons. I don't like this building or this neighborhood, I'm chasing a serial killer who likes women who look like Sierra, and she's got a crazy ex who's basically an unknown to me.

She heads up the stairs, with me closely following, and when we reach the last flight of stairs, I catch her hand. "Let me go first."

She turns to face me. "Why? Did I miss something? Did you see something?"

"No, sweetheart. Hero complex remember? Just being a macho ass who needs to save the world and you. And I figured you might want to look at my ass again."

She ignores my joke, as if it wasn't as amusing as it was. "Are you armed?"

"Yes," I say. "Does that make you feel better?"

"Since you seem worried about what's upstairs, yes. I didn't bring the mace on my outing. I brought you."

"And I'm better than mace. I've got you covered and later you can feel around and figure out where I hide that weapon." I kiss her temple, and move in front of her, beginning the walk up the next flight of stairs. The steps are long and ridiculously narrow, but it's not long until I silently declare the foyer between her apartment and one other safe and empty.

I take the bag Sierra is holding and step to the side of her door, giving her room to approach her apartment and unlock the door, but that's not what happens. Instead, she flattens against it and looks up at me. "You aren't coming in with me."

"That's a cock block if I ever heard one," I say. "I'm here. We're here."

"Thank you for today. Thank you for everything, but you aren't coming inside with me."

I set the bags down and step closer to her, pressing my hands to the door above her head. "Sierra."

"Don't say my name all low and rough like that. Like I'm your woman. I'm not."

"And if I want you to be?"

"You just met me."

"And I've never wanted to know a woman like I want to know you," I say, speaking a truth I don't even try to understand. It just is what it is.

"I'm *married,* Asher. What part of that do you not understand?"

"Let's go inside. I don't want your neighbor listening in."

"She barely speaks English and sleeps all day. She dances at some topless bar, which I know because she offered to get me a job. I'm married, Asher. I can't change that. I wish I could. I *so* wish that I could, but he will kill me before he divorces me. So, I can't ever be free."

"I'm crystal clear on your marital status and while no, I do not fuck, love, play with, or engage with married women, this is not cheating. You've been separated nine months while the man hunts you like an animal and it's time I hunt him."

"See," she says, poking my chest. "That's why we're over."

"Because you think I can't beat him when I can?"

"Because," she clutches my shirt again, "I'm saving your macho hero-complex-ass from getting killed."

I cover her hand with mine. "I know you think he's dangerous."

"I don't think. I know. I'm not emotional. I'm not irrational. I'm not damaged. He doesn't get to do that to me. And you don't get to downplay my intelligence."

"I didn't mean it like that, Sierra," I say. "I'm sorry."

"You're sorry?"

"Yes. I'm sorry. I'm not trying to be an arrogant prick. I'm just wading through the swampland here with you."

"Are you sorry enough to hear me and believe me?"

"I heard you. I believe you, but—"

"No buts," she bites out angrily and exhales, lowering her voice to calm again. "I'm rational, Asher, and I'm a smart person. I've stayed alive nine months that most people would not have survived, considering who he is and the connections he has. This isn't a man who wants to bring me back home. He wants me dead."

"Why?" I ask, assuming this is one of those me-or-nobody kind of crazy fuckers.

"I found out things about him and other very powerful people."

That wasn't the answer I expected. "What things?" I ask. "What people?"

"Go home, Asher."

I shackle her hip and walk her to me. "Let me be clear. I could have already run your fingerprints. I could have already looked into who you are, and based on what you're telling me, I'm going to. I have no choice."

"He has red flags set up. He found me in Texas and I did everything right. Almost everything right. That's another story. The bottom line though is that I barely escaped. The minute you dig around, he will come for me. And if he finds out that I'm with you, or your people, he'll kill us all. He'll make it look like a robbery or a terrorist attack, but he will kill us. He knows how to do it and survive it."

Holy fuck, I think. I believe her. "We have people high up in all of the agencies and in the government."

"Which means you could have people who are corrupted by his people," she counters.

"No one on our team is corruptible. I believe that one hundred percent."

"I thought that, too. I thought there were people I could trust. I can't take that chance again with your people. And neither can you. You need to forget you ever met me."

"I know you need time to trust me, Sierra. We'll find a path to get there."

"I already trust you, Asher. Maybe beyond reason but I do. It's not about you."

"Then give me time. Give me two weeks, until the baby shower, to show you my inner circle is trustworthy. Let me show you that we will keep this in that circle and find a way to take this guy down."

"Whatever you think I mean by that, you aren't thinking big enough. This runs too deep, too high for even you and Walker Security."

"If that's true, which I doubt, there are other options besides this damn apartment and that bar." I cup her face and stroke her cheek. "Let's go inside, sweetheart. This is not a conversation we should be having in the hallway."

Her lashes lower, dark circles on pale, creamy skin, torment in her expression before she turns to the door and flattens her hands on the wood. "Oh no," she whispers, before turning around. "I lost my key. Please tell me you really did keep a key."

"I did not."

"I never do stupid stuff like this. You're distracting me. You're making me crazy."

"As far as I'm concerned," I say, "it's fate. Now you have to come home with me." I settle my hands on her waist. "Let's go to my place. I want you there. I want you in my bed, Sierra."

"You know—"

"I heard everything you said."

"What little I have to my name is in this apartment."

"I can get you back in, but I don't have time tonight. I have to meet with my team before we head to the bar."

"It'll be like four in the morning when we get back here."

"I'll get you in tomorrow, *after* we sleep. I have to focus on the reasons I'm at the bar with no time distractions." I cup her face. "I'm of the opinion we should just fuck and get past any barrier your fuckhead ex puts between us. But I have a spare bedroom. I want you with me, but I'm not going to pressure you."

"He'll kill me before he'll let me divorce him. You get that right?"

"The only one that's going to end up dead is him, Sierra. That's a promise."

"That's the problem," she says. "He won't stop coming for me until I'm dead or he is."

"Then he gets to die."

Chapter Thirteen

Sierra

We're still standing at my apartment door when Asher pulls out his phone. "I'll get us an Uber," he says, pulling up the app.

I watch him keying information into his phone, while I question myself instead of calling the thrift store to see if they found my key. What am I doing? I can't involve him in this. I should be taking what money I have left and getting on a bus, running again, hiding. Keeping everyone but myself out of harm's way.

"Done," he says, sticking his phone in his pocket. "We'll have a ride in about ten minutes. We can wait at the door downstairs."

I nod and both of us latch on to one of my bags, but I drop mine again. "I can't do this. You don't deserve to get pulled under with me. I won't do this to you."

"Sweetheart, you already pulled me under and I wouldn't have it any other way. Let's get out of here."

"I'm not talking about whatever this is happening between us and you know it."

He sets his bag down again, closing the small space between us, and cups my face. "Fate, sweetheart. The way we met. The locked door. You belong with me."

"Fate isn't always good."

"Mark my word, and my word is golden. It's good for us and bad for that prick chasing you. Come home with me."

"Asher." I breathe out, a knot of emotion in my chest.

"I'm his worst nightmare, sweetheart. Let's get out of here."

I inhale a breath and let it out, tormented with this decision, but my gut says to stay with Asher. "Yes," I say, praying that it's the right choice.

He takes my hand and kisses it. "It's the right decision." He grabs both bags this time with one hand. "I'll go first again."

Shielding me, I think. That's what he does. He protects people. He has honor. I follow him down the stairs, with the understanding that he is so much more than tattoos and muscles, and even brains and a sense of humor. He's a man of honor who makes life choices based on that honor. A man who would die to save a life, while Devin is a man who would kill to save his own. Asher is like no one I have ever known. I like him. I could maybe *really* like him and yet, I'll never be free. Ever. *Ever.*

We reach the small foyer inside the apartment building and Asher catches my hand, leading me to the door, where he pauses to eye the street. "Our car's already here," he says, opening the door.

He exits first again, guiding me forward and keeping me tightly positioned at his side, his hand settling possessively, protectively, at my back. We walk toward a black sedan, and I sense his protectiveness. He heard me. He knows how dangerous The Beast is now. Maybe his awareness is why I don't have that sense of being watched I'd had earlier. Maybe that feeling was paranoia, which at the moment is consumed by how big Asher has suddenly become in my life. Asher holds the door for me and I slide into the back seat.

He joins me, sliding in close, me on one side of him, the bags on the other.

His hand comes down on my leg, possessive again, and in a way his touch had not been before our conversation upstairs, and I feel that touch radiating up my leg and through my body. He confirms the driver knows where he's going, and finally we're in motion, headed toward his apartment. We don't speak or even look at each other right then, but there is a shift in the air between us, as if my confessions have torn down a wall instead of placed one between us as I'd feared. We're combustible together, and I'm not sure where that leads. I was arm candy to Devin, a possession he used to soften his image. What am I to Asher? Sex? A challenge? Duty? That's all I can be at this point. I have no right to ever ask for more.

I press my hand to his and I don't even know why. *Control*, I think. I need to control where this thing between us leads. He looks over at me and without moving my hand, laces our fingers together. "Stop," he says softly.

"Stop what?"

"Thinking whatever you're thinking."

I don't know how this man reads me this well, but then, reading people is part of his job. What I used to do in a different setting, only he does it to survive and save lives. Still, I ask, because I need to know, "How do you know what I'm thinking?"

"You have the same look you had right before you bolted at lunch."

"I'm not going to bolt." *I hope*, I add silently. Running is old.

His phone buzzes with a text and he leans in and kisses me before pulling it from his pocket. I like that he does this.

I like how it makes me feel, how present he is with me. He reads the message, frowns, and types a reply.

"What's wrong?" I ask.

He types another message and then looks at me. "Something is off with Blake. I just texted his wife to ask what the hell is going on."

My unease is instant. "What do you mean by 'off'?"

He squeezes my leg. "Don't read into that. It has nothing to do with you, and if I thought it did, I'd tell you. Blake is a good man who has a hatred of disloyal, corrupt people. I promise you, he's the last person you have to worry about. Okay?"

I nod. "Yes."

"He's just cranky and unreasonable," he adds, as if I've asked. "That's not like him. I noticed it last night at the office."

"Is the job going badly?"

"It's not going well, but he rolls with that shit all the time. It's something else. Something's wrong and you don't even want someone on a job with you that isn't one hundred percent, even if they're the boss."

His phone buzzes again and he looks at the message. "Okay," he murmurs, his lips thinning. "Well, fuck." He surprises me by showing me the message that reads: *Five-year anniversary of Whitney's murder.*

Murder.

I hate that word.

"Who's Whitney?" I ask.

"His late-fiancée, and any further details are not for this car. But holy hell, Royce is losing his mind over Lauren's pregnancy and now this with Blake."

"Why is Royce losing his mind? Was the pregnancy a surprise?"

98

"No. He and Lauren have been trying to start a family for a while now. She's miscarried twice."

"Oh well, that explains it completely."

"It leaves me with Luke, the one sane brother out of the three of them right now." He leans in and whispers, "I'm either going to have to drink or fuck a hell of a lot to survive this."

My cheeks heat and I squeeze his fingers. "You're bad."

A low, rough laugh rumbles from that broad chest of his. "You'll like how bad, I promise." I never get the chance to respond. He sits up and taps the driver's seat. "This is it."

I glance out of the window to discover a red stone building in what looks like the Battery Park area, which makes sense. Asher said this is where he runs. It's also one of my favorite parts of the city, where a short walk allows you to watch the ocean crashing against a man-made shore lined with sidewalks and restaurants. Asher hands the driver a twenty-dollar tip and exits the car, with the bags in one hand again, before offering me his hand. "You live here?" I ask, scanning what is about a twenty-story half-moon-shaped building that I suspect frames part of the park.

"I do," he says as we walk toward the door. "My first contract job out of the SEALs was a job from hell that almost got me killed, but it paid for the down payment."

"One job paid your down payment in this building?"

"Not all jobs pay that well," he says, waving to the doorman as we enter the lobby with floors in gray and brown marble, chandeliers and towering high ceilings.

I glance up at him. "Am I allowed to ask what the job was? Or is that top secret?"

"A billionaire's daughter was kidnapped by a Mexican cartel and held for ransom. Blake and I had both done work in Mexico, so we teamed up and went in and got her." He motions to the security desk and we stop at the counter, where a tall, black man in a blue jacket greets us. "David, meet—"

"Kelli," Sierra supplies, obviously using a fake name. "Nice to meet you."

"Kelli can come and go as she pleases," I continue, following her lead. "And no. She doesn't have her ID. Her purse was stolen, but I need her on the approved list anyway."

He glances over at me. "I need a last name."

"Vincent," I say, which is, of course, a lie.

He has me sign a form and Asher slides his arm around my neck and pulls me close as we walk toward the elevator. "Is Sierra your real name?"

"Yes," I say, "but my apartment lease says Kelli, but I stupidly let my real name slip to the bar manager. And then I needed the job too much to turn back."

We stop at the elevator and he punches the call button. "Did you fill out any paperwork at all?"

"None," I say, "which is why I figured I could play it off and tell the manager he confused me with someone else tonight."

"Yes," he says. "Become Kelli."

The elevator dings and opens and our eyes collide, while my heart begins to race. Asher laces our fingers together and guides me into the car, punching in the code for his floor. I back against the wall. He's in front of me in an instant, and the minute his hands are on my hips, I admit, "I'm nervous," my palm settling on his chest, and I can feel his heart thundering beneath my palm, as if he's nervous, too.

"Because this matters," he says. "Because we matter."

"It's too soon to say that."

"Too soon and yet it's now. Right now, Sierra."

"I think I hit some hero complex button you have."

"Maybe I hit some hero complex button you have."

"No."

"But that's what it is for me?"

"I don't know," I say.

"I do. I don't fuck a woman who I see as my duty. You're not my duty, Sierra. And you don't belong to him anymore." He presses his cheek to mine, his lips finding my ear. "I'm going to make you forget he ever touched you."

I feel those words in every possible way. My sex clenches. My nipples tighten. My body is tingling all over, while my fingers close around his shirt, and when I would respond, the elevator dings. Asher pulls back, and he kisses me hard and fast before lacing our fingers together.

We exit the car and he slides his arm around my shoulders, and settles me close to his big body. We round a corner that way and I'm taken off guard by how immediately we're at his door. He keys in a code at his door, pops it open, and reaches inside to flip on the light. When I expect us to simply enter, he drops the bags and pulls me in front of him, his hands on my arms, mouth back to my ear. "I have about ten different places that I could take you to keep you safe. You're here because I want you here." He releases me, his hands going to either side of the door, and I understand why. He wants me to be here because I want to be here, too. There's no question in my mind that I want to be with Asher.

I walk inside and on some level I know that's the moment that our fate is sealed, his to mine and mine to his.

Chapter Fourteen

ASHER

Sierra walks into my apartment. I enter behind her, dropping her bags inside the doorway, and flipping the locks, my need for this woman a thundering rush of adrenaline that doesn't just surge. It pumps through me every second that I'm with her, and I pause just inside the entryway, inhaling the sweet floral scent of her lingering in the air around me, on my skin. I don't know where tonight leads, besides a whole lot of us fucking and me fucking up her ex, but those are good places to start.

I rotate to find her walking into the kitchen. No, she's *running*. That's the word that comes to mind. She's afraid of me and us because she's afraid of *him* and that's a barrier I have to remove. I follow her, closing the space between us, and she steps behind the island, the wall of appliances behind her, her hands on the wooden counter top. "I love your apartment," she says as I stop at the end cap. "The island is beautiful."

She's beautiful and breathless for the wrong reason: she's still nervous. I round the island to her side, and she attempts to dart the other way. I catch her hand, and she turns to face me. "Hi," she says, her cheeks flushing a pretty pink.

"Hi," I say, walking her to me and turning her to press her back to the island, her body between me and the counter.

She laughs, a soft, sweet musical sound that I feel in my cock and about ten other ways. In my fucking chest, and I don't try to understand it now. "Did I really just say 'hi'?"

"Yes," I say, cupping her face. "And it was actually perfect."

"Asher," she whispers. "You—"

"Need to kiss you really fucking badly," I say, and I make it happen. I kiss her, a deep stroke of tongue against tongue that ignites fire between us. I deepen the kiss, molding her closer, and we're on fire. Kissing, touching, my hands caressing her waist, her breasts, wanting her next to me. But when I slip beneath her shirt, my palm pressed to the soft skin there, she grabs my hand. "Asher, wait," she pants out.

"Wait?" I ask, pained just saying that word.

"I'm married. I suddenly feel very guilty."

Brakes officially on. I press my hands to the counter on either side of her and lift my body from hers. "You still love him." And fuck that idea punches me in the chest.

"God no," she says, flattening her hand on my chest. "No. I don't remember ever loving him."

"You married him."

"I know I did. He was—He is a decade older. I met him at a party, a charity event I was hosting. He was the eligible bachelor everyone wanted and he wanted me. I feel like I was worlds younger then. The billionaire rockstar businessman."

"Billionaire." My lips thin. "I suddenly wish I hadn't given away all my money."

"Don't say that," she says, her hand settling on my cheek. "I don't want your money. I hated his money. I hated it and

104

him beyond words, but I was trapped. He threatened my mother long before I even knew the things I know now. I didn't love him. At most, I was stupidly young and enamored."

"How long were you with him?"

"Two years. I dated him for one of those, but he traveled, and he was different then. A gentleman. Someone who cared. He introduced me to my mentor. He got me the internship."

Her mentor that is a forensic psychologist, I think. He's law enforcement or government. And a billionaire. She's right. He's dangerous.

"The minute I married him, though," she continues, "he changed. The minute I crossed him, he threatened my mother and gave me reason to believe him."

"He hit you."

"He did a lot of things."

"But you feel guilty with me."

"My guilt isn't about him, Asher. It's you. I can't get rid of him. Ever. I don't want you to regret this. I don't want you to—"

Brakes off. I kiss her again, a deep, kiss-the-hell-out-of-her kiss, and then I say, "Does that taste like regret?" But I don't wait for an answer. I kiss her again, licking into her mouth and this time, she doesn't pull back, there is no reserve in me or her. I need her. She needs me. I taste that on her lips. And I don't like to be needed, but I do now. I do with her.

I press her shirt up, and cup her breast again, pulling down the lace of her bra to stroke her nipple. She arches into the touch, and I caress her shirt upward, intending to take it off, but she catches it. "I need to tell you something first."

"Can you tell me naked?"

105

"No," she says. "Not this."

I inch back and look at her and she adds, "I have a scar."
I go stone cold still. "Did he—?"

"No. It was a car accident three months after I married him. I almost died."

And now his ability to control her makes sense. That's when he changed. That's when he shifted the power between them. "Sweetheart, I have a train wreck of scars on my body. I'll show you mine, if you'll show me yours."

"I'm not an insecure person, but this—"

I kiss her. "I'll go first." I pull my shirt over my head, toss it on the counter and then present her with my right arm, and trace the deep scar there. "Did you not notice it?" I ask.

She reaches up and traces the line. "No," she says, looking up at me. "I was too busy noticing...other things."

"My ink."

"That too," she says. "I like it, but it's just a bonus. Did you ink up to cover the scar?"

"No. I had to have the ink fixed after the damn thing healed."

"How did you get it?"

"How else? A dirty bastard with a knife." I reach down and unbutton and unzip my pants, pulling them down enough to show her the deep scar on my hip. "Shrapnel," I say.

She presses her hand under my pants and covers the scar. "The battle wounds of a hero."

I pull her to me, my hand under her hair at her neck. "Careful where you touch."

"Does it hurt?"

"No," I say. "But you'll make me forget we're doing show and tell right now." I kiss her. "I have another on my ass.

You ready for that one, or do you want to show me yours first?"

"I'm pretty sure the entire female population is ready for that one," she says.

"You're the only woman who I want to be ready for anything."

"Asher, you're..."

"I'm what?"

"Different."

"Different than him."

"Oh yes. So different. But different than anyone I've ever known."

"Show me the scar, sweetheart. Okay?"

"Why don't I care when you call me sweetheart now?"

"I don't know. I'm still asking you to get naked."

She laughs. "Yes. You are."

"Show me," I say gently.

"It's on my stomach."

I lower myself to my knee in front of her. "Can I?" I ask.

"Yes," she says, pulling her shirt up.

I unbutton and unzip her pants and as I pull the zipper down she trembles with anticipation and not the kind I want her to feel. This scar really bothers her and I'm more curious than ever now. Her jeans are low on her hips and I easily slide them down just enough to see the damage done to her skin from hip to hip and up to her belly button. I don't react, but fuck. It's bad. Really bad. I look up at her. "Metal or glass?"

"Both," she says.

I press my lips to her belly and she trembles again under my kiss. And holy hell, my mind flashes to war scenes I've lived, to images of shrapnel in bodies that killed innocent people I couldn't save. She could have died from this. I can't believe she didn't. "It's okay, Asher," she says when I don't immediately react. "I know it's ugly and—"

"No," I say. "It's not ugly." I kiss her belly again and stand up, my hands settling on her shoulders. "I've seen people with metal in their bodies, and it's too easy for me to imagine metal and glass, in your body. It's not something you want to know someone you care about experienced." I stroke hair from her face. "But, sweetheart. You're beautiful. Stunning. That scar does nothing to detract from that. In fact, it just reminds me what a survivor you are."

"I can't have kids. It damaged me. I can't—I can't *ever* have kids."

"Then I don't have to use a condom, right?"

"Asher, please. This is a big deal to me."

"I don't want kids. I've seen too many people die. *Kids* die. I can't have one of my own that could die. If you want kids—"

"Don't say adopt. I've heard that. I don't want to hear that, and I don't want to adopt. I don't want kids."

She doesn't have to say more. The bastard husband wanted kids and made her pay when she couldn't have them. He probably mocked her scar. He probably did a lot of things I don't want to think about until I stand in front of him, and I will. "This is us. We decide what matters for us. Yes?"

"Yes," she says.

"So," I say, trying to shift the mood. "No condom, right?"

She rewards me with that soft, sweet laugh of hers. "No. We don't have to use a condom."

"Then it's official," I say. "You're the perfect woman."

She surprises me then and leans into me, pushing to her toes and pressing her lips to mine, her hand on my cheek. And for a moment, I let her mouth linger against mine, just enjoying the first time that she's actually kissed me, but I am too hungry and hot for her to last long. My mouth slants over hers, my tongue licking into her mouth, at the exact moment the doorbell rings.

"Holy fuck," I murmur against her lips. "I feel like I'm never going to actually get you naked."

"You do know we only just met, right?" she teases. "It's not been long."

"It feels like a lifetime of me wanting inside you, sweetheart. And since I only have a few people on my approved list, this is a Walker keeping me from being there." I kiss her. "Fix your clothes. You're for me, not them." I grab my shirt.

"Did you miss your meeting?" she asks, attending to her zipper, which she pulls up while I really just want to pull it back down.

I pull on my shirt and glance at my watch. "I have an hour and a half before I have to be at the office."

"Should I go someplace?" she asks. "Another room or—"

"You stay right here, with me. That works just fine." I kiss her and head to the door, zipping up my pants on the way. The bell rings again and I open the door. "Hold your fucking horses," I say as I bring my father in his six-thousand-dollar blue pinstriped suit into view.

"Hello, son."

"You're not on my approved list."

"I bought the building. I'm on everyone's approved list."

"Of course you did," I say, considering he's always trying to own me. "What do you want?"

"Invite me in."

"Not really feeling that kind of love right now."

"Invite me in, son."

I open the door wider and leave him there, walking back toward the kitchen. Sierra's behind the island and she mouths, "Your father?"

"Unfortunately, yes," I say, rounding the island to stand next to her.

"Should I go somewhere?" she asks again.

"Stay with me," I say again as well, right as my father appears at the other side of the island. I look at him now the way Sierra might see him, a fifty-five-year-old version of me when I had no tats, and my hair was short. I hate that image. I hate anything that reminds me that this man and I are blood.

"I see we have company," he says, eyeing Sierra. "And you would be?"

"With him," she replies, repeating what I told her, which is not only a smart response considering her circumstances, but an amusing one. No one talks around my father but me, and now Sierra. He intimidates the damn wind, but not her. But then, she has practice with men like him. Her ex, I realize now, is someone quite like my father. And I'm his fucking son, who many think is a flip of a switch from becoming his father. Or, to Sierra, a clone of the man who is trying to kill her.

Chapter Fifteen

ASHER

I look at my father, who is looking at Sierra and I don't like it. "Why are you here?" I demand.

He cuts his gaze to me. "Right to business," he says. "A chip off the old block. The company is doing a Wounded Warrior Project black tie fundraiser just before Thanksgiving. We've sent you two invitations and left you four messages. It would be appropriate, as my son and a veteran, as well as a distinguished SEAL, to attend."

"Distinguished," I say. "Now I'm a distinguished SEAL? Is that what you're feeding the stockholders when you explain why I'm not working for you?"

"They're impressed, as they should be."

I laugh without humor. "Should we tell them that you disinherited me for becoming a distinguished SEAL?"

"Is that what you want? The money? I'll write you a damn check if you'll put an end to this silliness. Take your seat at the table where you belong."

"Yes," I say. "Please write the check. Then I'll show up at the event, where I'll re-write the check to the Wounded Warrior Project charity. Then all will be well in my world."

He reaches into his pocket and sets the invitation on the counter. "Be there. It would look like shit to your fellow servicemen if a distinguished SEAL couldn't spare a few hours on their behalf. And bring your plus one, if you can afford to buy her a dress. She's a hell of a lot prettier than you these days."

He turns to leave and Sierra calls out, "Because what woman could afford to buy her own dress, right?"

And there it is. Every nerve my father can hit for Sierra, which her ex must have hit, too, already surfacing. I know my father and I know exactly what comes next. *Words are weapons,* he used to tell me. *They can be used against you. Speak less and listen more.* And that piece of advice is what he uses against Sierra now. He stops and turns to look at her, giving her an amused, arrogant look, before he simply says nothing and leaves. Translation: You poor pathetic little girl are simply beneath a reply.

I don't pursue him. I don't look at Sierra, not yet. I stand there, hands pressed to the counter, and listen to his footsteps, waiting for the door to shut. The minute it does, I push off the counter, and walk across the room and lock the door. *Fucker.* He's smart enough to assume Sierra matters to me or she wouldn't be here. He was jockeying for a way to use her against me and he did. He messed with her head. I cross the room and Sierra is now at the end cap of the island waiting on me, leaning on the counter. She watches my every step, her expression unreadable.

I stop in front of her, and before I can speak, she says, "I'm sorry."

"Why would you be sorry? He's the ass."

"I know what just happened," she says. "He used me against me and me against you. I can see it now, but I still let it happen."

"That's not on you, Sierra."

"Yes, it is. Because Dev—The Beast, that's what I call him in my head—my ex—my fucking husband I can't get rid of, is just like your father. And I know, I know so well, how he watched me from the moment he got here and looked for a trigger. And I let it happen."

She almost said his name. Dev. That has to stand for Devlin or Devin, or hell, maybe the devil, but right now he isn't the issue. Right now, I need her to see me, not my father. Not The Beast, as she apparently calls him. I pull her to me, my hand sliding under her hair. "I'm not him. I'm not my father."

"I know that."

"You can't know that, Sierra. You don't know me well enough to know that, but you will. I promise you, you will." I close my mouth over hers, tongue stroking hers, and there is no resistance in her. She gives a soft little moan, and melts into me, her soft curves pressed against me, ensuring I'm hard all over. And holy hell, I could get lost in her, I could forget everything I hate about my father right now, and I want to, but I don't let that happen. I don't make her an escape fuck. Not Sierra. Not the first time. "We don't have time to do this right and I want to do it right," I say, tearing my mouth from hers.

"We both have anger issues right now we need to deal with," she says, "and you said, we needed to just fuck and get past it. So, let's just fuck and forget and then—"

I don't need to be told twice. I kiss her and this time when my hands slide up her shirt, I don't stop and she doesn't stop me. I pull it up and over her head and follow with mine again. Her hands are on my chest before I finish tossing it away. "I really do like your ink," she says, her hands traveling down my arms.

"Show me," I say, removing a money clip just below her bra and tossing it aside.

"I will," she promises, as I reach up and unclip the front clasp of her bra. I part the silk cups and my gaze lowers to her high breasts and tight little pink nipples. Her body is perfect. Everything about her is perfect. My eyes lift to hers, and caress the straps from her shoulder, and then flatten my hand between her shoulder blades, and mold her naked breasts to my naked chest. "Show me now."

"I will," she says, her voice a raspy, sexy, desire-laden turn on that makes me want to kiss her and fuck, even more than I wanted to kiss her and fuck her before. I kiss her again, drinking in the taste of her, all sweet honey and passion, my lips to her lips. My tongue to her tongue. My hand on her backside.

"Asher I need—"

"I need," I say, scooping her up and her legs wrap my hips, which is exactly where I want them. Where I want her. Next to me, pressed to me...*riding me.* She clings to my shoulders, and I carry her into the living room on the opposite side of the stairwell, a room hugged by red brick with high-arched, deep windows that don't quite reach the floor or ceiling. I set her down on the thick pile of the brown rug in front of a leather couch.

Her hands caress over my arms, tracing the colorful designs in my ink, one of her palms flattening on my stomach, just above my jeans, fingers slipping into the very top of my waistband, then down over my zipper. I inhale as she strokes the thick ridge of my erection through my pants, the image of her soft little hand wrapping on my cock, a perfect fantasy, she will no doubt make real, and yet I want something indefinably more with this woman. I slip my hand under her hair and pull her to me. "More," I say, voicing that thought, my free hand unzipping her pants. "Give me more." I kiss her, a fast, deep, passionate kiss that ends with me setting her away from me. "Undress," I say, planning to do the same. I sit down on the couch and she sits down on the ottoman just behind her. She takes off her shoes.

I remove my ankle holster and show it to her. "The hidden weapon."

"And I didn't even have to look for it," she says.

"Next time," I say, setting it on the couch and pulling off my boots.

I stand then, digging my phone from my pocket and tossing it on the couch. She's still sitting, watching me and I let her. "I'll go first again," I say, and she doesn't argue. She just watches me with big blue eyes while I watch her, looking for any signs she feels she's in over her head, or moving too fast, but I find none.

I strip my jeans and my underwear away in a fast, swift move. My hands out to my sides, my cock hard between us. "I'm all yours, *Sierra*."

She doesn't look away. She's bold with her inspection, her gaze traveling my body before reaching my eyes. "Am I allowed to say you're beautiful, or is there some other word I'm supposed to say?"

"For a guy, you get naked and you show him with your hands and your mouth."

She laughs, just like I hoped. "The things you say."

"I say it how I see it, and I'm not seeing it, not all of it." I step to her, and take her hand, pulling her to her feet. "Come on, sweetheart. I want time we don't have, and I need those pants of yours off."

She reaches for her pants and I consider sitting down, watching her like she watched me. And I would any other time, but not when I am aware of anything that might make her feel she's performing for me, aware that The Beast demanded much of her. Threatened her. Controlled her and I have zero doubt that extended to sex. No. The time for me

115

to sit and watch Sierra is not now. It's when she makes that decision or gives me some signal that she's ready for more and she's not now. Not this first time. Not until she really does trust me.

She slips her pants and panties down her long legs and then off, and I'm left with creamy white skin and perfect curves. I mold her to me, my cock at her hip, one of her breasts in my hand, my fingers tweaking her nipple. I'm rewarded with her arched back, and a tiny, sexy pant. "I'm going to make him hurt the way he made you afraid."

Her hands grip my arms. "You can't—"

"I can," I say, "and one day you'll understand that the good guys aren't less brutal or deadly than the bad guys. We're still killers. We're just the killers who do it for the right side of the law. Maybe that will give you peace. Maybe that will make you hate me, too, but I can't change it. And neither can he."

I don't give her a chance to reply, and I don't let myself think about how ultimately, a killer to her might really be the enemy no matter what. Because I have killed. Because I'll kill again. And so, I kiss her again, long and deep, and then I sit down, pulling her between my legs, looking up at her, searching her face, and looking for the answer to what it is I feel with her, why I feel anything but lust, when lust is all I ever feel. Looking for the answer to the question I just kissed her to avoid asking: While I fall for her, and she gets to know the killer in me, will she hate me?"

She reaches down and cups my cheek. I lean into the touch, and then take her hand and kiss her palm. I release it and my attention goes to her scar again, and I trace the deep and brutal edges of it, before glancing up at her again. "I can't tell you that the scar is sexy, Sierra, because nothing that hurt you is ever going to be sexy to me. But you are. So fucking sexy." I press my lips to her belly and caress my hand over her hip and then down between her legs, until my finger teases her clit. She gasps and arches into me and I press into the wet heat of her sex. And while I want to just think about how wet and hot she is, I noticed that she's shaved, and I can't help but wonder if she's hiding her real hair color. I don't even want to think why she fears anyone would get that close.

She grabs my shoulders, and just when I would slip two fingers inside her, she pants out, "We have no time, remember? We're supposed to just fuck and—"

I pull her into my lap, straddling me, my erection between us, and I am hit with how much it must have taken for her to trust me, to be here like this with me right now. Nine months of trusting no one. Years of what he did to her. "I won't ever hurt you."

"I know that," she says, "and don't tell me I don't. I do. I see who you are. I feel who you are. And I—I just know."

She doesn't, but that's okay. She wants to believe she does, but I want her to *know* it. I want what she knows to be real and that's a contradiction to how much I need her to know that I'm the killer that can kill him. Those things fall to the side now though. Now I just want inside her. Now I just want to fuck her. I drag her mouth to mine and lift her, pressing my cock inside of her. She grabs my shoulders and does this slow, driving-me-wild slide down my cock, until I'm buried inside her, all her wet, tight heat, clamping down on me.

"And now we did it," she whispers. "We're past it."

"No," I say, pulling her down while thrusting into her, "now we're just getting started."

She pants out a breath, her lashes fluttering, and I want to kiss her, but I want to watch even more. "Ride me, sweetheart," I say. "Show me you know I'm here."

She laughs. "Like I could not know that fact right now, Asher."

"I'm not sure you do," I say, thrusting into her, making sure she damn well does know. She leans into me and holds onto my shoulders, and we start this slow bump and grind that I could savor for a long damn time, but we really don't have time. I pull her mouth to mine and the minute our tongues touch, we snap. We start a frenzied thrust and ride, and I wrap my arm around her waist, dragging her down against me, pumping into her, until she stiffens on the edge of release, and tries to bury her head in my neck.

"No," I say, pulling her forehead to mine. "Stay right here with me." I pause, and remembering my promise, I add, "*Sierra.*"

"*Asher,*" she pants out in a raspy laugh before sucking in a breath as she starts trembling and quaking, her sex clenching around my cock. And oh yeah. That's just what I need. I am there with her, holding onto her, and pulling her down on top of me one last time as I thrust into release. We go up together and we come down together, and I know the moment we're present, outside those moments of intense pleasure, again, our foreheads still melded together.

"Now we did it," she says and we both laugh.

"Yes," I say. "Now we did it."

She cups my face and leans back to look at me. "Any regrets?"

"Regrets? Sweetheart, I'm ready to go again. Okay. Well. In a few minutes."

She laughs and my phone rings on the couch where I'd set it. I groan and reach for it. At least they waited until afterward."

She tries to get up and I hold onto her. "I'll carry you to the bathroom," I say.

"But your call—"

I answer the line. "Yeah, Blake," I say, standing up with Sierra in my arms, me still inside her, as I walk toward the downstairs bathroom, under the stairs.

"I pulled Kyle off the job," he says.

"Why?" I ask settling Sierra on the stone countertop in the spare bathroom and flipping on the light before handing her a hand towel.

"Just get to the office." He hangs up and I set the phone down next to Sierra. "I need to get to the office."

"I cannot believe you were talking to whoever that was while inside me."

"I like being inside you," I say, but I pull out of her and she presses the towel between her legs. "We need to go, though," I add. "Hurry and dress. My bedroom and bathroom are at the top of the stairs." I set her on the floor.

"*We* need to go?"

"I told you. I want you to get to know my inner circle and so yes. We need to go."

"Asher, I don't know about this."

"Do you trust, Luke?"

"I have a good feeling about Luke, yes."

"You'll feel the same about the rest of the team. Scout's honor. Okay, SEAL's honor. I was never a fucking scout. That uniform was ridiculous." I kiss her. "Hurry up."

I exit the bathroom and walk back into the living room, pulling on my pants. Sierra joins me and picks up her clothes. "I'm going to grab my bags, and go dress upstairs."

I nod and she hurries away. I'm pulling on my shirt when I hear her walking up the stairs. Normally I would follow her to my bedroom, but my mind is on Blake's odd behavior and his secrecy over pulling Kyle off the job. There's more of a problem going on here than the anniversary of Whitney's murder. And problems with the Walker clan are dangerous.

Chapter Sixteen

Sierra

For the first time in what feels like years, I can't feel the nightmare of Devin's hands on my body. I feel Asher's. I feel a sense of freedom from The Beast that I didn't believe possible, and I have Asher to thank for that. But at what price to Asher? I don't let myself think about the implications of that question for too long. Not now when I'm naked and charging up a set of stairs with bags in my hands. Not even when I reach his bedroom, which smells all earthy and spicy like him, and now me. I can smell him on my skin. Not even when I rush across the brown wooden floor with a sanded finish to pass his massive bed, framed by a brown leather headboard. A bed I will sleep in with him tonight.

I hold my thoughts at bay until I'm standing inside his bathroom, fully dressed, with my new, used lace-up boots on, my money belt back around my waist, and my wild mess of hair brushed. A mess created by Asher's fingers. Hair brushed with his brush that I found in a drawer of the dark brown cabinets beneath his double sinks. That's how entwined my life has become with his in a blink of an eye. I'm sharing his brush, which is somehow far more intimate than just fucking. Because what just happened downstairs, which was supposed to be just fucking, wasn't just fucking at all. My hand goes to my belly, to the scars there that run far deeper than the surface. Asher knew that, he understood, but he doesn't know why, even if he suspects. That accident, the way the scars messed with my head afterward, those things weakened me for long enough to empower Devin, every nasty part of him, of which there are many.

I shove aside that thought and push off the counter, snatching my new, also used, black leather purse from the thrift store bag that I've set next to the dark wood edged egg-shaped tub. I study the purse, as I did in the store, almost certain it's a real Chanel, which is a real treat for a girl with a bar tip trust fund and nothing more.

I slip it over my head and chest and let the small bag rest at my hip, despite it being ridiculously empty. I have no make-up with me. I have no key, but it serves a purpose. I lift my shirt up, and unzip the money pouch, removing a twenty and sticking it in the side pocket of the purse for easy access. I then take some cash and stick it in my boot. I straighten and I'm suddenly aware of Asher standing in the archway of the door. "You carry the cash with you because you're afraid you'll have to run," he says.

"Yes," I say, one part of my brain thinking about those colorful inked arms of his holding me, while the other thinks about Texas and the stupid moves I'd made there that cost me thousands of dollars. "I carry a purse so that anyone who tries to steal from me, thinks they got everything I have."

"All smart decisions most people wouldn't think about. I'd never leave cash in that shithole of an apartment regardless of the lock I installed, but you're here now. Keep a couple hundred dollars with you. No more until I can make other arrangements for you." I'd ask what arrangements he means, but he's already continued with his thought. "You can leave the rest in my safe."

He pushes off the archway and motions me to the closet, leading the way inside, where he flips on the light. I join him in the large walk-in with a bench in the center and built-in wooden cabinets. He stops in front of one of them, a row of suits beside him that I don't expect, but I should. I've met his father. I know he went to Harvard. Asher opens the cabinet and displays a safe, turning the lock's circular combination. "50-11-33," he says, opening the door to display a wooden box with a gun sitting on top.

I remove two hundred dollars for my money belt, and then stick the belt in the safe, and the cash in my boot. "If you get into trouble," Asher says, "you call me. If you can't call me, meet me at the Hard Rock in Times Square. Sit in the bar. Wait for me and don't take public transportation of any kind to get there. That's where they'll look for you. Walk there."

"Why the Hard Rock?"

"It's busy, with multiple levels, and not where anyone would expect you to go. They expect you to be on the move, and when you're on the move, you might find them, and miss me. Stay put. Be the needle in a haystack and New York City is one hell of a haystack."

"That haystack is exactly why I came here despite the high cost of living."

"It's expensive, but still a good decision." He taps the box in the safe. "My emergency funds, ammo, and travel documents. If at any time you think you need to leave, take the cash and the gun, and leave my documents in case I need them to help you. I'll get you documents for your fake name and I'll teach you to shoot."

"You can get me documents?"

"Yes, I can, and I will, and one of the reasons I want you to come with me today is to see Blake. He's a world class hacker. My father is going to look into you. He'll ask for the name at the security desk and since he bought the building, he'll get it. I want him, and anyone else looking, to find you. The Kelli version of you, and Blake can make that happen."

"Thank you, Asher. I hope I don't ever need the emergency resources, but there is more comfort than I can express in knowing that I have them."

"The only way to ensure that never happens is to destroy him before he comes for you." He shuts the safe. "And when you trust me enough to give me his name, I will."

"Know your friends and your enemies," I say. "That's a lesson I learned the hard way in Texas, when I called someone I thought could be trusted. Someone in law enforcement, Asher. High up and well-respected. I knew him for over a year. I've given you my trust in a blink of an eye. To ask me to trust your inner circle as fast is a wall I just can't climb at the same speed."

He studies me for several beats, his expression unreadable but obviously tense. "Let's go." He doesn't touch me. In fact, he steps around me and starts walking. He's angry and I get it. I have secrets. He's protecting me despite those secrets and I don't know what to do. I've already gone so far out of my comfort zone with Asher, but then, he is doing all of these things for me without any demand for anything in return. Even my secrets.

I follow him and by the time I catch up he's already halfway down the stairs. I rush down them and he's on the phone at the door when I reach the living room. "Twenty more minutes," Asher says, glancing at his watch. "It's only seven," He unlocks the front door but doesn't open it. "I'll have an hour when I get there. Yes, Blake." He turns to face me as I join him. "I'm aware you're in a pissy mood and since that hasn't happened since you've been with Kara, we obviously need to talk." He ends the call and slips his phone back into his pocket. "The code is 2379," he says as he opens the door and we step into the hallway. "You don't need a key. I'll install the app on your phone tomorrow."

"You're angry."

"No, Sierra. I'm not angry. I'm just thinking."

"But you're feeling that regret now, aren't you?" I ask, deciding that is worse than his anger.

"I'm just thinking, Sierra," he repeats.

"About what?"

"Know your friends and enemies. That's a profound and accurate statement. I understand what happened in Texas. I get it. You were betrayed by someone that resembles the people in my circles. But if you judge me and my people by him and his people, we're over before we started and we're also all going to end up dead." He steps to me. "Think outside your box."

"I have. That's why I tried to walk away from you."

"If that's what you want, Sierra, I'll let you go, but it's not what I want, and someone alone is not better. It's just alone." He turns to open the door. I catch his arm.

"I'm about to take you to the Walker offices. I'm about to invite you into their safe zone. And I'm about to ask my boss, who despite his asshole mood is a good man, to give you the documentation you need to leave the country, while I've given you access to the cash. I'm doing this despite the fact that when you're the kind of good guys we are, we make a lot of nasty enemies that could use someone like you to attack us. And I'm doing it, because you, despite all logic and time, already matter to me. Because I choose to trust you even if that makes me a fool, but I cannot allow that to hurt my friends who are my family."

I press my fingers to my temples. "I don't know what to do, Asher. I see your point of view. I see it clearly, but if you really see mine, you know why I can't just blindly trust anyone, and yet I have you. Don't ask for the documents yet. Wait until you trust me, and I'll wait to ask for that kind of help when you trust me."

"You didn't ask. That's the thing, Sierra. I'm not holding my help ransom."

"I don't know what to do, Asher. We're trying to get someplace together that defies time but requires it. Either let me go, at least for now, or don't involve them. Actually, I need to go."

He steps to me, his hand at my hip. "Is that what you want? Do you want me to let you go?"

No, I think, but I know that's me being selfish, so I say, "Yes."

His hand falls away and he takes a step back, as if I've slapped him or hurt him. I don't expect his reaction. I don't expect the moment he turns around and presses his hands on the door, his head lowering, as if grappling with what to do next. Nor do I expect to feel the loss of his touch. Or the promise of losing so much more by losing him. I can't leave him, and us, like this. I move toward him, and slide between him and the door, pressing my hand to his chest. "Not because I don't want you. Not because I don't want to see what this is between us. Because this is the only way I can keep you and them safe."

His hand slides under my hair and cups my neck and he drags me close. "That's not a good answer. I don't wake up any day of my life expecting to be safe and neither do they. We expect to make a difference. And let me be clear: You can choose not to be in my bed, but I won't let you end up dead."

"You know that I want to be in your bed, Asher."

"I'll give you time Sierra, but remember this. Every minute I give you is a minute I give your Beast."

Chapter Seventeen

Sierra

Every minute I give you is a minute I give your Beast.

Asher says those words and then kisses me. One of those curl-my-toes, feel-his-tongue-all-over-my-body kind of kisses I'm coming to expect from Asher. When it's over, he takes my hand and leads me to the hallway, and once he's keyed in his door code that he has me repeat, we head to the elevator. We don't speak on the ride down because there are two things in the air. That kiss and his words. No, not his words: The Beast. He's the threat that both divides us and pulls us together.

Once we're in the lobby, Asher links the fingers of one of our hands and leads me to the shop just inside the exit. "Fill your purse with things women fill their purses with. That way if anyone grabs it, it won't raise questions. Put what you need on my account and get what you need for the morning. They'll send it to the room, but hurry. I need to get to the office." He kisses me. "I need to call Luke about tonight. I'll be just outside the door."

I start to walk away, but I'm aware of him telling me who he's calling and why. I'm aware of him trying to earn my trust and I turn around and kiss him. "Thank you."

"For what?"

"Everything," I say.

Now, I turn away from him and walk into the store. I grab random items and I make it fast. I charge Asher's account because it's faster and easier, but I keep the receipt. Asher meets me at the door, obviously done with his call. Hand in hand, we head outside into the dark, and judging from the thunder, a potentially stormy night. Asher guides me right and we head down the sidewalk.

"Walker Security is three blocks down," he tells me. "The brothers don't just own the building and the garage I mentioned. They live there. I'm telling you this for a reason. There is always someone present in their location who is as deadly as anyone chasing you. I'm going to make sure you have about ten numbers in your phone you can call."

I don't argue. I've claimed to be smart. I'm going to back it up with actions and having a resource of people to help me is smart, but I've also been taught by way of my near capture in Texas, that you never assume that association, job title, or even brief encounters means someone is honorable or safe. I'll pick whose number I'm willing to use and do so cautiously.

We reach the Walker building which is a white stone structure that is high and narrow, like so many in the city. Asher uses a security code and a key to open the door. We enter the business office to find the lobby, which has several mahogany desks and a waiting area with leather chairs vacant. "My meeting is in the conference room," Asher says. "I'll come get you to meet them when we're done." He glances at his watch. "We need to be at the bar in an hour."

"I'm fine waiting. I want to freshen up anyway. Where's the bathroom?"

"I'll show you," he says, leading me down a hallway.

We stop at a doorway and he motions to an open door. "I'll be there if you need me." He kisses me—he's always kissing me, and I like it—and then heads toward his room.

I open the bathroom door and flip on the light to find a simple single-stall bathroom with a sink and mirror, and a fancy marbled counter top. There is also a fancy soap dispenser on one side of the sink and a small vase of flowers on the other. I smile with the certainty that there has been a female intervention in an all-male environment. Not that men can't be in touch with their feminine sides, but I've met Asher and Luke so far and talked to Blake. None of them strike me as the types that would do flowers and fancy soaps.

I start to shut the door, but I'm just fixing my make-up and the idea of being in a strange place and not knowing what is sneaking up on me stirs the claustrophobic sensation I've battled since the car accident. Or maybe since The Beast entered my life. I'm pretty sure it started then, and the accident drove it to full realization. I leave the door open and walk to the sink, applying a rose-colored lipstick when I hear footsteps pass the door, as if there are people joining the meeting. A minute later, Asher's voice lifts in the air. "Why did you pull Kyle off the job? What aren't you telling me, Blake?"

I suck in a breath with the realization that I can hear their conversation. "I have intel that Alvarez might be alive," a male voice that I recognize as Blake's replies.

"Our worst fear when his body wasn't discovered," a female says.

"I was there, Kara," Asher says. "Your sister pushed him out of a chopper. He couldn't have survived that."

"Unless he did," Blake says.

"No," Asher says. "That can't be true. I'm telling you. No one could survive that. You're both letting your fears that he'll come for Myla again affect you. What does Kyle say about this?"

"I sent Kyle and Myla to Rome on the pretense of doing a job for Kayden Wilkens."

Asher grimaces. "Pretense? Does that mean you mislead him? Did you even tell Kyle what's going on?"

Blake's jaw sets hard. "Not yet."

"You're fucking kidding me," Asher snaps. "Myla's his wife."

"And my sister," Kara chimes in.

"And," Asher says. "The woman Alvarez picked out of a harem of kidnapped women to make his own. She was brutalized by that man. She and Kyle have a right to know."

He's right, I think, leaning on the wall. Though, of course, I don't completely understand what is going on, but if Myla was kidnapped by this man, she needs to know she's at risk.

"We don't want to create panic," Blake says. "And Kayden Wilkens is not only a friend to Walker Security, he's the equivalent to the mafia in Italy and Rome, if the mafia had a good version. He's the balance keeper there and he's far more powerful that Alvarez and his cartel have ever been. They're staying with him and his wife, Ella, and Kayden knows he's protecting them."

This is Kara's sister. How can she leave her in the dark like this?

"This is your sister," Asher says to Kara, following my thoughts exactly. "This is okay with you?"

"Myla went through hell," she says, her tone high, defensive. "If this is fake news, I don't want her traumatized. We need to know for sure. And she's using this time to push her clothing line in Europe. She's excited."

"Right now," Blake says. "We have a serial killer to catch and a schedule to keep. Let's talk about Ju-Ju."

I straighten. Serial killer? Ju-Ju is a serial killer?

"With the time in mind and five dead girls to think about," Asher says, "we'll talk about Ju-Ju now, but tomorrow, we're talking about Kyle, Myla, and Alvarez."

I suck in a breath. Five dead girls? There are *five* dead girls? That is all I need to hear. I don't think about my next move. I just make it. I exit the bathroom and walk down the hall and into the conference room. Asher is standing on the side of a long mahogany conference table. A tall, dark and good-looking man who resembles Luke, and is obviously Blake, since he's the only other man in the room, is standing directly across from him. Kara, a pretty, petite brunette, is standing next to Blake.

"Sierra?" Asher says, a question in his tone.

"I can help," I say, focused on him for now. "I want to help."

"I don't want you involved in this," he says. "I don't even want you at that bar."

"I'm here," I say, stepping to the end of the table. "And I know what this is now, and I can't not help."

"Are you law enforcement?" Blake asks.

"I don't want you involved in this, Sierra," Asher repeats, his tone sharper now.

"I'm *already* involved," I say. "I know. And I'm not going to freak out or blink at the bar. I understand killers. I've had to survive living with one and working with one. Ju-Ju doesn't scare me."

"If you mean some crazy ex, that doesn't make you qualified to help," Blake says. "So I repeat. *Are you law enforcement?*"

"No," I say, "but I've worked with one of the most sought after forensic psychologists in the country, and I've actually investigated several serial killers, and a great number of murders that wouldn't be classified as serial murders, with him. And I've interviewed the Son of Sam and the D.C. Sniper as well as studied every serial killer that has ever been documented."

"We're all good at catching killers," Blake snaps.

"If good was good enough, then the FBI wouldn't call in people who are experts. They wouldn't need Sherriff Rogers, just to name one expert, who isn't even FBI, but travels the country to consult with the FBI."

"And you think you're one of those experts?" he asks.

"No," I say. "I'm not one of them because I've come to know that those people have a little Dexter in them that I do not. They're people who understand a killer's tendencies a little too well to turn your back on them, even if you think they're heroes, like you all are. But I know this because I've been around my share of Dexter-like people and maybe, just maybe, if not now, one day, that makes me as good as them."

"Sierra," Asher says tightly. "Are you saying that your ex is—"

"I'm saying that I can help," I reply quickly, cutting him off. "We're talking about Ju-Ju."

"Yes," Kara says. "And if you can help, I say help, but you need to know that there are not only five victims, they all look like us, Sierra. Brown hair and varied eye colors. All the same age range and build. All single. None of them were in active relationships. And his mother, who died when she was right about our age, looked like them, and us."

I glance at Asher. "Now I know why you were so touchy-feely with me in front of him. Thank you."

"That was all my pleasure," he assures me. "I really don't want you involved in this."

"How does he kill them?" I ask.

"He taints the drugs he gives to the victims," Asher says, "but thus far law enforcement can't tie the drug sales to Ju-Ju. They can't call him a killer, let alone a serial killer, and the deaths by drugs isn't reading serial killer to the FBI."

"Proof law enforcement likes to repeat mistakes," I say. "There's a case history on just this type of killer. Charles Cullen. He was a nurse. He killed at least forty patients. He overdosed them or contaminated their medications. There were signs that he was a killer. There were opportunities to stop him that were ignored by the medical facilities to avoid liability. They fired him. They didn't report him and that happened more than once. But there was another killer that used drugs as well."

"Harold Shipman," Kara says.

"The killer drug doctor," Blake adds. "We're both ex-ATF so we know how drugs are used as a weapon, and we both know those people who use them as such."

"Which is why this client came to us," Kara says.

"I've killed killers no one else could kill," Asher says, looking at me, a point in that statement. "That's why I'm involved and I'm a fast study. Who was Harold Shipman?"

"He was technically not a doctor," I say, "but a general practitioner who ran a private practice. He killed fifteen of his patients with drugs. He won awards in his field and was highly regarded in his community. There were no signs that he was a killer except for dead bodies that his practice justified as natural or medical causes. In both of those cases, neither left notes or taunted the police like Son of Sam or the even the D.C. Sniper, though I'm of the opinion he was trying to cover up killing his ex-wife." The way The Beast would cover up killing me.

"Those kinds of killers, the ones that taunt people and brag, resemble the drug cartel killers we know," Kara says. "They kill and brag about it. I find the ones that don't brag, that just kill to revel in it privately, far more terrorizing."

"Agreed," I say. "And Ju-Ju most resembles these types of killers, and most certainly Cullen and Shipman. He's got a drug connection as they did, and drugs are his weapon. It's not quite the perfect crime with the perfect cover, as it was for Cullen and Harold, because they chose legal professions, but they could have inspired him."

"Which means he'll be hard to catch," Kara says. "But we wouldn't be involved if this was easy."

"Maybe I'm thinking about this wrong," I say, thrumming my fingers on the table. "Maybe he's not like Cullen and Shipman. Maybe he's using the illegal drug trade as a taunt. He can do whatever he wants, and we still can't catch him."

"That's a good point," Blake says. "He's breaking the law right in front of our faces, and still getting away with killing, too."

"If that's the case," I say. "Then he'll keep pushing, trying to get noticed, until he can't push anymore. Then he'll go underground. Can I see his file?"

"We have a time issue here," Asher says, tapping his watch. "We need to continue this later."

"If you want my help, I need the file," I say. "I've studied enough killers to look at their history that ties to their actions when they killed. Maybe I can find something you haven't that will let you catch him before he kills again."

Blake, Asher, and Kara share looks before Blake nods his head. "Asher will give you what you need."

"And in exchange for her help," Asher says, "We need you to create a digital identity now, tonight for Kelli Vincent. My father showed up tonight and took an interest in her. He'll look her up and soon. I need her to clear his review and anyone else who looks."

"Done," Blake says, pinning me in a stare. "But I have questions."

"That you'll ask me," Asher says, his tone steel. "And to be clear. She is not, and will not, become bait."

"No," I say, pretty sure I sense a prior conversation in play. "I won't be bait for a serial killer. I'm already living that. Though I might be perfect for the job. I'd kill him and it wouldn't matter. I don't exist anymore and then we're rid of a killer."

"Holy fuck," Asher murmurs.

"I don't know if I love you," Blake says, "or if you scare the fuck out of me."

"By the way," Kara says, as if I haven't just suggested I'd kill the killer. "If you notice the tendency for Asher to say 'fuck', you can blame Blake. They've worked together too much, and Blake doesn't seem to have another verb or noun for any sentence."

"Who has Kyle's role tonight?" Asher asks, ignoring her, clearly not looking to lighten the mood. He glances at Kara. "I mean, who the fuck has Kyle's role tonight."

"Luke's following Ju-Ju, but he's out in a week for an airport project," Blake says. "Royce is out of town in meetings, but he'll be on this team when he gets back."

"What about the surveillance truck?" Asher asks.

"Jacob, and Cooper, the new guy, are covering it for the rest of this job."

"Then let me go full circle to the start of this meeting," Asher says. "Let me, Luke, and Royce, handle the rest of this case. You and Kara use Kayden Wilkens and take care of Alvarez. Take care of Myla and Kyle." He presses his hands to the table and pins Blake in a stare. "Because if you don't, I'll call Kyle myself and tell him everything."

Asher doesn't wait for a reply. He straightens, takes my hand, and leads me out of the conference room and doesn't stop until we're on the street. The minute we're there, though, and the door shuts, he presses me into the corner, his hands on the surface above the door. "I need to know and I need to know now: Is The Beast a serial killer, Sierra?"

Chapter Eighteen

Sierra

"Answer me, Sierra," Asher demands. "Is your ex a serial killer?"

"Your cartel leader, Alvarez," I say. "He's like him, only he's sought after and praised by the elite, and everyone who would openly condemn Alvarez."

"That doesn't answer my question. *Is he a serial killer?*"

"Killing isn't his motivation," I say. "He kills to get ahead and get people out of his way, so no. Technically, he's not a serial killer. He's just a killer."

"And you found out."

"That and more," I say, "which is why he wants me dead."

"And yet you want to take a run at Ju-Ju."

"I'm not running at Ju-Ju, but so far, I've survived my monster. Five girls have not survived theirs. I don't want there to be a sixth."

"I don't want number six to be you."

"It won't be," I say. "You already kissed me and claimed me, remember?"

"We can't know that's enough to dissuade him," he says. "He's shown interest in you when he won't even look Kara's way."

"Yes, but—" My brow furrows with a thought.

"But?"

"If you're right, and he's shown interest in me, despite you obviously staking a claim, then you don't have his formula down."

"I can see you thinking," he says. "Where are you going with this?"

"You told me that refusing a paycheck made me look vulnerable, and that essentially makes me a target for any kind of predator. Maybe being single wasn't why Ju-Ju chose his victims. Maybe it was more about them being vulnerable, or in trouble, in some way."

"In other words, Ju-Ju talked to someone at the bar that knows you are working for tips only."

"Maybe. That's my thought."

He pushes off the wall. "We need to move and I need to make a phone call." We start walking and he digs his phone from his pocket. "The subway is the only way we can make sure no one knows where we came from."

"What about after work? Aren't some of the subways closed?"

"Yes," he says. "Which is why we walk to the ones that are open." He punches in an auto-dial in his phone. "Luke," he says and then listens a few beats, before adding, "Sierra and I have a hunch that someone at the bar is aiding Ju-Ju in some way." He glances at me. "Yes. Sierra knows about Ju-Ju. I'll explain later if Blake hasn't already." He listens a minute and they have a drawn-out conversation I can't keep up with, especially when we head down the subway stairs. "I'm headed into the tunnels," Asher says. "We're going to cut out. We'll be there in fifteen minutes." He ends the connection and sticks his phone in his pocket and pulls out two subway cards, one he hands to me. "That has plenty of money on it. Keep it, but not in your purse."

We both swipe, and for now, I stick the card in the pocket of my jeans. The minute we are on the other side, Asher's hand is on my back, a protectiveness and intimacy in the way he steps close. We head down the stairs just in time to catch our train, which is virtually empty. In unison, we both gravitate toward the end of the car, claiming the side-by-side seats there that allow us to keep our eyes on the entrances.

"What did Luke say about Ju-Ju?" I ask.

"He doesn't give a lot of opinions on the fly. He just gets the job done. He's putting a man on Terrance, the manager, since he's the one most likely connected in some way to Ju-Ju. And I'm not of Blake's caliber when it comes to hacking, but I can hack pretty damn well. Between Blake and I, we've already done a basic fingerprint for everyone at the bar. Tomorrow I'll dig in deeper, especially where the manager and the owner are concerned."

"I think it has to be Terrance," I say. "He's the one I've dealt with, and since I don't have a file, I'd say it has to be him. I really hate that I told him my real name. I can't believe I was that stupid."

"Running gets old and exhausting," he says. "And so does pretending to be someone you're not. You think your cover has become so real, even to yourself, that you can't misstep, but we're all human. And in your case, you've had to change identities several times in nine months."

"Yes," I say. "Sierra with blonde hair in Denver. Leslie with black hair in Kansas. Jenny with red hair in Texas. I used wigs, clinging to the idea of one day being me again. Until I got here. I had no time for a wig and after Texas, I knew it was time to embrace a new me."

"Have you?"

"Not really."

139

He reaches up and brushes hair from my eyes. "Believe it or not, I get it."

"Because you've had to pretend to be someone else?"

"Yeah well, that's part of it." There's a flicker of something in his eyes I don't quite understand, and he cuts his gaze, his jaw set hard. "Let's talk about Terrance and damage control," he says, changing the subject, and when he looks at me again, that flicker of something is now gone, wiped away. "It's Saturday night and the busiest night of the week at the bar. One of the two of us needs to go to Terrance, on your behalf, we'll play it by ear on which one."

"And say what?"

"A demand that if you prove yourself tonight, you want to be on payroll for your next shift. Play it off as if you always believed that would be the case."

"As Kelli Vincent?" I ask.

"Yes. When he calls you Sierra, ask him if he gives nicknames to all the girls. Make him believe he got confused about your name."

He means, convince him that I'm not vulnerable, therefore, Ju-Ju, a serial killer, shouldn't target me. Because apparently, somewhere in the process of studying crazy killers, I became a magnet for them.

———— ∞∞∞ ————

Asher and I arrive late to work at the bar.

We enter the building through the back entrance and we're about four steps past the break room when we come face-to-face with the bar manager, Terrance, who is big, bulky and maybe thirty-five. Or forty-five. He's one of those people that you just can't guess the age for, even if you are one of those who always gets it right. I think it's the shaved head or perhaps the unibrow and bad attitude, and in that order. "Why the hell are you two late and walking in together?" he demands.

"We were fucking," Asher says, "and if you don't like it, fire us. Carlson down the road at Red Roof Bar offered us both jobs, and they promised Kelli a real paycheck."

I'm contemplating punching Asher, at least twice: Once for the "we were fucking" comment and once for putting my job on the line, but Terrance steals the show, with a scowl and another demand. "Who the *fuck* is Kelli?"

"Me, of course," I say as if in disbelief. "*I'm* Kelli," I add, and I just decide to go with it, and follow Asher's lead. "And Carlson knows that."

"I thought you were Sierra," he snaps.

"I thought you just gave everyone a nickname," I say. "And mine was Sierra."

"How's this for a nickname?" he asks. "Get your *asses* to work or you're fired."

"Do I get a paycheck?" I press.

"You were late," he says. "Ask me when you prove you can be on time."

"She gets a paycheck," Asher says, he and Terrance staring each other down.

Terrance clenches his jaw and looks at me. "We'll do paperwork if you survive Saturday night." He turns and walks away.

I turn and face Asher. "We were *fucking*? You couldn't be more discreet?"

"Terrance isn't exactly a discreet kind of guy, and we need to get the point across. You're with me."

"I'll punish you later," I promise, but for now, I move on. "You pushed him to fire us and knew he wouldn't," I say. "What do you have on him?"

LISA RENEE JONES

"Walker paid a couple of the bartenders to quit over the past week," he says. "He can't afford to fire us." His phone buzzes with a text and he pulls it from his pocket and reads the message. "Ju-Ju just had an Uber drop him in the parking lot two blocks away."

"Why would he—" I stop myself. I know why. "A drug deal," I say.

"Yes," he confirms, sticking his phone back in his pocket, "but he's not selling to anyone that fits his victim profile."

"*Hello,* assholes," Terrance shouts at us, reappearing in the hallway. "Get to work."

"On it, boss," he says as if he's actually compliant, instead of a smart ass, his arm settling around my shoulders as he sets us in motion down a hallway. "Punish me, baby," he murmurs in my ear. "I didn't want you to think I missed that promise."

I smile, despite the fact that Terrance glares at us for several of our steps before he disappears into an office. We cut left, and round a corner to enter the dimly lit, crazy crowded bar considering it's still early. Asher snags my hand and starts walking, leading me through the tables and bodies, the sound of Kelly Clarkson's "Love So Soft", blasting through the speakers. *Kelli.* My name is Kelli. I can't forget that. I don't know how I forgot with Terrance. Maybe I really am tired of running but a fight just isn't always the answer. A reality I already know Asher won't easily accept.

I lose that thought as we near the bar we work behind, and I bring the two half-naked asses attached to two half-naked women dancing on top of it into view and I'm thrust into the past. To one of the many times The Beast forced me to go to topless bars. Forced me to watch him get lap dances and even get them myself when I just wanted to leave, wanted to run. But, I was forced to run. Forced to take this job, but it's money, and it brought me to Asher, and I can't regret either of those things.

Asher and I head to the end of the bar and he unlatches the wooden counter, lifting it and creating an entrance. I pass through the opening, stepping behind the bar. Asher joins me, and as soon as I turn to face him, he pulls me close, and presses his cheek to mine, "Watch for Ju-Ju," he says, and when I expect his arms to fall away, he instead adds, "You don't belong here. We're going to talk about that."

He releases me and walks to the bar to attend a customer, leaving me behind to digest his words with a mix of emotions, both good and bad. Yes, I like Asher's alpha protective nature, but no, I do not want to be controlled by another man.

An hour later, Asher has dispelled any negative his statement created in me by paying zero attention to the dancers, while managing to touch me as much as he has his orders. On one quick pass behind me, his hands settle on my hips, and he leans in close. "Luke just texted me. Ju-Ju is at a diner down the road, and on a separate, immensely important note, your ass looks fucking perfect in those jeans."

I laugh as he moves away and attends to a customer, while I too serve up drinks.

Over the next hour, Asher and I have many intimate little moments before he steps behind me again, his hands back on my hips, as he leans in and finally offers an update on Ju-Ju. "He's somewhere in the bar, and we can't be out of here, and naked in my bed together, soon enough," before he moves away.

That naked and in his bed comment isn't missed, but I'm also quite certain it's meant to distract me from some anticipated freak-out over Ju-Ju, and him being undercover to catch him. I'm not freaked out. I'm not going to blink. I want to catch a killer. Exactly why I greet a customer, and discreetly scan the crowd to find no signs of Ju-Ju. For another full hour, which then turns into two, there is still no sign of Ju-Ju in the crowd, by me or Asher, even though the Walker team insists he's here.

I've just shared a look with Asher, confirming that hasn't changed, when a bald dude, with a bald dude that is not him on his shirt, orders a beer. Which is weird, while him dragging out the transaction to attempt to ask me out, is irritating. Ultimately, he hands me a twenty-dollar tip and finally walks away. I stick the cash in the money jar, just as the girl dancing to my right suddenly squats down in front of me, her ample breasts pretty much falling out of her top. "I'm Jesse," she calls out, over the exceedingly loud music, that at present is *What Lovers Do* by Maroon 5, I think. "I can't afford to take a break without Terrance firing me," she adds. "Any chance I could get some water?"

Her fear of Terrance reminds me of a much smaller version of my fear of Devin, and I happily grab my sprayer and fill a glass for her. She gulps it down and hands the glass back to me. "Thanks," she shouts out as she shoves some guy away. "Lucky you," she says, after he backs off. "I wish I was behind the bar."

I wouldn't ever be on that bar, but I get it. She's using her assets to survive. As if proving that point she tugs her top down a bit more and stands, only to have the guy she shoved away grab her leg. I use the water hose in my hand and spray the drunk asshole, who curses at me, but backs off. Jesse gives me a thumbs-up thank you and we both laugh.

She turns away and I glance over at Asher to find his side of the bar packed with people while the other dancer is kneeling in front of him, facing him, her legs spread wide. He motions for her to move, but she grabs his arm and bites her bottom lip, and actually tries to drag his hand to her panties. My stomach knots with a flashback of me watching Devin feel up a dancer, because if I didn't—

Asher jerks his hand back, and points up at the dancer. I don't know what he says, but her face falls hard and fast, and she stands just as hard and fast. He turns in my direction, and I quickly face the other way before he knows that I was watching. Hating how much seeing that woman offering herself up to him bothered me. I just met Asher. I have no right to feel this way. I don't want to feel this way. I *won't* feel this way.

I step to the counter and take an order, but Asher is suddenly next to me, pulling me to him, his cheek pressed to mine, hand on my lower back. "That was her, not me," he says, making it clear that he knows I saw what happened. "You have my full attention, and no one has *ever* had my full attention."

The minute he says those words, I know that I have the option to reject them as sweet talk or to choose to trust him and he's made that decision remarkably easy. My hand goes to his face, my lips pressing to his lips, and I've just touched my tongue with his when someone grabs my arm. I look up to find Jesse squatted down again. "Trouble!" she shouts, pointing down the bar.

Asher and I follow her lead to discover two guys on top of the bar grabbing the dancer I will now forever think of as "crotch girl." Asher curses, and in a swift move and a jump, he's on top of the bar, yanking one of the men off crotch girl. He tosses the guy off the bar, but that doesn't end it. The other guy lunges at Asher, and crotch girl jumps off the bar, and to my side of the counter, just in time to avoid the impact of a fist. Jesse jumps too, and joins us, but I'm not focused on them. I'm focused on Asher, and the two new guys that jump onto the bar, and go at him. I suck in air, and watch as Asher struggles with them but ultimately wins out. I breathe out in relief. He's virtually unscathed, and they look like the drunk fools they are who stupidly chose an ex-Navy SEAL to fight.

"I hate when this happens!" Jesse shouts over the music, her complaint telling me that this fight is a version of normal to her. The fact that there are people standing around the bar, still drinking and dancing to the music, confirms that yes, this is a normal Saturday night, and Lord help me, I don't want it to be my normal.

Thankfully though, the fight begins to die down and a couple of guys approach our end of the bar, waving Jesse and crotch girl forward. Both dancers rush toward the obviously familiar men, while the bouncers, along with Asher, now have the final troublemakers off the bar, and they're dragging them toward the exit.

Terrance parts the crowd and charges at Jesse and crotch girl. "Dance!" he shouts. "Now!" They both scramble to the top of the bar, as he leans across it and focuses on me. "Get busy!" He seals that barked order to me by turning to the room and waves people forward.

I'm rushed by customers, and I start taking orders, but freeze with what seems to be a flash, like a camera. My head jerks up and I scan the area, to spy no one taking pictures, but then, I'm swamped with people. "You're paranoid," I murmur to myself, filling another order, but Asher hasn't returned, and I have this sense of being watched, this unease that I can't shake. It's nagging at me and I ignore the guy in front of me demanding a buttery nipple and laughing while he does. I focus on the seating areas, scanning for the source of my unease and I find it: Ju-Ju is sitting at a table halfway across the bar, staring at me. Asher's right. I have Ju-Ju's attention and my only comfort in that is that maybe, just maybe, while focused on me, he's not focused on another innocent girl. Because I'm not innocent. I might not know how to use a gun, but there's at least one asshole in Texas who most likely knows my knee more intimately than he's ever known pleasure.

I turn away from him and my gaze lands on Asher, two bouncers, and a cop, standing near the front door, the cop my real focus. My heart starts to race at the sight of that uniform, which has a connection to my past that is far more dangerous than Ju-Ju. I cannot risk being recognized. Not when Devin has his cronies looking for me, while the many random press photos I've been forced to smile through, by his side, make me easier to recognize than I'd hope. Decision made, I jump up on the bar next to Jesse and grab her arm. "I have to pee. Send people to the other bars!"

She gives me a thumbs-up and I jump down on the other side of the bar and that's when Ju-Ju steps in front of me and holds up a photo, a taunting smile on his face. A photo that he would be paid large sums of money for supplying to Devin. I reach for his phone, and he pulls it away, waggling a finger at me before he disappears into the crowd, holding it and me hostage. I want to go after him, knee him, and take his damn phone.

I take a step toward him but he's already walking toward the door, and my gut says that he's luring me out of the bar, where he could have one of Devin's cronies waiting on me. My heart now wants to beat right out of my chest. I need out of this bar. I head to the employee exit where Asher and I had entered the bar, and I don't stop until I'm down that hallway and in the bathroom.

My phone rings and I grab it, finding Asher's number on the caller ID. "In the employee bathroom," I say, "and I need to see you now."

"I'm on my way." He disconnects the call and I slide my phone back into my pocket, wishing I had the mace I left back in my apartment.

Instead I lean against the wall, my mind racing as fast as my heart. "Think, Sierra," I whisper. "Calm down and think." I inhale and exhale and my mind actually starts to work. Ju-Ju can't know who I am. He's just playing games with me. He's not connected to Devin. He doesn't know what that photo is worth.

The door opens and Asher is immediately in front of me. "What's wrong?" he asks, his hands settling at my waist, a huge cut down his cheek. "What happened?"

"Ju-Ju took my picture and he could sell it for big money. He could hand it to the wrong person and it's the end for me and us."

Asher's jaw sets, determination and decision in his face and actions as he releases me and moves toward the door. "No," I say, stepping with him and grabbing his arm. "Wait. Don't go after him. We need to think about this."

"No thinking required," Asher says. "I'll beat his fucking ass and take it."

"No," I say, my thoughts coming full circle now. "You can't do that."

"Hell if I can't."

I step in front of him, blocking the door. "If he's the serial killer, and you spook him, he'll retreat. That means you won't catch him until he kills again, and that could be a long time. You can't take my photo from him."

"You were completely panicked when I called you."

"Now that I'm calming down, this isn't the problem I thought it was. There's no way he took that photo to sell."

"Unless someone has been asking around about you."

He's right. There is that, but I'm back to logic. "We can't risk letting a killer get away," I say. "Most likely he takes a picture as part of the game he plays with his victims."

"Are you fucking serious? Am I supposed to be comforted by the idea that a serial killer targeted you as his next kill?"

"Yes. He's nothing compared to The Beast."

LISA RENEE JONES

Chapter Nineteen

Sierra

"Did Ju-Ju use a phone or a camera to take your picture?" he asks, when I'd expected him to push for answers about Devin, the devil, *The Beast*, who I've just told him scares me far more than Ju-Ju.

"A phone," I say. "He showed it to me. He taunted me with it, and he obviously, in my assessment, tried to get me to follow him, but I'm not that young and gullible."

"No," he says. "You are not, which makes him targeting you feel off."

He's right. It does, and yet Ju-Ju has most definitely targeted me, but I don't get the chance to say that. Asher has already pulled out his own phone and hit the auto-dial. "Blake," he says, obviously throwing the idea of excluding Blake from this conversation to the wind.

"Talk to me," Blake says loud enough that I hear him, no hesitation in reply either, as if he doesn't remember the conflict with Asher any more than Asher remembers it with him.

"Ju-Ju took Sierra's picture," he says. "And while it's most likely one of the ways he taunts his victims, we all know she's on the run. She can't have that photo go public."

"You could always beat the fuck out of him and take it," Blake says, still loud enough for me to hear. "Of course, based on Sierra's earlier assessment that might not be in the

151

case's best interest, but for the record, man, if she's your woman, I get it. He'd be pulp fiction if this was Kara."

"No," I say firmly. "You can't. You won't."

"I heard that," Blake says. "Just do it anyway."

"Stop, Blake!" I call out.

"It's not off the table," Asher says to both me and Blake.

"You can't," I say. "And you know it. That will—"

"Send him underground," Asher states. "I get it." He hits speaker. "You're on speaker, Blake."

"Nothing on his cloud," Blake says. "I'll look for other ways he might upload."

"I have to get back behind the bar," Asher replies. "I need someone to text me his location now and any time it changes."

"Done," Blake confirms. "And I'll get you an update on the photo."

"For the record," Asher adds. "Your ass is off this case after tonight."

"We'll talk," Blake agrees, surprising me with the rather compliant reply, when there is nothing about the man that is compliant at all, before he disconnects.

Asher sticks his phone back in his pocket. "Ju-Ju is either using a phone in someone else's name to take those photos or a throwaway."

"How do you know he even uses the cloud?" I ask.

"Blake hacked his MacBook and turned it on. And he has an alert set up to ensure it stays on."

"Is that possible? That can't be possible."

"You'd be surprised just what a hacker can do." He presses his hands on the door on either side of me, his expression and tone turning harder. "And you'd be surprised what a serial killer will do. There's a big difference between sitting in a room with a restrained killer, and facing one who is walking the streets and wants you dead."

"I know that," I say.

"I don't think you do, but I do. Just as you're an expert at analyzing killers, I'm an expert at keeping the right people alive and killing the bad guys. Which is why you will do what I say the rest of this night, or I swear to you, I will drug you myself and take you out of here. And before you get the idea in your pretty little head that I'm strong-arming you like your ex, stop and think. I'm going to keep you alive. He's trying to kill you."

"I know that, too."

"You better," he states firmly, "because I'm the difference between you living and dying. We need to get back behind that bar." He pushes away from me.

I don't move, intentionally remaining the block to him opening the door. "Are the police still here?"

"They left and you can explain to me why you're afraid of them when we get out of here."

"I'm not a criminal," I say. "I told you that."

"Later, Sierra."

"No," I say. "I cannot stand the idea of you thinking that you're helping a criminal. He's close to law enforcement and he's a public figure. He filed a missing person's report and I've been photographed with him too often to not be worried about being recognized."

He studies me for several beats and while his expression has not changed, his energy is sharp, angry, even. "Let's get back out there," he says.

There are so many things I need to process right now, maybe even say to him—admit to him—but I need that processing time, and he's right. If we plan to keep our jobs here, we need to go back out there. I step away from the door

LISA RENEE JONES

and Asher opens it. Once we're in the hallway, he takes my hand, and while I feel the touch, and the burn, between us just as much now as ever, he's distant, withdrawn. Maybe he's even regretting helping me.

We round the corner, back into the crush of people, and the blast of music, this time Van Halen's "You Really Got Me", the song rocking the walls. Asher has my hand again, leading me through the crowd, and when we reach the bar, it's to find Terrance standing in front of the entrance. He scowls at us, but he couldn't speak if he wanted to, not and be heard. He moves and lifts the bar. Asher pulls me in front of him, and I enter, hurrying to my spot, where I start taking orders. I glance left and find Asher in his spot as well. He doesn't look at me. He doesn't talk to me. He doesn't touch me.

It's making me crazy. He's making me crazy. I want him to talk to me. I want him to touch me. An hour passes and I have a lot of thoughts in that time that come down to a few: He has taken risks for me, invited me into his life, his home. His trust and even willingness to give me two unconditional weeks to confess everything to him while he still offers me protection. But he feels the danger of the unknown those two weeks represent, and if I take them, I've taken and taken, and given him nothing. That doesn't work.

I glance at the time on some dude's watch. Last call is about ten minutes away, which means a rush at the bar, and I can't take it anymore. Asher is filling an order and I walk toward him. The minute he sets the drink in front of the guy, I stand between him and the bar. My hands come down on those gorgeous colorfully tattooed arms of his, arms that tell a story of his life that I want to know. My eyes meet his and I not only register the question in his eyes, I feel the connection between us like a live charge through my body. I

154

know what I have to do and I push to my toes, pressing my lips to his ear. "I will tell you everything, but only you. You can't tell anyone else. Not without—"

He pulls back and suddenly his hand is at the back of my head and he's kissing me, a deep, possessive, intense kiss that is over too soon. "We'll figure it out," he promises, his lips now at my ear before he's staring down at me and giving me a nod that is a question.

I nod back, relieved, certain now that he's right. Fate brought us together, but he decided to keep us together. And he needed to know I did, too. The ten-minute final call is announced and he brushes his lips over mine before releasing me. Ten more minutes, and we can get out of here.

The minute drink service ends, Asher grabs the tip jar and my hand, once again leading me through the crowd, and we don't stop until we're in the break room where thankfully no one else is right now. "Let's get your cash and get out of here," he says, pulling a wad of bills from the jar.

"My cash?" I ask. "Don't you mean our cash?"

"Tattoo boy."

At the sound of Terrance's voice, Asher grimaces and glances to the door. "What do you want, baldy?"

"A minute," he bites out. "Alone."

Asher stuffs the cash he's holding back inside the jar and then glances at me. "Do not leave this room."

"I won't," I promise, with absolutely no hesitation. I might be willing to battle Ju-Ju to save other people's lives, but I'm not foolish enough to want to die in the process.

He studies me for several beats, as if weighing my flight risk, which has me adding, "I'm not going anywhere without you."

He steps closer. "If you do, I'll come for you, and unlike others, I'll find you." He turns and walks away, and I'm surprisingly comforted by the certainty that he would indeed find me. Hopefully, he'll never have to prove that to be true.

He and Terrance disappear into the hallway and I pull the cash from the tip jar a little at a time, and start counting. Five minutes later, I've determined that tonight's take is twelve hundred and sixty-two dollars and tonight was busier than last night. I stuff it all in my purse, because I don't need mace. I have Asher, who walks back into the room, his expression all hard lines and irritation. "What did he say?"

"Nothing I didn't expect," he says, glancing at the empty tip jar and then back at me. "Are we ready to get out of here?"

"Before we ever got here," I say, not about to bring up the tips he obviously didn't share last night, now. He's tense and we both want out of here. "I put the money in my purse," I add, and trying to drive home my promise to stay with him, to tell him everything, I add, "I decided that you're a better weapon than mace."

"I am, sweetheart. Bet on me."

"Like you've bet on me?" I ask, starting to really grip the magnitude of that trust.

"That's the idea."

"I *will*," I promise. "I am. Asher, I—"

He leans in and kisses me, his hand on the side of my face. "I want you to finish that thought, but later, when we're alone." His thumb strokes my cheek. "I want you out of this hellhole."

"I want *you* out of this hellhole."

He laughs, the tension in his expression easing. "Come on," he says, taking my hand and leading me out of the room and the instant we're in the hallway, he walks me to his side. Not behind him. Not in front of him.

We reach the exit, and he pauses, looking over at me. "Eight blocks to the train station," Asher says, his arm sliding around my shoulder and pulling me close. "Four north. Four east. And not only do I have men monitoring our exit, one of them has our backs, making sure we get on that train without company."

I want to ask where Ju-Ju is now, but he's already answered that question with his promise that Ju-Ju won't follow us. Ju-Ju isn't here. Devin isn't here. Asher is and that matters more than he knows. I need him to know. After all he's done, he needs to hear that. He deserves to hear that.

We exit the building into the alleyway and the night is starless, stormy, the smell of rain in the wind, the sound of thunder in the not so distant distance. Asher slides his arm around my shoulders and pulls me close, my side molded to his, and I have this sense that he's sheltering me. He's been sheltering me from the moment he stopped being the asshole that told me to take off some clothes and get up on the bar and dance. I'll analyze how we went from that to this another time.

Right now, we turn a corner, onto an even darker street, and Asher is quiet, his body tense, and I have this sense that he's listening, on edge, and ready to act if needed. I don't think that it is about Ju-Ju either. His men are watching for him. Asher trusts them, but he's as aware as I am of the unknowns he battles in my name. And so the silence between us continues until finally the subway is in view and his phone buzzes. Asher stops us in our tracks and I stiffen with the fear that this is a warning of some sort.

"Relax," Asher says, releasing me to pull his phone from his pocket. "Jacob is supposed to text before we go underground. This is a sign they have eyes on us." He glances down at the text and then shows me the message that reads: *All clear*.

I breathe out. "Thank God." I glance up at him. "I didn't realize how nervous I was until right now."

He sticks his phone back in his pocket. "I know you don't know it yet," he says, as we start down the subway stairs. "But everyone on my team would die for you."

"I don't want anyone to die for me, Asher."

"No one is going to die, Sierra." And with that vow, he takes my hand and settles it on his, and sets us back in motion. It's not long until we're through the payment gates, and hurrying down the second set of stairs into the subway tunnel. Hurrying toward his home, because his life has become intertwined with my life.

We reach the entrance to the tunnel and it's not long until we've passed through the payment gates. Asher motions me forward, toward one of only four track options for this location. We hurry across the concrete paved path and then down two flights of steps, that lead to one of the cave-like terminals where a half dozen people mill around, waiting on one of two trains to arrive. Asher and I claim a spot just beyond the tracks, both of us facing forward. "What did Terrance say to you?" I ask, glancing over at him.

He looks over at me. "He wanted to know how long we'd been fucking."

"What did you say?"

"Longer than his dick," he replies, "right after I jacked him against the wall and told him to stop thinking about my woman."

The muted sound of the train approaching is my one-minute warning. "It makes no sense that he's that interested in our bedroom habits," I say.

"I handled him," he replies.

"That's not an answer."

"You didn't ask a question," he says, as the explosive roar of our train pulls to a stop. The doors buzz with a warning before opening and Asher and I step into the empty car, but even with all the seats empty, I am too wired to sit. I step to a pole, and Asher steps to the opposite side of it, our hands aligned. Our legs pressed together.

"You want a question?" I ask, as the doors shut. "Was Terrance asking for himself or Ju-Ju?"

"I don't know that answer," Asher says.

"You have a gut feeling," I insist as the train starts to move.

"Yes," he says. "I do."

"Don't do that," I warn. "Don't shut me out when I've promised to let you in."

"Are you going to let me in, Sierra?"

"Yes. I am, so answer."

"I believe Terrance asked for Ju-Ju."

"Why?"

"It's a gut feeling," he says. "That's all I have to offer."

"Right." I look down, suddenly overwhelmed with just how easily these beasts hone in on me.

Asher cups my face, and tilts my gaze back to his, his free hand snagging my hips and walking me to him. "Did you wake up to the fact that Ju-Ju is a monster to be feared?"

"I'm not, nor have I ever, downplayed how dangerous he is."

"You were practically smiling in that bathroom when you realized he was stalking you, instead of your ex."

"My ex *is* stalking me and if I seemed unfazed by Ju-Ju in that bathroom, I wasn't. I'm not."

"And yet you want to be bait."

"No. I told you no. I just don't want to let fear be the reason someone gets hurt."

"And because The Beast scares you more than Ju-Ju."

"Actually," I say, "the idea that a serial killer is targeting me is no longer overshadowed by my relief that he wasn't taking photos for The Beast."

"We don't know that."

"He doesn't connect to my ex," I say.

"He just kills women who look like you."

"I told you. I know how dangerous he is."

"How long has your ex been The Beast to you?" he asks, shifting the topic.

"Since my accident," I say. "That's when I gave him the name. But he'd already started showing himself as that monster. I think my accident just sped it up."

"When I told you no one was going to die, I reserve the right to exclude The Beast and that monster, Ju-Ju, from that statement."

Alarm bells go off in my head and I grab his shirt, stepping into him. "You cannot go after him."

"Running isn't the answer."

"You're going to end up dead. You will not go after him and I'm not telling you who he is, until you make me believe you mean it."

"I don't die easily. I'd give you references, but they're all dead."

"There you go with your arrogant, macho hero complex again. Damn it, Asher. I want to tell you who he is. I want my secret to be our secret, but you cannot go after him."

"I won't promise that."

"But you still expect me to tell you."

"Sweetheart, we obviously have a miscommunication. I want your trust. I want to do this right but I'm resourceful. I'm going after him, whether you tell me who he is or not."

LISA RENEE JONES

Chapter Twenty

ASHER

The announcement for our stop sounds and Sierra releases the bar and turns away from me, standing in front of the door to wait for it to open. I step behind her and I'm about to settle my hands on her arms when she turns and points at me, holding on to one of the steel bars framing the door. "You *do not* touch me. I can't think when you touch me. You make me crazy."

"How firm are you on that no touching rule?" I ask, grabbing both of the bars, and bringing our bodies close, if not touching.

"I wouldn't suggest you touch me and find out."

The doors open and she rotates, charging forward into the empty train station, and I am quick to step to her side, keeping pace up the stairs. "For the record, the feeling is mutual, sweetheart," I say. "You make me just as crazy. I've broken every rule in my book for you."

She stops walking, and whirls on me. "You've broken rules? Really? I've broken every rule of survival in my book for you and those rules exist for a reason. I want to stay alive and I want everyone else to stay alive." She points at me and firms her lips. "That means you, hero boy." She turns and starts moving up the stairs again.

"Hero boy?" I ask in disbelief, keeping pace with her. "Sweetheart, I haven't been a boy since I gave up my virginity to Ashley Cameron when I was fourteen and she was seventeen."

"Don't call me sweetheart," she says.

"Are we back to that again?"

"Yes, and I'd bet money that Ashley Cameron gave it up to you, and not the other way around."

"Is that a compliment or an insult?"

"It's a simple observation," she says.

At that point, I decide to do what the Walker men rarely do with their women: shut up before I dig a deeper hole. We clear the stairs and walk across the expanse of the terminal. She doesn't look at me, which is probably good. I'm pretty sure looking at me would just piss her off all over again right now.

We reach the final set of stairs that lead to the street and I pull my phone from my pocket, readying auto-dial for the moment I have bars. Once that happens, I violate Sierra's damn rule by catching her arm. "Don't exit to the sidewalk until I get the all-clear."

She turns to face me and gives me a lethal stare, but follows it with a nod of understanding, which is when I punch the auto-dial and release her arm before I get punched. Which would be okay if I could make her kiss me and make it all better. But that time isn't here yet.

"Update," I say when Jacob answers.

"All clear," he says. "And uneventful. Ju-Ju went home. No guests."

Because he doesn't need to hunt anymore, I think. He's already picked Sierra, and I don't like that answer. "Let me know if that changes, no matter what time it is," I say.

"Copy that," Jacob says, and we disconnect.

I motion Sierra forward and stick my phone back inside my pocket. We clear the tunnel, and start the short walk to my building. Sierra doesn't ask for an update, but our status is fairly obvious. We're safe. She's safe, the way I intend to keep her. That's the entire goal here. Well, not the entire fucking goal. I want her with me when I've never wanted any other woman with me beyond a fuck. And yeah, sure, I want Sierra naked. Sooner rather than later, but ultimately, with me, in my home, in my bed, and I don't question why. I've watched three Walker men go from highly single, to obsessed with a woman, and I now accept their explanation, which is: There is no explanation for how one woman, one chance meeting, changes everything.

I follow her rule. I don't touch her, but the idea of Ju-Ju sitting at home and fantasizing about killing her has me walking really damn close to her. We cross the street and enter my building with her silent treatment rock solid and going nowhere. I don't like it. I'm going to end it. Once we're at the elevator I punch the button and the doors open instantly.

We step into the car and I key in the code. Sierra flattens on the left wall. I don't go to her, or pull her to me and kiss the fuck out of her. I want to. I really fucking want to, but my gut says that would be a mistake with Sierra in her current state of mind. Instead, I claim the opposite wall, my hands on the steel rail behind me, a way to occupy them before they end up all over her.

We stare at each other, and where there had been anger minutes before, now there's combustible anger, the kind of anger driven by how much we want to fuck again. In my book, that's progress. "Come here, Sierra," I order, thinking about how much I really want my fingers in those long strands of brown hair.

"No," she says.

"Please," I say.

165

"No. You come here."

I smile and with zero reservation, push off the wall, closing the space between us to stand in front of her. "Here I am. Now, what are you going to do with me?"

"How is it that I told you what to do, and I still feel like I did what you wanted me to do?"

"Because getting closer to you again, no matter how it happens, *is* always what I want and not something I'll ever turn down." The elevator dings and I push off the wall, backing up and motioning her forward. The doors open, and she gives me an intense look and then exits the car. I follow, and I really don't mind the way she's charging forward and leaving me. I do enjoy her ass in those jeans, but I'll like it better naked. I catch up with her and step to her side, and when we reach my apartment, she does the unexpected. She doesn't wait on me. She keys in the code and I love it. She's pissed but she's not running from me. It shows a commitment level I doubt she understands, but I do, and if she was anyone else, I'd be objecting, not celebrating.

But *I am* celebrating, damn near ready for party hats and balloons. Or the alternative version with whiskey and sex. She enters the apartment and I join her, shutting the door and locking it. She flattens on the door beside me. "I'm not going any further than right here until we talk."

"Okay," I say, stepping to her, my legs framing her legs, my hands at her hips. "Let's talk."

Her hands go to my wrists. "I told you. I can't talk when you're touching me."

"That isn't exactly what you said, but close enough. And I'm going to fucking lose my mind if I don't touch you."

"You don't get to be in control. That's the entire point."

"Sweetheart, I'm not one to just lay back and let you ride me, but if that's what makes you happy..."

"Asher!" She grabs my shirt, which actually turns me on, but I don't think now is the time to tell her that. "You know I'm not talking about sex. You are trying to take over my life."

"I'm saving your life," I say.

"And I'm saving yours. What part of 'I won't let you die' do you not understand?"

"I told you—"

"Don't say you won't die," she says, her voice vibrating with emotion. "*Do not* say it again. You're human. Just like I was when my car crashed."

There is panic in her voice, real fear, and I pull her close, my hand at the back of her head. "Easy, sweetheart. We can do this together."

"We won't work if you—"

"We already work," I say, my mouth slanting down over hers, my tongue licking into her mouth, a deep slide of tongue followed by another. She resists at first, her hand pressed to my chest, her arm stiff, but then comes her soft moan that is hot as hell, followed by the softening of her arms. I deepen the kiss, drinking in the taste of her, sweet and fierce all at once, molding her closer, but she pushes against me, tearing her mouth away.

I don't give her time for the objection sure to follow. I scoop her up and she yelps. "What are you doing?" she demands, but at this point I'm already at the steps and climbing.

"Taking you to my bedroom, where I've wanted you all night."

"I said I wasn't leaving the doorway until we talked."

"We did talk," I remind her, "and we'll talk some more."

"Let me go, Asher."

"Never."

167

"Put me down."

"Almost," I say, clearing the top step and walking into my bedroom, where I elbow on the light. "I brought you up here for a reason."

"To get naked," she says

"Well yeah, sweetheart," I say, setting her down with me between the bed and her. "That's a given, but we could have done that downstairs and that's the point." I catch her hand where it's landed on my chest before she can escape. "Let's talk about those broken rules. I'll tell you mine. You tell me yours. Deal?"

"Yes. Okay. Deal. I'll go first. Don't get close to anyone. Don't even make eye contact. Don't let anyone in my personal space. Don't ever say his name. Your turn."

"Don't get close to anyone. Don't bring women here. Not to my home. Not to my bedroom. Ever. I tell women up front. I fuck. I don't fall in love. And we've already agreed that you're going to tell me his name." I slide my hand under her hair and drag her mouth close to mine. "I want you here, Sierra. You belong with me now. And I don't know what this is between us, but I want to find out."

She closes her fingers around my shirt. "You have to stay alive to find out."

I cup her face. "That's the point I'm making. I'm not going anywhere. In fact, I've never been so present in my life." My mouth closes down on hers once more, and the minute my tongue touches hers, she is right here with me this time. She kisses me, she melts into me, her soft curves all snug against me, making me harder, and hotter. I tangle fingers in her hair, wanting her submission in a way I have never wanted another woman's. And where I'd resisted demanding too much of her earlier, now, I want it all.

I tear my mouth from hers, and back her against the bedpost, one hand at her hip, the other on the post above her head. "He doesn't own you."

"He does or I'd be free."

"No. You're with me now. You know it. I know it. I'm all in, sweetheart. *Sierra.*"

"Asher," she whispers, slipping her hand under my shirt, soft skin that is cool and yet hot. Everything about her makes me hot. "I don't mind if you call me sweetheart. I actually like it, unless I'm mad at you."

"Easy solution. Don't be mad at me."

"Don't make me mad."

I laugh. "Right. Well. Let's resolve to not stay mad for long."

She laughs. "Probably the best choice."

Our laughter fades, the air around us charged. "All in, Sierra. That's the only way we do us. Say it."

"I can't. He does own me, Asher."

"No. If he owned you, you wouldn't be here." I kiss her, a quick, deep, passionate kiss, my hands pressing under her shirt, and caressing it up her body until I pull it over her head. "If he owned you, I wouldn't be doing this." I toss her shirt away, and unhook her bra, sliding it off her shoulders. "Or this." I reach up and tease her nipples. She arches her back and I cup one of her breasts, while my other hand slides between her shoulder blades and molds her to me. "Who owns you, Sierra?"

"Stop asking me that."

"Not until you let go of him."

"I'm not holding onto him."

"As long as you say he owns you, he does."

"And you think you do?" she challenges, anger sparking amber in the depths of her beautiful blue eyes.

"*You* own you," I say, turning her to face the bedpost, forcing her to catch herself on the wood, before I lean into her, my lips at her ear. "But if I have to own you to get you to let go of him, I will."

Chapter Twenty One

ASHER

"No man will ever own me again, Asher," she whispers.

Those words, delivered with an emphasis on my name, hit me with a hard punch of reality. She is too insistent that he owns her. She hasn't let go. Maybe she doesn't want to let go. Fuck. I've become too attached to this woman, too fucking fast. It's like the Walker brothers and their obsession with their women have become a contagion and there is no damn vaccine. I release her and grab the bedpost above her head. "You won't ever be owned by anyone but him," I say. "Got it."

She faces me. "No," she says, her hands flattening on my chest. "That is not what I'm saying."

"Then what are you saying?"

"I left him for a reason."

"To belong to him from a distance? Because you're choosing to belong to him. To fear him, or maybe it's not fear. I don't know what the fuck it is."

"You don't understand."

"Make me," I say.

"No."

"Then let go of me, Sierra." I push off the bedpost and when I would move away, she grabs my belt loops.

"I'm not letting you go," she says. "I don't want him."

"But you want me?"

"You know I want you. You know I want to know what this is between us just like you."

"Then who owns you, Sierra? Because you're about a fuck and good morning away from owning me, and I'm not going there if you belong to him."

"I don't belong to him."

"*Who* do you belong to?"

"Me. I belong to me."

"Are you sure?" I press.

"Yes. *Yes.*"

"Say it," I order.

"I belong to me."

"That's not what I want to hear."

"He doesn't own me."

I cup her head. "Say it like you mean it."

"He doesn't own me, *Asher*. And I'm saying your name to make sure you know that I know who I'm with."

Where she belongs. That thought comes to me, and I don't try to understand it or fight it. It's the Walker way. Women are fuck buddies until one woman explodes into your life and overnight, changes that. There is no doubt that I caught that bug and I have none of the regret Sierra has feared. I take her in my arms and I kiss her—a deep, drink-her-in-and-fucking-*own*-her, kiss. Her hands press my shirt upward and I pull back and drag it over my head. Her hands are immediately on my arms, her eyes on the scar where it blends into my tattoo. She leans in and kisses it, her lips warm on my skin, while I'm hot with a variety of fantasies about where else that mouth can go. For now, I press my mouth to her mouth, and the instant my tongue touches her tongue, there is a surge between us: hunger, need, lust, my hands everywhere I can touch. Her hands everywhere she can touch. Her boots come off and then mine. She reaches for my pants and I reach for hers. It should be fucking perfect, but perfect is ruined by her voice in my head saying: "he owns me," which leads to me thinking about her mouth on him, right when it's on me, and I don't like it.

I tear my mouth from hers, my hand sliding under her hair to cup her neck. "There are two ways to own someone, Sierra," I say. "The wrong way. His way. Or the way I'm going to own you right now, tonight."

"And your way is the right way?"

"I'll let you judge." My cheek slides to hers, lips to her ear. "My way means that you moan. You sigh." My fingers lightly touch her nipple and she arches into me. "You tremble," I add, cupping her breast. "You want more now, and yet you don't want it enough to make it end. And I already don't want it to end, Sierra."

She leans into me, her head resting on my shoulder, emotion that isn't pleasure radiating off of her and crashing into me. I cup her face and tilt her chin up, my thumb stroking her cheek. "What are you thinking?"

"Nothing. Everything. Can you kiss me again already?"

"Where, Sierra?"

"Where?"

"Where do you want me to kiss you? Tell me."

"Everywhere." She pushes to her toes, and her lips find mine, looking for an escape, trying to drive her demons away.

I want to demand her answer, make her tell me where she wants my mouth, but I feel her desperation, her need to escape whatever is in her head. And so, I press my lips to hers, I kiss her mouth, drinking her in, and I don't taste him this time. I taste her. I taste us. I taste need and hunger and passion. "I want you naked," I say, my hands sliding inside her jeans and panties. "In every possible way, Sierra."

173

"I'm pretty sure I'm already there, and it's terrifying." She flattens her hand on my chest. "If you turn into an asshole, I swear—"

"You can punish me," I promise, "and I'm still willing to offer suggestions."

"If you turn into an asshole after I trusted you," she says. "I won't need suggestions, Mr. Ex-Navy SEAL who won't be able to hide from my wrath."

Fuck, I'm crazy about this woman. "Good thing I'm not going to turn into an asshole. I want you naked," I repeat, and this time, I make it happen. I lower myself to one knee and take her jeans and panties with me. My arm wraps her waist and I lift her, dragging her clothing away, and setting her back down. My hands settle on her hips then and I look up at her. She stares down at me, the simmering look in her eyes all about arousal, submission. And I want that from her and not because it's some sex game, of which I could play and play well.

I press my lips to her belly and just that easily she trembles, and it only makes me want more. Everything is more with her. I drag my mouth lower and lower until I linger a lick from her clit, my breath a warm trickle meant to tease. She reaches for me and that's when I turn her to the bedpost, forcing her to catch herself, and presenting her perfect heart-shaped backside for my pleasure. I give it a little smack. Not the kind that hurts, but it surprises her and she yelps. I stand up and do it again, my hands resting on her cheek. "Have you ever been spanked, Sierra?" I ask, leaning in close.

"No," she says.

"Tied up?"

"No."

"Flogged?"

"*No.*"

"Had your nipples clamped?"

"Oh, no," she says, sounding shocked.

I laugh. "Oh, yes. You'd like it. I promise"

I don't—"

"You do. You will. You'll like it." My hands settle on her shoulders. "I'm going to step back and undress."

"I can't stay like this."

"Just for a minute," I say. "This is about trust. I'm not going to do anything but undress. I promise, Sierra." I drag my hands down her arms, my fingers catching hers before I let them fall away.

I step back, and I'm undressed in about thirty seconds. Just that fast, Sierra turns to face me, her gaze raking over my naked body. Her attention lingering on my cock that is now jutted between us for long enough to distract me, and have me thinking about her, on her knees, in front of me, before her eyes jerk upward to mine.

My fantasy blow job has ended with a reality check. "Obviously we have less trust than I thought," I say.

"It's not about trust."

"It *is* about trust," I insist.

"Actually no. It's about claustrophobia. It hit me right after my accident. I was trapped in the car and I just have these random triggers and—" She cuts herself off and tries to walk away.

I catch her and pull her to me, my erection at her hip. "What triggers?"

"He used to turn me around like that," she whispers. "I know it's you, not him. It's not that I'm with him right now. It's just these triggers that I have no control over and I hate it *so much.* I hate that I'm weak enough to have something I can't just turn off."

My desire to kill this man grows stronger every minute. "We all have demons, sweetheart. I have a clusterfuck of my own. So I'm going to give you advice. I'm going to tell you how to make that feeling go away."

"SEAL training?"

"Most definitely."

"Then yes. How?"

"Kiss me. Fuck me. Go to bed with me."

She smiles her way into a laugh. "Is that right? That's SEAL training?"

"It is," I assure. "I recommend you try it immediately."

"Then kiss me. Kiss me now and—"

I do. I kiss her, my tongue licking her mouth, and in that one stroke, we're all over each other again. Touching. Tasting. Wanting. I cup her backside, squeezing that sweet little ass of hers and dragging one of her legs to my hip.

Her hand closes around my cock, and I'm not sure if it's her or me that presses me inside her. I'm just there, in the sweet, wet heat of her body. I lift her then, and her hands grip my shoulders, but I don't thrust into her. Not here. Not like this. I carry her to the mattress, and I go down with her, on top of her. We have a moment where we just look at each other and it's combustible. And then I'm thrusting into her, driving, pumping, my hands still cupping those sweet cheeks and lifting her into me while she arches her back. We're wild, primal, and it's exactly where the fuck I want her. With me, and making these soft, sexy sounds, that tighten my balls every damn time she moans into my mouth or against my cheek.

She's here.

She's present.

But so the fuck am I. I'm with Sierra, not just some woman, and even now, driving into her, I register how insanely different that is for me. How insanely different she is to me. How mine she is in the moment now, when later she may withdraw. I want to keep her here, in the moment, outside her beast and her demons, and I force myself to pump slower, to calm my body and hers. I roll to my side and take her with me, kissing her as I do, my lips trailing to her cheek, her neck, my hand on her breast, my mouth on her nipple. I lick it, suckle it, and repeat before kissing her shoulder, her neck. Her lips. I tangle rough fingers into her hair and she breathes out, "Asher, *please*."

Please, she says.

Thank you, I say.

I drive into her and we're burning hot all over. Wild. Back to primal needs, but this time there is no turning back. We're touching, kissing, moving, hungering for each other, and I can't get deep enough, or close enough to this woman. Too soon, and yet just in time, she digs her fingernails into my back and tenses. A second later, she spasms around me, and I'm driving into her with the quake of my body, and that damn near rocks me. I don't even know where she begins and I end, or where I begin and she ends. Time is some elaborate scheme to force us back to reality, but it wins. We're suddenly out of the lust-filled, pleasure-laden bubble. Back to the world where The Beast has to be named, but not tonight.

I stroke hair from her face and kiss her. "I'll be right back. Don't move or the wet spot is all your fault."

She laughs. "Of course. Blame the one who doesn't have a rocket launcher attached to her body."

"That's what you're calling my personal gear now?"

"Personal *gear*?"

"It's better than rocket launcher and hero boy."

"I was mad when I said that, but I got your attention, now didn't I?"

"You had my attention the minute you showed up at the bar." I kiss her and pull out, walking to the bathroom, where I clean up and grab a hand towel for Sierra.

I return quickly and offer it to her. "Thank you," she says, taking it, and then quickly scooting off the bed to dart toward the bathroom. I turn to watch that cute ass that was just in my hands, shaking just the right amount. "I have to pee," she calls out at the door, over her shoulder "so *do not* come in here." She shoves at the door but it doesn't quite shut.

Smiling, I turn on the bedside lamp, and then walk to my dresser and grab a pair of sweats. Once I've pulled them on, I flip out the overhead light. I've just yanked back the blankets on the bed when Sierra appears in the doorway, wearing one of my shirts, her energy and mood ten shades of sober now. The Beast is back with us. "I hope you don't mind," she says, indicating the shirt.

"I like you in my shirt, Sierra. I like you in my bed. Come join me."

She doesn't move. "Asher, that talk."

"It's nearly five in the morning. Let's sleep. We have all day tomorrow."

She wets her lips and nods, crossing to join me. She climbs into the bed, and I follow, flipping out the light and pulling her back to my front. My hand settles on her hip. "You okay?"

"Yes. I'm perfect, actually."

But she's not perfect. I can feel her thoughts beating at her, The Beast working her over. For a half hour, I listen to her thinking, without a word spoken. I lay there, holding her, making sure she feels safe, and it's an hour after we lay down, with the sun beginning to lighten the room, that she whispers, "Devin Marks," so softly that it seems that she thinks I'm asleep and she's simply testing what it feels like to say his name.

I don't reply, but holy fuck, there it is. The Beast has been named and he's the real life Tony Stark of the world, if Tony Stark was a monster not a hero. She's right about him. He's well-connected with the highest levels of government, here and in other countries. I know much about Devin Marks and the many corrupt acts connected to him but unproven. And the real kicker. As a SEAL, I saved the fucker's life. A wrong I'll happily undo. My hand settles on Sierra's belly, where the scars of that car accident will never heal. I wonder now if they were an accident at all. Maybe even then, she was targeted to die, but she survived.

LISA RENEE JONES

LISA RENEE JONES

180

Chapter Twenty Two

Sierra

I blink awake to sunlight and the scent of Asher, a heady combination that has me caving to the heaviness in my limbs, and the call of more slumber. I shut my eyes again and snuggle deeper into the luxurious sheets and comfortable mattress and Asher except—wait. I open my eyes again. Where is Asher? I roll over and my hand hits a piece of paper. I grab it and read: *Downstairs, drinking coffee and working. Your shopping bags are all in the bathroom.*

I glance at the clock and read: one twenty-five. My eyes go wide and I jolt to a sitting position. I slept until one twenty-five? No wonder I have to pee so badly. I throw off the covers and dash across the room to the bathroom, where I first answer nature's call, and wash up. My bags are on the counter and I open them and dig out a toothbrush and toothpaste, and quickly brush my teeth. I open a drawer to find a brush that I use to untangle the mess on my head. I set it back in the drawer, and stare down at Asher's razor and various aftershave products, the intimacy of being here, in his bathroom, replaying his words in my head: *Don't get close to anyone. Don't bring women here. Not to my home. Not to my bedroom. Ever. I tell women up front. I fuck. I don't fall in love.*

He doesn't bring women here, but I'm here. He doesn't fuck women that he considers his duty. He doesn't fall in love. I need to make sure I don't foolishly fall without him. I pat my cheeks, trying to keep myself firmly planted in that reality. Images of the prior night start running through my head, and working against that goal: the passion. The deep connection I share with this man, which is terrifying and wonderful, all at once. Falling asleep in his arms had been— oh God. I grab the sink. I said Devin's name. I thought we'd be together when we woke up, we'd talk about him and what to do next. What if he's already talking to other people about this? We'll all end up dead.

I turn to the door and Asher is standing there, fully dressed in black jeans and a black T-shirt that contrast the bright colors of his tattoos, his broad shoulders filling the frame. His blond hair tied at his nape. His green eyes simmer with heat and the intimacy of the night before, while a cup steams in his hand. "Caffeine?" he asks, lifting the cup slightly.

I have a moment that is an out of body kind of experience. I flash back to a similar moment with Devin standing at the bathroom door. He'd been equally as good looking, Mr. Tall, Dark and Debonair, in a tailored suit and tie. But he wasn't holding coffee. He was holding a jewelry box because that was how he apologized for his verbal bashings. This time, I was a broken woman who couldn't even bear a child. Thanks to me, he would have no heir to his throne.

"Sierra?"

I blink Asher back into view, and I'm taken aback by how certain I am that yes, he could kill, he has killed, and yet he is gentle, good. He is all man in ways Devin will never be. I cross the small space between us and stop in front of him, my body warming with the heat of our connection, the smoldering embers in the depths of his green eyes. "I'd love some caffeine," I say, accepting the cup, the brush of our hands electric, and I am suddenly aware of my missing underwear, and him saying: "I want you naked in every possible way."

I'm there, I think. I've been there with him since the moment I met him.

I glance down at the cream-colored liquid in the cup, and then at him, the sexy one-day shadow on his jaw conjuring some rather naughty thoughts, but I still manage to say, "What is this exactly?"

"Cream with a little coffee. I like it as sweet as I can get it."

"And here I thought you'd want it so strong it grew hair on your chest."

"Then it might grow hair on your chest, too," he says.

I smile at his never-ending wit, and take a sip that proves to be a sweet, yummy flavor. "Is that caramel?"

"Yes," he confirms. "I have a thing for caramel." He takes the cup from me and sets it on the counter before pulling me close. "And for you, Sierra."

There is something in his voice or maybe it's his eyes, a kind of possessiveness, or anger, or both really, that tell a story that I understand. "You were awake. You heard."

"Devin Marks," he confirms, his voice hardening on the name. "I heard his name, loud and clear, sweetheart."

My heart starts to race and I grab his arms. "Please tell me that you haven't told anyone."

"I told you I wouldn't. I haven't."

"You also said you were going after him no matter what."

"Yes, I did. I am."

"He's—"

183

"I know who, and what he is." He moves on. "Do you like pancakes?"

"We aren't talking about pancakes."

"Yes. We are. Because Devin Marks doesn't get to fuck up one more moment of your life, including breakfast." He sets me away from him and starts to leave, but then pauses. "I had Kara do some shopping for you. The new bags are in the closet. Claim whatever spot you want to hang your things up, and a drawer or two or whatever you need." This time he leaves and after a brief stunned moment of processing, I race after him.

"Asher, wait," I call out, catching up with him at the top of the stairs, while he is a few steps down.

He turns to look at me. "Would you rather have waffles? An omelet? A hamburger? I love a good hamburger."

"I can't accept whatever is in those shopping bags," I say. "I appreciate you doing this, but I can't accept."

"Nothing in those bags fit me and I don't think either of us wants to see me in pink lingerie."

I'm too resistant to the way money and gifts can change us, to laugh. "I don't need gifts from you."

He walks up the stairs and stands in front of me, but he doesn't touch me. "What do you need from me, Sierra?"

"More than I should."

"And yet, I'd define it as not enough." His hand settles on my hip and he pulls me to him. "Nothing with you seems to be enough. He doesn't get to make you live like you've been living. I won't let that happen. That's not how I'm wired, but I don't expect anything in return."

"I can't take and give nothing in return."

"Eat pancakes with me. That sounds pretty damn good to me, but then so does going back into the bedroom and getting naked. In which case, we'll be forced to eat Funyuns and drink beer."

I laugh. He always makes me laugh. "Funyuns and beer?"

"That's about all I have in the house. We have to go shopping." He turns me to face the door. "Take that pretty little ass into the bedroom before I take that pretty little ass back to bed." He smacks my ass and I yelp and head into the bedroom, laughing, something I'd almost forgotten how to do before meeting him, even before leaving The Beast. I told myself that was about the killers I investigated, the horrors I studied, but that was my mind game that I used to justify everything with Devin.

I walk back into the bathroom, and more than a little eager to find out just what Kara picked out for me, I head to the back of the bathroom and flip on the closet light. I step inside the large walk-in space, my gaze captured by the rows of clothes lining the walls that seem to divide out pieces of Asher's life. The left side is suits, which are clearly expensive, with a row of drawers that separate them from blue military fatigues. The right wall is all jeans, T-shirts, jackets. There are so many dimensions to this man, so many complexities that I want to understand and know.

My rules are broken. I'm here. I've involved him. I've not only looked him in the eyes, I could get lost in those eyes and forget why I'm supposed to be a loner for the rest of my life. My gaze lowers to the center of the room to count at least a half-dozen bags, a Victoria's Secret logo on one of them. I sit down on the bench and start looking through each of them. There is so much here. Make up. Jeans. Shirts. Dresses. Shoes. Boots. Bras. Panties. Even a flat iron and a curling iron. There is easily two thousand dollars in purchases here. Guilt stabs at me as I think of my first reaction to his generosity, my push back, that was all about Devin, and his gifted manipulation, not Asher. Asher didn't do this to control me or to own me any more than he was when he changed my lock and bought me pepper spray, then taught me how to use it. I know this. Any other thought back there on the stairs was unfair to him. I need to say that to him. I will say that to him.

He didn't just buy me clothes though, he invited me to claim part of his closet. What this tells me is that he's also invited me into his life, while I've invited him into a war, without that being my intent. But he's in it now. He's not walking away from it, I know that, too He needs to know how dirty this gets, how deep it runs, how possible it is that someone in the Walker operation could be on Team Beast.

And I know what I have to do to make that happen.

Chapter Twenty Three

Sierra

Feeling the urgency to talk to Asher about The Beast, I shower quickly and dry and flat iron my hair, apply minimal make-up and a new soft scent. I then dig through my new items, and hang some of them up on hangers beside Asher's fatigues. Next to that part of him that is a soldier and fighter. I dress in faded, distressed jeans after trying on several pairs in different sizes. I pair them with an emerald green, long-sleeved V-neck sweater. My bra and panties are black. My boots are black Christian Louboutins with a red bottom. My hair feels soft. My clothes feel like mine, not someone else's, even though I didn't pick them out myself. No one else has worn them. Just me. And feeling like me is empowering. I'm not hiding anymore.

With that thought in mind, I rush to the stairs and pause with not just the sound of music but more so, to the sound of Asher singing Chris Young's *Losing Sleep*. His voice is whiskey smooth perfection and the lyrics, bittersweet: *Fall into me, let me breathe the air you breathe. I can take you anywhere you want to be.*

I want to be here. I want to be with him, but more so, I want to do it without fear for him and everyone around him, which reminds me of my purpose. Tear down the cocky in him that might be driving him in the wrong direction. Give him the hard reality of what war means with Devin Marks. I inhale and start down the stairs, determination in my steps. I clear the wall to find Asher to my left at a high-top wooden kitchen table that is wide enough that he has three MacBooks in various positions and high enough that he's sitting on a barstool. He grabs the remote next to him and lowers the music, his burning green eyes fixed on me.

I stop in front of him, on the opposite side of the table, but I don't sit. I mean to say something about Devin, but the way he's looking at me, all warm and wanting, has me backtracking. "Thank you. For all the things you bought me. I love them."

"So that's a yes? You'll eat pancakes with me?"

I smile with his unassuming humor. "Thank you for that, too."

"They aren't here yet."

I laugh. "I mean, for being you."

His smile fades. "And not him?"

"Yes, actually. He's a monster."

"Good," he says, his voice hardening. "Then I can't be The Beast."

He's too confident. "You're too confident." I pull the tiny recording device I've been carrying around with me for nearly a year from my pocket and set it on the table. Asher glances at it and then me. "What is that?" he asks.

"A reality check you need."

The doorbell rings. "That's going to be our food," he says, pushing to his feet, but instead of walking to the door, he rounds the table, and pulls me to him, his hand on my face, thumb stroking my cheek. "You checked my reality the minute I met you, but check it again and again all you want." He kisses me. "After we eat." He starts to walk away, but I grab his shirt.

"Tell me you know how dangerous he is," I order.

"I know more about Devin Marks than perhaps even you do."

"What does that even mean?"

"We'll talk. Let me get the food."

"I don't care about the food." My stomach growls.

"Let me get the food."

"Asher—" The doorbell rings again and Asher's hand comes down on the back of my head and he kisses me, a sexy slide of tongue before he says, "Damn woman, what are you doing to me?" He kisses me once more and heads for the door while I silently answer his question.

What am I doing to him? Quite possibly tying him down to get him to listen to that tape, and really hear it, if that's what it takes. I contemplate the many benefits of such an action, when the door opens and I hear, "What the fuck are you doing here, Blake?" And then, "Hey, Kara."

Oh God. He didn't. He wouldn't. Did he tell Blake and Kara?

"I deliver you pancakes and that's the thanks I get?" Blake demands.

Asher apparently leaves him at the door because he's walking back toward me now with two bags in his hand. I stick the recorder in my pocket and turn away from him, pressing my hands back on the table and willing myself to keep a cool head. If he's done this, he's done this, and I have to head off any fallout. I'll deal with him later. The door shuts, and I can hear Blake and Kara murmuring to each other. Asher sets the bags on the table and suddenly he's beside me, turning me to him, but I don't look at him. "I didn't say anything," he says, his voice for my ears only. "I keep my word."

I look up at him. "You didn't?"

"No. Okay?"

189

I nod and he laces his fingers with mine. "Come over here and eat with me." He leads me around the table and pulls the stool next to his out for me. "Water or beer?"

And just like that I laugh. "Water. I'll save the beer for the Funyuns."

He winks at me while Blake says, "I'm in for the beer."

"Oh, I love that green on you," Kara says, claiming the seat across from me and indicating my shirt. "I knew it would look amazing on you."

"Thank you and thank you for shopping for me. I love everything."

"I'm so glad," she says. "Next time we should go together."

A knot forms in my belly at the idea of forming a friendship, any friendship. Something I didn't have time for between school and my internship, and even if I had, Devin screened everyone. He called it a necessary security assessment that I later knew to be all about control. His control wiping away mine.

"I know things are challenging for you right now," Kara adds when I don't immediately answer.

"Yes," I say. "They are, but at some point, maybe—I'd really like that."

"This would probably be a good time for me to speak up," Blake says, as he and Asher claim the seats across from each other. "I was an asshole to you, Sierra. I'm not normally an asshole, well, except to jerk-offs that deserve it, and that's not you."

"And to me," Asher chimes in. "Where's my apology?"

"Like I said," Blake replies. "Except to assholes who deserve it." He reaches into the leather bag he's settled on the arm of the stool and then places a folder in front of me. "Consider this a peace offering. That's your new identity."

He glances at Asher. "It hits all the hot points we talked about this morning."

I don't ask what the hot points are. I don't want any conversation that leads them to talk about me. I simply flatten my hand on the folder. "Thank you. Sincerely. Is it live now?"

"Not only is it live," Blake says, "I've got it set up to ping me any time you get a search. Which I can do on your real identity if I ever get to know that identity."

"I know," Asher says. "Leave it at that."

Blake's gaze shoots to his, and I don't know what passes between them, but there's a conversation there, and once it's complete, Blake doesn't push me. He moves on, glancing between us. "Both of you look over the file and make sure you don't have questions," Blake says. "But it's done." He eyes Asher. "Your father's people already pinged Kelli Vincent."

"Of course he did," Asher says dryly. "Good ole' pops."

"And good thing we handled her," Blake says. "I got it loaded thirty minutes before it was pulled."

"What does that mean?" I ask. "Handled my ID?"

Asher turns me to him, in profile to Blake and Kara, hands on my knees. "Don't freak out. Blake pulled a couple of photos from the Walker Security cameras. He will not, *I will not*, let it go elsewhere, but we had to attach a driver's license to your new identity."

"I doctored a few of them to create a high school and college history as well," Blake says. "I gave you copies of everything that will pull when you're searched for in that folder."

"It was necessary," Asher says.

"You can trust us," Kara adds. "Whatever it is—"

"I'm not a criminal," I say, turning to them and because this feels like it's leading places I don't want to go, at least not yet, I change the subject. "What about the photo Ju-Ju took of me?" I ask.

"Nothing has changed," Blake replies. "He hasn't uploaded it anywhere I can track, and I can track just about everything."

"And he hasn't left his house today," Asher adds. "I've been in touch with Jacob."

"That's his typical behavior," Kara says. "He stays in until he leaves for the bars."

"What about food?" I ask. "Shopping?"

"He has everything delivered," she says. "Have you looked at his file?"

"Not yet," I say.

"Well, hurry the fuck up," Blake says, and sets an envelope in front of me. "That's your first consulting check, in the name of Kelli Vincent. We want you to take on the Ju-Ju case with us. Otherwise, we'll do what you already pointed out as an obvious next move. Call in an expert."

"I didn't do this," Asher says softly. "Blake is just an ethical guy. He does right by people despite the fact that he wanted to use you for bait."

"Ju-Ju decided to make that a reality," I say. "He's targeted me."

"Which is why you take the job with Walker," Asher says, "And you walk away from the bar."

"I can't walk away," I argue. "We've had this conversation. I'm not one of you. I study killers. I don't go to war with them." I laugh without humor. "Well, not by choice. It seems I'm pretty good at getting their attention. Ju-Ju terrifies me. He does. But how do I sleep at night if he targets someone else and actually kills them?"

192

"I don't want you to become bait," Asher says. "No. Correction. I *won't let you* become bait for a serial killer."

"I have a suggestion to help us evaluate Ju-Ju's intentions toward Sierra," Kara says, looking at me. "You're staying here, right?"

"Yes," Asher says, answering for me, his hand squeezing my leg under the table. "Sierra is with me now." It's about as alpha and controlling as it gets, but then he does this Asher-thing he does and he looks down at me. "I want you here, Sierra," he adds, and it is a statement and a question.

"I'm here," I say, offering no timeline for that reply. He hasn't had that reality check and if he's as smart as I think he is, it's a game changer. I look at Kara. "What is your suggestion?"

"We need to know if Ju-Ju really is targeting you for multiple reasons. Is he really focused on you or not? If he's not, and we decide he is, we could miss another target. And if he is, we need to make informed decisions about how to ensure that he doesn't find you beyond the bar."

"You obviously have a plan," Asher says. "What is it?"

"I'd like to dress to appear as if I'm you," Kara says. "Jackets. Hats. I'll go in and out of your apartment." She looks at Asher. "And don't tell us to go to Europe. And don't make me feel fear and guilt over my sister, who is with Kyle and all of Kayden's men. I'm the only victim look-a-like we have. I'm not leaving when a killer is on the loose."

"Actually," Asher says, focused on Blake, not Kara. "We're going to need you here."

"Good," Kara says, ignoring the obvious undertone of something more than Ju-Ju that I know is Devin Marks. "Our plan to have me dress up and move to and from the apartment works but there's one catch."

"What's the catch?" Asher asks, his gaze jerking from Blake to her.

"We have no reason to believe that he's followed her and found her apartment," she says. "Maybe that is simply because he never goes to his victim's homes. But if Sierra doesn't go back to the bar, and he hasn't found her, he might then."

"Then I have to go back," I insist. "We need him to stay focused on me, not someone else."

"You're not bait, Sierra," Asher says. "End of discussion."

I twist around to look at him. "We have to catch him."

"We aren't due back to the bar until Friday night. If he doesn't show up at that piece of shit apartment before then, we'll discuss what comes next." His tone says we won't, and his attention goes to Blake. "Let's go to the balcony." He stands up.

Blake pushes to his feet and rubs his hands together. "Oh goodie. I always do love a good balcony chat."

The minute they walk away, Kara looks at me. "I know you know that at one point Blake suggested making you the bait, but that is not what this plan is about and that was not what it seemed. He was thinking of you as someone that was already bait. Someone we could save while catching Ju-Ju."

"I am. He was right. I'm going to help with Ju-Ju. Whatever it takes, and no matter how much I have to fight Asher over it. But my experience is where I'm a real resource. Once I look at Ju-Ju's file, I feel like I'll have more to offer."

"We'll protect you, Sierra."

I don't think she's talking just about Ju-Ju right now, but I don't lead her any other place. "You mean, Kelli, right?" I open my new file and start to read. "Brunette with blue eyes," I say. "Check."

"Except that you need to do your roots. I see your new growth. You're blonde."

It's a stupid sore spot that shouldn't matter as much as it does. "I'm brunette," I say, swallowing a knot in my throat and looking up at her. "The file says so." I exhale and start to read again. "I'm also twenty-five and born April 11th." I look at her again. "At least I got younger, not older."

"Your parents were killed in a car accident when you were eight. This all checks out under inspection too, just to put your mind at ease. The new you was in foster homes, and bounced around, until you were eighteen. Again, that all checks out."

I nod and flip to a new page in the file only to shake my head at what I find. "No. This doesn't work. I can't have a degree in criminal justice. It's too close to my problem."

"Hide somewhere in the middle," Kara says. "That's the point here. People who have to hide tend to go to one extreme or the other. Being too close to your past or too far apart is what gets you caught. The bar is actually dangerous. It's the kind of place people on the run hide. We need you out of there."

"The middle is the safe zone," I say. "You're sure?"

"Very sure and Blake knows how to fool-proof your identity. He does it for every Walker that goes undercover. He doesn't trust anyone else to do it. Everything you're seeing is a piece of a puzzle. Read more detail. You'll see what I mean."

I'm still not sure how I feel about that degree, but I glance down at the notes and try to take in the entire picture that's been built for me. "I worked for a PI for the past three years," I say, seeing the connection to the degree. "Is this a real PI firm I see listed?"

"Yes. The owner is a friend of ours and he only hires contract employees, all of which rarely know each other. The job will check out. And the story is this: You were working for the PI and crossed paths with Asher on a job. You two fell for each other and we recruited you to our team three months ago. You have payroll records for both jobs and an active bank account." She slides the check in front of me. "Take the paycheck. We need your help with Ju-Ju and we'll pay someone else if not you. And this not only supports your cover story, it reinforces it."

I shake my head. "This isn't going to work. This cover aligns me too closely to you and your team. It's dangerous, especially to Asher. This makes him a target."

"It's what he wanted. He called us early this morning and asked us to connect you to him."

"Why would he do that? He knows what, and who, I'm dealing with."

"Don't let his sense of humor fool you. That man is not just brute force. He's cunning. He's sharp as a razor and he will cut his enemy in creative ways that they never expect. He has a reason for everything he does and if he wants to hurt you, he will."

I'm reminded of Asher's father, and Asher's certainty that he could and would destroy him had he not gone into the Navy when he did.

"And I've never seen him look at a woman like he looks at you," Kara adds. "I would not want to get between him and you."

But Devin Marks does, and he's not just cunning, he's evil. Asher said himself I could leave when I had my new identity but if I leave, Ju-Ju is still free to go after someone else. I look up to find Asher standing at the other side of the table, staring at me and I know he's reading my mind. I know he knows that I'm thinking of leaving. "It's time to go, Kara," Asher says, without looking at her.

Kara sets a card on the table. "That has my number if you need me." She stands up and Blake joins her.

"We'll lock the door on the way out," Blake says, and they head to the door.

Neither Asher nor I move or speak until the door shuts. "You have the resources to leave, Sierra. I made sure of it. Now you have a choice. Stand with me and fight, or run. Which will it be?"

"Don't say 'run' like I'm some sort of cowering fool," I bite out, angry now. "I'm not, but despite Kara calling you smart and cunning, you might not be." I grab the recorder from my pocket and set it on the table. "Your reality check."

LISA RENEE JONES

Chapter Twenty Four

ASHER

Sierra punches play on the recorder and then grabs the back of the kitchen stool, as if bracing herself for what comes next.

"Your wife called the Ridell offices," a familiar male voice that I can't quite place, says, but I know Ridell. They make military robots. *"She asked questions we don't want asked,"* the man adds.

"When?" Another male voice I know to be that of Devin Marks's asks. *"What questions?"*

"Today," the other man says. "She called from a payphone, but we used voice recognition. She pretended to work for you, and tried to find out when a delivery was going to happen. How the hell does she even know about Ridell?"

"I'll handle her," Devin bites out.

"That's not an answer."

"It's the only answer you're getting," Devin snaps back. "I don't answer to you."

"Wrong answer, because if the wrong people find out there's a leak, we're all dead. Make her go away or they'll make you go away." The sound of movement fills the recording. Paper. Clothing. Shuffling. "Do it my way this time," the other man says, clearly handing something to Devin. "Use this."

"What is it?" Devin asks.

"Poison. It won't show up on tests. It'll look like she had a stroke."

The tape ends while my fury is just getting started. "That's when I ran," she says. "I was afraid to stay another moment."

"You recorded this?"

"Yes," she confirms. "He was working. I went by his office to get a check for a charity event I was coordinating. Everyone else was gone. I was terrified, but I stayed that night. I assumed he'd need to plan my murder before he made it happen. I needed to plan as well. If I had any chance of escaping, and getting my mother out of there safely, I needed time to get to the bank without him suspecting anything."

"That meant waiting until morning," I supply.

"Exactly," she confirms. "And that meant I had to wait until he went to work. I had to act like nothing was wrong. Fortunately, he woke to some emergency at work and barely spoke two words to me that morning. The minute he left the house, I packed what I could, went to the bank, and then picked up my mother with thirty grand in my pocket. It was the most I could risk, what I could take without them calling Devin."

I press my hands on the table directly across from her. "Where is your mother now?"

"I told her the truth and then put her on a cruise ship with twenty-five thousand dollars. I wanted her as far away from me as I could get her. From there, I had her get off at one of the ports, an island with a low cost of living."

She gave her mother almost all of her money. "What island?"

"Las Terrenas, in the Dominican Republic, and I was worried about her passport being tracked, but my mother proved resourceful. She met some man who got her a new identity. She never used her passport."

I don't tell her how common an escape path she's chosen, or how likely The Beast will be looking for her, and her mother, through that route. Nor how dirty most of those island officials are, and how quick they'd take a pay-off. "Who was the other man on the audio?" I ask.

"He's your reality check. His name is Norman Casey. He's—"

"Deputy Director of Intelligence at the CIA," I say, the voice on the recording clicking now. "I'm aware of who he is. What is it that you suspected you knew or actually do know and about who? Aside from the fact that they plotted your murder?"

"It started with a few of Devin's phone conversations that I overheard, but didn't quite make sense. Until one did. He ordered the murder of a man I knew who worked inside his operation. I was in denial until the man had a car accident."

"Before or after your car accident?" I challenge, more certain than ever that it was no accident at all.

"After," she says, "and when I was still bedridden. When I heard him order that killing, his tone said that this wasn't the first time. I did my research and tracked a series of apparent accidents that I could tie to him in some way, shape, or form."

"Why were you calling Ridell?"

"I started putting together a file of documents that detailed those people that I believed had been murdered and what I thought might be illegal sales of arms to foreign governments. I was trying to tie Riddell to Devin."

"Do you have those records?"

"Yes, I do," she says. "I wasn't leaving without them. I kept them in a lockbox in Colorado, but I took them with me when I ran. I got nervous, though, carrying them with me. I put them in a new lockbox in Dallas where I planned to turn them into the FBI. Obviously, that went wrong and I had to leave so quickly that I didn't dare go after it."

"We have men there," I say. "I can have—"

"No," she says quickly. "We cannot have random people involved in this."

"My people are not random people."

"No, Asher. No. No. No. That is everything I have on him besides this tape."

"All right," I say, holding up my hands. "Then we'll go together."

"How do you even know Norman Casey?" she says, changing the topic, and I let her. For now.

"I was SEAL Team Six," I say. "We worked so closely with the CIA that we were—they are—often called the CIA's Praetorian Guard."

She blanches. "You were Six? *The* Six?"

"Yeah. I was Six and so was Luke, but neither of us want the attention that announcement gets us. That aside, sweetheart, what you just told me explains a helluva lot."

"What does that mean?"

"Five years ago, the CIA sent my team to Mali to recover a civilian hostage as well as a load of weapons that were supposedly stolen while being delivered to our military. That hostage was your bitch-ass whimpering Beast. Only he wasn't a beast, then. We had to escort him through a hostile village where women and children lived. We were attacked and he freaked the fuck out and grabbed a militant's gun. He killed a woman and two children."

She swallows hard. "Killer. He's a killer. I knew that. I just didn't realize he could pull the trigger himself."

"With ease," I say. "And without remorse. He said they got in the way."

"What did you do? Could you do anything?"

"We escorted him to the extraction point and I put him on the cargo plane that they sent for us. Once he was inside, I joined him, threw him against the wall, pulled my service weapon, and pointed it between his eyes. I proceeded to tell him that if I ever saw him outside of my duty, I'd kill him. Luke was the next on board and he joined me. He repeated exactly what I'd done and said. Every member of our team repeated my actions and my words."

"What did he do?" she asks. "How did he react?"

"He threatened us. He said he'd report us. I told him that he'd murdered those people and that was a war crime, but I told him I wouldn't bother reporting him. I'd just kill him."

"And then what?"

"He shook like a baby, as well he should have. We all took our seats across from him. We left him in a seat alone on one side of the plane, and not one of us spoke. Not that we could over the engine noise. We all just stared him down. So you see, sweetheart. If he finds you next to me, and Luke for that matter, I promise you he'll think twice about coming at you. Because if one of our SEAL team goes down, the rest will go after him. All I have to do is put them on alert."

"It's not just him," she says. "It's the CIA. You know that now."

"I get it. I do. But I have friends inside the agency that I trust."

"Like I had a friend in the FBI in Texas? I did. That's who I went to for help. I knew he would know what to do about Devin. But he was Team Devin. He gave me up. That's what

I'm telling you, Asher. Devin's reach is wider than you're giving him credit for. CIA and FBI, and even broader."

"We have the team and resources to handle him and to take him down. He needs to be taken down."

"CIA and FBI, Asher."

"Royce and Kara are ex-FBI and I will tell you that there isn't a naive or stupid bone in either of their bodies. They get it. They know corruption exists. We have the right team to beat Devin Marks."

"I need to think," she says, standing up and pressing her hands to her face.

I round the table and catch her hips with my hands. "Every minute I give you on this, I give him."

"I know that, but by being here, I'm the magnet that could be drawing him to you, Asher. I don't doubt that Luke and Blake are good men, but they have families. I don't want them hurt and one mistake, one trusted person inside your circle that's disloyal, will get everyone killed."

"I need you to trust me," I say. "For now, we'll isolate our trust to just the Walker brothers themselves. We'll talk through the risks with them."

"Not yet. It's too soon. I told you. I need to think."

"I have to call my SEAL team and alert them that there's trouble with Devin Marks, and that means Luke, too. I need—*we* need them on alert."

"*Not yet.*" She curls her fingers around my shirt. "What part of that do you not understand? Not yet, Asher."

"Sierra—"

"You can't tell me none of those SEALs are corruptible."

"I won't tell you that there is no SEAL that is corruptible, but my team, the men I worked with, are not. I would bet my life on it. I *have* bet my life on it. I don't have to tell Luke, or any of my SEAL team, that this is about you. I just need to put them on alert that Devin Marks may need to be dealt with, once and for all."

"Luke isn't stupid," she argues. "If you put him on alert about Devin Marks, he'll know it's about me. So I repeat: *Not yet.*"

Not yet.

I drag her to me. "I am trying not to push you, but 'not yet' is a phrase I don't accept readily with lives on the line, including yours. We're going to have to get by them now."

"Let go of me, Asher."

"That's not going to happen. I'm all in, remember?"

"And what if I'm not?"

Anger burns in me hard and fast, and I tangle fingers in her hair. "Let's find out." My mouth closes down on hers, tongue stroking deep. She makes a frustrated sound and that turns to a moan and in an instant she's kissing me back, wrapping her arms around me, melting into me, holding onto me like she's afraid I'll escape. But it's her that keeps wanting to run, her that I'm not going to let escape. I'm not leaving her exposed. And that's what she's about to find out. "Call me him if you want, but I'm not letting you go."

"You aren't him," she says, her fingers pressing into my arms. "I don't think you're him."

"Prove it. Trust me."

"I do trust you."

"No."

"Yes. I do. That isn't the point."

I cup her face and tilt her head back. "You have to let me do what I need to do."

"I just need to breathe."

"Breathe with me," I say, and I cover her mouth with mine again, and that's when I snap. When I want to own this woman like I know she doesn't want to be owned. But I need her. I want her. I have to have her, and protect her. She kisses me like she wants the same. Like she needs me, and wants me just as fucking badly. We are wild, hot, desperate. We are all over each other, touching, licking, biting. And it isn't long until her pants are gone and mine are down. I'm lifting her, the thick, hard length of my erection pressing inside her, *all the way* inside her, and she is tight and hot and soft, and strong in all the right ways. I hold her like that, our bodies connected, and she holds me. I don't know for how long, but with her weight against me, our bodies molded close, my need for this woman burns deeper, sharper than any evil she believed Devin Marks holds. She buries her face in my neck, and she smells sweet and floral— too sweet for the war she's now forced into. War that consumes and leaves no escape unless you fight and win. I know that feeling well, while she knows it only now. I understand that now, here, holding her, buried inside her. I understand the fear, the anger, the need to make the right decisions and the fear that you will not. And the need to escape the pressure, if only for a short while.

It's that need that has me pumping into her and pulling her against me. She holds on, panting next to my ear, and when I feel her snap, feel her slip into this moment with me, I lose everything but her, and this, and I do not even know where we start and end. It's a whirlwind of passion, and a near desperate grinding of our bodies, until we are both shaking, quaking, trembling.

I come back to the present with the memory of that recording, and the man who is supposed to be her husband plotting her murder. With the memory of the scar on her belly that I know was that bastard's doing. That bastard will pay. He will hurt. He will suffer.

I bury my face in her neck and whisper, "He will burn in hell before he touches you again."

Chapter Twenty Five

ASHER

I ease Sierra to a stool and we both quickly put our clothes back in order. I'm about to reach for her when she steps to me first and jabs a finger in my chest. "You push too hard, too fast."

I catch her hand between us. "It's necessary. It's about protecting everyone near this."

"I know that. I want that, too, but I know none of these people well. My husband, the man I married, whose bed I shared, wants to *kill me*. That is the kind of betrayal I've experienced, and yet I told you everything. You Asher. Just tonight. Give me a few hours, to process that. To talk to you about. To breathe. Do you understand at all?"

And there it is. The reality check she told me I needed. She's right. She's been cut and cut deeply. Even an FBI agent turned on her. "I do," I say, my hands settling at her waist. "You're right. I'm wrong. Let's breathe. And eat while we do. I'm starving. Are you starving?"

"Yes. I'm starving."

"Good. Because someone once said that pancakes make everything better."

"Did you say that?"

I laugh. "Yes. You're catching onto me." I kiss her firmly on the lips and then release her, but the minute I start to move away, she catches my arm. "I know we need to tell the

Walker brothers, and soon. I just want time to talk through how that looks with you. Okay?"

"Completely fucking okay. What else?"

"Can I look at the Ju-Ju file now while we eat?"

I decide right then with that turnaround and refocus that going after Ju-Ju somehow gives her purpose, which I get. She needs to feel like she's doing something and that something is good. It's the entire fucking reason I joined the SEALs. I kiss her temple. "You got it." I release her and walk around the table, grabbing the file from the paperwork beside my computer and setting it in front of the seat next to mine. "It's all yours." I grab the bags and turn to the counter. "This may not warm up well," I say over my shoulder. "But we'll give it a try. We might need to order something new." She doesn't reply, and I stick a plate in the microwave.

"This is the entire file?" she asks.

"That's a big file," I say. "What are you looking for?"

"More information on his family," she says, turning in her seat to face me.

I lean on the counter next to the microwave. "There's basics in there, though I admit that's not an area I focused on. What is it you want that isn't there?"

"Just more," she says. "Maybe it's here." She turns to the table again and starts digging through the pages.

The microwave buzzes and I pull out the food inside, only to find it rubbery. "This is not going well." I throw the food in the trash.

"Ju-Ju is rich?" she asks, sounding astounded. "As in he doesn't have to work, let alone sell drugs?"

"That's right," I say, grabbing a box that holds my favorite muffins and joining her. "He inherited a ton of money from his stockbroker father." I set the muffins on the table between us. "That's one of the reasons they wanted me on this case. Because I come from a wealthy background. Blake felt I might have some insight someone else might not."

"You might," she says. "If the right situation arises."

I lift the top to the box and show her the contents. "Chocolate chip."

Her eyes go wide. "Those are the biggest muffins I've ever seen in my life and they look amazing."

"They taste like Tollhouse cookies."

"Sold," she says, tearing off a piece of the muffin while I grab the rest of it. "Does Ju-Ju live like he has money?" she asks before taking a bite of her muffin, which immediately distracts her. "Okay, wow," she says, pointing into the box. "These are incredible and probably a thousand calories a muffin. I really need to get back to jogging."

"I'll take you in the morning," I promise. "Or even later tonight. And as for Ju-Ju. He lives in a place off the Hudson River that is valued at five million and we traced the funds. It's not bought with drug money."

"In other words," she says. "He has no logical reason to sell drugs. This has to be driven by something in his past that isn't in this file. It says nothing about his mother. There is no career. No details on her beyond age and birthdate, with a few random, inconsequential facts. But she, who is petite with brown hair, like the victims, is not inconsequential. Did she have a job that I don't see listed?"

"She didn't work outside of the home is my understanding," I say. "There is not much to know about her."

"If Ju-Ju is the killer, in theory and usually in application, there's something in his past that will connect him to these murders. It has to be related to her. Can you use your hacking skills and find out more?"

"We've hacked. We've looked."

"Have you looked up his old school friends? His old neighbors? Have you asked them questions about Ju-Ju and his family?"

"No. We have not. We've been focused on who he is now and what he might do next."

"Which is logical, of course," she says. "But if we talk to the people in his past, someone will know more about his family and maybe even him. If he's really your guy, there is something in the past we can use to link him to the murders before he kills again."

"Our guy," I correct, opening a bottle of water. "You're in this now, too." My cellphone buzzes with a text and I grab it, only to laugh. "Blake says he forgot to get the key to your apartment." I type a message.

Sierra laughs. "Did you tell him to try the thrift shop or the subway?"

"I told him to take a tool kit."

"If I'm staying here, I need my things from there."

"If? And what things do you really need?"

"I didn't mean if, and I guess nothing. I have nothing."

"Now you do have things," I assure her. "And a paycheck that will be regular. They'll use you for other jobs."

"I don't want them to feel obligated to pay me because of you. That's not how I need, or want, to operate my life."

"I didn't tell him to pay you. Let me see the check." She grabs it and hands it to me. I open it and look inside before setting it back down. "That's our standard consulting fee, and it's exactly what they'd offer someone else. The Walker men are good men. They don't screw people. They do what's right." I hand her back the check.

"It's ten thousand dollars. That's standard?"

"They're billing the client, and if your role grows, they'll pay you additional fees."

"I don't even have my Ph.D."

"You have more experience than any of us with serial killers and we're all pretty damn experienced. That's the thing about Walker. We run a deep pool of experience and when we come up short, we fix it. We win. Turns out, we fix it and win with you this time."

"About that." She reaches for her own file and opens it, digging through it to find her new driver's license. "This and the money. You know I could leave."

"I've asked you before, and I'll ask you now: Is that what you want?"

"No. I don't want to leave here. Not as long as you're here, but am I being selfish? Because I want to be here with you? Because it feels good and safe to have you and your people around me?"

"No. You are not."

"If anyone dies because of me, I will never forgive myself."

I stand up and take her hand. "Come with me."

"Where are we going?"

"You'll see." I lead her back up the stairs and down the hallway to the left and I don't stop until I'm at the locked door at the end. I key in a code there and look at her. "5571," I say. "Got it?"

"Got it."

I open the door and lead her inside, where there is a long wooden table facing us with chairs on either side. I point at the walls left and right. "Both have nearly invisible panels built in that lower and open. If you know they are there, you can see them." I motion to the one on the left and lead her across the wooden floor. I drag a finger down a small line in the wall. "That's the seam."

"It's nearly impossible to see. This really opens?"

"It really opens." I move to the center of the wall and point down. "Step on the seam in the wood that is at the exact center of the wall. It's a sensitive pressure point. You touch it, it responds." I lower my foot and tap it. The wall folds down, as if we've opened a suitcase lid, to display my collection of small firearms.

"What is all of this?"

"Every member of the Walker crew has a collection of weapons that could supply at least a half dozen of our staff if ever needed."

"Is all of this legal?"

"Every last bit of it."

"Then why hide it?"

"This is no different than the caution I gave you with the mace. Anything you can use to hurt someone, they can use to hurt you. Protect it. Protect yourself." I remove two small firearms from the shelf that I know will be suitable for her and motion behind us. We move to the table and I round it to sit facing the wall, and at my prodding she claims the seat across from me. I settle the weapons between us, resting side-by-side on the wooden surface. "What do you know about guns?"

"Nothing except the idea of holding something that can kill someone is rather intimidating."

"It is to most people but knowledge and hands-on experience eases that feeling, as does the peace of mind, in knowing you can protect yourself."

"I want to learn," she says. "What's the difference in the two guns?"

"This is a Ruger LCR Revolver," I say, indicating the weapon on the left. "Small, light, and it's going to have a small kickback when you fire, which you should be able to handle with ease. It's the best choice for you now, until you learn to how to handle a semi-automatic."

"Why is this my best choice now?"

"You don't have to load a magazine, which can be intimidating and make you freeze up if you have to reload. And you don't have to cock the gun under pressure. You'll just point and shoot." I open the cylinder. "This is where your bullets go, but we're not going to load it right now." I close the cylinder. "It's basically point and shoot, but it's not as easy to hit a target as you think. We're going to work on hand position and target practice. Once you master the revolver, we'll move to a semi-automatic."

"Why use the semi-automatic over the revolver?"

"Semi-automatic weapons will recoil, or punch back, less. The triggers are easier to manipulate. The sights are usually much bigger and better. They're prone to less malfunctions and failure than the average revolver. And most importantly, semi-autos have two to three times the ammo capacity of a revolver of equal size and weight. That means you can keep shooting if you need to."

"Then shouldn't I just jump straight to whatever this other gun is?"

"Sig Sauer PS238," I say. "And no. I've heard women say that a handgun is like a pair of shoes. It has to fit right and while I agree with that statement, what's more important to me is that handling it becomes as second nature as holding a pen in your hand to write. You need to be able to load fast and aim correctly. If you take a bad shot, or hesitate with the recoil, while you're recovering, the weapon can be taken from you."

"Now I'm intimidated."

"You won't be. We'll practice and practice until you don't even have to think to handle the weapon. Until you are so confident, and skilled, that if someone comes at you, you have a bullet with their name on it."

"You mean a bullet with Devin Marks's name on it."

"You're learning to protect yourself because it's smart. Because that skill erases a fear you don't want to live with the rest of your life. Because you're now one of the Walker staff and that is a mandatory part of working with us. As for Devin Marks, he's mine. I have a bullet in my gun with his name on it. You can count on it."

Chapter Twenty Six

Sierra

Asher and I spend the next few hours in the gun room, working on my skills, among other things. Once he feels that I've mastered the basics of a classroom revolver lesson, we move on to the semi-automatic. He teaches me how to load the semi-automatic and has me practice with blank bullets until my hand randomly hurts and forces a break. In between that practice, we eat Funyuns and drink beer, and he drills me about the details of my new identity to ensure I don't slip up in public, the very existence of Kelli Vincent driving me to replay Devin's plot to kill me in my head. In turn, I become more and more motivated to protect myself, to start learning how to handle a gun like the way a pro like Asher can handle a gun.

Eventually Asher grabs his computer and starts researching Ju-Ju's past and the results at least present options his file does not offer. "We have a long list of schoolmates, and neighbors, even co-workers of Ju-Ju's father to try to connect with now," he announces after about an hour of work. "Our best bet is to plan a roundtable with the team tomorrow and all of us start making calls. You can dissect the information as we get it in."

"Sounds good," I say, trying to load again, only to have my hand freeze up, and I growl. "I don't understand how I'm getting worse at this." I set the weapon down. "I should be getting better."

"Your hand is tired," Asher says, glancing at his watch. "And it's late for Sunday shopping anyway. We need to get to a store to buy you a purse that you can carry that in."

My gaze catches on his watch, an Omega with a thick silver biker-style look with a wide black leather band. It's stylish, about seven grand, and it fits him. It also reminds me of the past I want behind me. "Sierra?"

I blink and look up at Asher. "Yes?"

"Why are you staring at my watch?" he asks, his arm resting on the table near my hand.

"I like it. It's very you." I reach out and cover his arm with my hand. "Like the tattoos. They fit you." I stroke the image of a skull that wears a scarf and looks like a pirate. "A Navy pirate?" I ask.

"Yes." He covers my hand on his arm with his hand. "Why were you staring at my watch, Sierra?"

"It's not important."

"It is to me, so humor me."

"The Beast had me buy Omega watches for his inner circle last Christmas. An extravagant gift meant to win their loyalty. That's what he does, Asher. He buys people or he threatens them. Or he kills them like he wants to kill me."

Asher stares at me for several beats, his lashes half veiled, and pulls his arm back and starts to unbuckle his watch. I cover it with my hand. "What are you doing?"

"We're getting rid of him in every way."

"He doesn't get that much control. Keep the watch, Asher. I really do like it on you. I want it to be about you. It is about you. The only reason that man is on my mind is because he's dangerous, and I don't even have the evidence to prove it. I left it in Texas. Okay?"

"No," he says. "It's not okay, but it's going to be." He leans over the table, cups my neck and kisses me, a deep, drugging kiss before he says, "Let's get out of here." He stands up. "Leave the weapons out for now. One or both will be on your person once we get that purse. There's a Bloomingdale's not far from here."

I stand up and study him, certain that Bloomingdale's and purses is not what's on his mind. I see that in his face. I feel it in his energy. I open my mouth to ask where that confession over the watch has taken him, but his cellphone rings. He pulls it from his pocket and glances at the screen. "Blake," he tells me and motions to the file laying on the table. "Grab your new ID."

I flip through the file and snap up my driver's license and stare down at the girl named Kelli Vincent who looks like me. The person I have to become if I let Devin Marks win. I stick the ID in my pocket and head out of the room and hunt down my purse and phone. Asher heads on downstairs, and I snatch my purse from the bathroom and follow him, but I don't hear a word he's saying to Blake. I'm thinking about Kelli Vincent, the girl with The Beast in the mirror, who has to find a way to break that glass.

———————⟨∞⟩———————

A few minutes later, Asher and I step onto the street and he settles his arm around my shoulders and pulls me close to him, our hips aligned. We walk at a decent speed, trying to hit the stores before they close, but still tucked in close, steps paced together, and I wonder if I ever walked a sidewalk with Devin in this way. If I did, I can't even remember it, and that's probably because it wasn't like this. I didn't feel safe. I didn't feel warm all over despite an early evening chill, signaling that late October is finally here. "What did Blake say?" I ask, since they literally didn't hang up until a few moments ago, even talking through the struggle of bad elevator service.

"Kara got into your apartment," he says. "So far Ju-Ju is at home and hasn't left."

"What about Terrance? He could be helping Ju-Ju? Or someone else, even?"

"You think that someone might be helping Ju-Ju with the actual murders? Not just feeding him information they think is related to his drug deals?"

"The Son of Sam insisted he was part of a cult. He even named the members, but waited until they died. I could name other examples. So do I think it's possible? Yes."

"If that's the case, Terrance would be an obvious target. Or someone from another bar. He has no other communications. He's a loner. But I told Blake about the work we've done on Ju-Ju. We're going to meet at the office at ten tomorrow. Luke and Jacob will be there as well."

"Who will be watching Ju-Ju?" I ask.

"Chance, our new guy, is proving stealthy. He's going to follow Ju-Ju, while Rick, another newer recruit, is watching Terrance."

"Kara will be watching for anyone suspicious, not just Ju-Ju, right?"

"She's sharp and smart, but so is Blake, and that man would die for her. No one is getting to her. Of that, I'm certain. Like no one is getting to you, Sierra." He kisses my head, and I swear, I feel a squeeze in my heart. I'm falling for this man. I'm leaning on him. I trust him and I didn't think I could ever trust again. But just as he's protecting me I need to protect him. I'm just not sure how to do that. I'm not sure I haven't already ensured I *can't* do that.

We head down into the subway and soon we're on a nearly empty train and sitting at the end of a bench. "Kara wants you to call her," Asher says. "Why don't you let me put her number and about half a dozen others in your phone."

I pull it from my purse. "Why does Kara want me to call her?"

"Blake didn't say." He keys in her number and tags it with her name before adding several more. "Okay," he says when he's done. "You have me, Luke, his wife, Julie, Kara, Blake, Royce, and his wife, Lauren." He glances at me. "I'm still going. You have Jacob, who you will meet tomorrow, and Kyle and Myla. They are gone now, but Kyle and I are close."

"Which is why you want to tell him about Alvarez."

"Which is why Blake and I have to have that conversation, and preferably tonight. As for the numbers I've put in your phone, consider these people your safe inner circle now. I trust them with my life and that means yours. Memorize them. If you get separated from me and you can't reach me, then you call them."

"In what order?"

"Luke first," he says, "but any of the brothers after him."

"Luke first because he's your SEAL brother?"

"Yes. Exactly. I know him and how he thinks better than anyone else on our team." The train stops and we exit, hand in hand. I'm getting used to my hand in his. I'm getting used to his gorgeous tattoos. I'm getting used to his kisses.

We climb the stairs and exit to the street, and it's not long until we're in the handbag section of Bloomingdale's with Asher giving me instructions on what we're looking for. "Pick something you like, but will be able to wear crossbody. That way it is always attached to your hip. You want it to be small enough that it doesn't impede you if you have to move quickly. You want it to have easy access to the weapon, with a top slit, but it needs to zip. That way no one can reach inside and grab the gun."

"Don't I need a permit to carry?" I ask as we start to look around.

"Yes," Asher says. "But that requires you go to the Sherriff's office. You aren't getting one now. We don't want that kind of attention."

That response is oddly comforting. He gets it. Law enforcement is a problem for me, *for us,* now.

A pretty redhead stops in front of us. "Can I help you find something?"

"Yes," Asher says, and if he notices how truly stunning she is, he doesn't show it at all. "We need a bag this size." He holds up a small bag. "But it needs to zip at the top and be large enough for a handgun."

I gape at him for repeating what he's just told me, including the part about the gun, but the woman is unfazed. "I know the perfect bag." She turns and starts walking.

"Did you really just tell her we need a bag for a gun?"

"Would you rather me say an umbrella?"

"Smart-ass," I chide. "And yes. Maybe."

"She's a carrier."

"How do you know?"

He winks. "I get gun mojo off of people." He takes my hand. "Come on." We hurry forward and meet the gun-carrying redheaded store clerk at the Prada counter. "This is the Quilted Bowler Crossbody Bag," she says, holding up a purse. "It has a zipper and a spacious interior that will hold a small handgun. And it's a steal at just under $1,800. The Paradigm tote matches it well, if you ever need more space. It's two thousand and you can fit a small computer inside right along with the smaller purse."

"We'll take them both," Asher says and then looks at me. "If you like them."

"I do, but—"

"We'll take them," Asher repeats.

The woman lights up. "Excellent." She motions to a register. "Let's head that direction." She grabs both bags and starts walking.

I, in turn, grab Asher's arm. "Four thousand dollars for purses?"

"Yeah. What about it?"

"It's too much."

"The bags work. You like them. We can get something else later in the week if you want."

"No. I don't. Asher—"

He kisses me. "I like buying you things. Another first for me. Don't make that a bad thing."

The way he says it, the roughness of his voice, the sincerity, undoes me. With Devin, everything was about his power and control. With Asher, it is something far different that I can't even name, but I also can't argue. "Thank you."

His eyes warm. "You're here. That's all I need."

Just like that, my heart squeezes again, and once again his fingers are linked with mine and we're headed to the register. After Asher has paid, and I've stuffed my temporary purse and the new smaller Prada inside the larger bag, which has a strap I use crossbody, we leave the store. We step outside into the chill of the now murky darkness outdoors, the stars covered by clouds. We start walking and a block down the street, with Asher by my side, and his arm back around my shoulders, I have a sudden realization. For the first time in nine months, I've forgotten to look over that shoulder. I'm far from out of danger, and yet, this man is the right kind of Beast. The kind everyone else should fear. The kind that makes Devin Marks quake in his shoes. Good versus evil. Asher versus Devin.

No.

Me versus The Beast.

Whatever the case, while moments ago, I'd felt safe, now I feel like this is the calm before the storm, and as if driving home that point, thunder rumbles in the near distance. Perhaps the too-near distance, and with it comes a sense of foreboding. The Beast is near. He will always be near unless I shut him down. But how do you shut down someone with a worldwide network? Even if you kill that person, that network exists. That network still keeps coming.

Chapter Twenty Seven

ASHER

It's all about the watch.

Sierra and I take the subway back to the apartment and I continue the mental path that I've been on since her reaction to me simply looking at my watch: time matters. I know all too well, from experience, that too much or too little of anything, most specifically time, can get a person killed. That, along with the vivid image in my mind of Devin Marks shooting two children and an innocent mother, killing them all, becomes a stark, sharp reminder that he wields a blade that he will use to cut anyone in his path. Sierra knows this. She's afraid and that fear is driving her actions. They can't drive mine, no matter how hard I have to push her.

We exit the subway and our path to the apartment takes us past the door of Walker Security where I pause. "I need to talk to Luke, and Blake, too, if he's back from your apartment, and then we can run by the grocery store."

"I thought we were going by the Walker offices in the morning?"

"Tomorrow we'll have a room full of people focused on Ju-Ju, as they should be. I need to discuss Kyle and Myla, among other things."

"Of course," she says. "But the office looks dark."

I unlock the door. "We'll walk through to the stairs. It's the only way to get to the living quarters outside of the garage." I flip on the light and hold the door for her.

She enters, and in a few minutes, we've locked back up and we're on the other side of the building, flipping the office lights back out and climbing the wide, wooden steps. "Do the brothers all live on the same floor?"

"Used to," I say. "With a baby coming, Royce and Lauren wanted more space. They just remodeled an unfinished floor and moved in. Kyle and Myla took their old place." We reach the floor that is our destination. "This is it." We take a few steps to the forked hallway directly in front of us. "Left is Blake and Kara. Right is Luke and Julie. Down the hall behind us is Kyle and Myla, when they're here."

I lead her to Luke and Julie's place and ring the bell. Almost immediately, Luke opens the door, in his typical uniform of jeans and a Walker T-shirt. "Come in you two," he says, his tone welcoming. That's Luke. Easygoing. Cool as fuck until you give him a reason to be deadly. Most people will never see the latter. I have, and right about now that latter is what I like most about him. "Julie and Lauren are in the kitchen." He backs up and I urge Sierra forward.

"Do I smell cookies?" I ask as Sierra moves down the hallway.

"Yes," Luke says. "Because apparently now Lauren and her baby can eat only cookies, cucumbers, and ranch dip."

"What happened to the ice cream?" I say as I join him in the hallway.

"It makes her sick now." He shuts the door.

"Sierra!"

At the sound of Julie greeting Sierra like she already knows her, I give Luke a quiet, "We need to talk in private."

"I assumed as much," Luke says, as our women disappear around the corner. Luke and I follow, bringing his newly remodeled apartment into view, the new floors some kind of dark grayish brown wood. The entire place looking like a spread from a magazine I've never read, nor will I ever read. The formerly flat ceiling is now inset low. The living area to the left is done in muted white couches and a boxy table. We head in the other direction toward the open kitchen where Lauren sits at the head of a long teakwood table, I've never seen before, with a glass of milk and cookies in front of her. I look at Luke. "To think you used to just have some brown couch and a glass table someone told you to buy."

Luke laughs. "Marriage changes things, man, and not for the worse."

"You want a cookie?" Julie asks, looking every bit the Marilyn Monroe twin people call her, as she carries a tray to the table.

"I would love a cookie," Sierra says, sitting down on a chair next to Lauren that looks like a damn tree trunk. Who wants a tree trunk in their house?

"I really need a damn cookie," I say, walking to the table and taking two, before giving Sierra a wink and then joining Luke at the island a few feet away. Both of us sitting on some fancy silver stools, facing the girls. "That's the new Prada release," Julie says, fawning over Sierra's new bags. "I didn't know this was out already."

"Can I see it?" Lauren asks.

Meanwhile I down my last cookie and interrupt with a more urgent matter. "Do I have to be pregnant to get milk around here?"

Sierra looks up at me at the same time Lauren does, both of them brunette beauties. A fact that has me flashing back to Royce's furious reaction to Blake taking the Ju-Ju case when the women look like Lauren and Kara, and now, Sierra. I'd thought he was overly protective. I don't anymore. Funny how a shot of mace and the woman who tortured me with it have quickly changed my perspective.

"About that milk, Asher," Lauren says, snapping me back to the present. "You get milk if you're pregnant or an asshole. You qualify as at least one of those two things."

"You've been hanging around Blake too much," I say. "You used to be so nice."

She laughs. "You know I love you and you can have all the milk you want. It's Julie and Luke's. I have my own." She looks at Sierra. "I hear you have a Ph.D. in psychology? And you've actually interviewed several living serial killers."

Sierra's gaze shoots to mine and Luke hands me a pint of milk. "That's my big mouth talking there, Sierra," Luke says. "Lauren's a criminal defense attorney. I told her I thought you might help her on a few of her cases."

"What's said in this room stays in this room," I tell her.

Lauren covers Sierra's hand with hers. "What happens in this building is like Vegas. It stays here." She smiles at Sierra. "Sometimes it's even just as exciting."

And there it is. One of the reasons I brought Sierra here tonight. I wanted her to feel the bond that is this family unit, be it family by blood or those extended members like myself. Sierra shares a look of understanding with me before she smiles at Lauren. "Thank you. And no, I don't have a Ph.D. Not yet. Close. Or maybe never."

"Never say never," I say. "Not in the Walker clan."

"We'd love to hear about the interviews you've done," Lauren says. "And we're going to help make calls on the Ju-Ju case tomorrow. Julie has client meetings, but I've been so sick that I've been taking Mondays and Fridays off when I can."

"You both practice criminal law?" Sierra asks.

"Isn't Royce back tomorrow?" I ask quickly, trying to avoid the topic of Julie's legal specialty of high profile divorces, that might hit a hotspot.

"He got delayed," Lauren tells me. "He won't be back until Wednesday."

Which means I'm going to need to call him. The doorbell rings and before Luke can even get up, Blake and Kara are walking into the room. "Do I smell cookies?" Blake says, making a beeline for the kitchen.

"Do not eat all of my cookies, Blake," Lauren warns while Kara sits down next to Sierra.

"Of course I won't eat all of the pregnant woman's cookies," Blake says, already at the table and taking two of them. "Why would you think I would be that cruel?'

"Because you're a pig," I say. "We all know it." Lauren and Kara chime in in agreement, and there is laughter that pretty much sums up the room's agreement on that point. There is also an exchange between Sierra and Kara that ends in more laughter, with their heads tilted low in conversation, in a budding friendship.

Conversation flows for a good fifteen minutes, and there is a point in the midst of many voices and more laughter when Sierra's lashes lower, a bittersweet look on her face. She likes them. She trusts them, but she's confused in some way. I eye Luke and he says, "Now?"

"Now."

"Blake?" he asks.

"Just you right now," I say, wanting to talk about Sierra, but also Kyle, and to do so with someone objective about Alvarez, which Blake is not.

229

We both stand and Luke indicates the cantilevered wood and steel staircase. I pause behind Sierra, my hands on her shoulders, and lean down to her ear. "I'll be just a few minutes."

She covers my hand with hers and nods, and I catch Lauren's warm look at our intimacy. They get it. I'm crazy about her. I have to free her. I lean in and kiss Sierra before I leave her there and follow Luke up the stairs that are just wide enough for one. We enter what equates to a den with a corner bar, pool table and a brown leather couch framing a stainless-steel fireplace, two matching chairs on either side of both.

Luke and I claim the pair of chairs that face the stairs, keeping any company in view. "Are we talking about Kyle or Sierra?" Luke asks.

"Both," I say. "What's your opinion on the Kyle-Alvarez situation?"

"I'm torn, man. The buzz about Alvarez being alive could be nothing more than the cartel trying to play a game with law enforcement or a rival cartel."

"In other words, these rumors could float around for a lifetime," I say. "Kyle and Myla can't hide for the rest of theirs."

"Agreed," he says. "But I do think that the two of them being in Europe while we investigate is a good idea. And Myla was traumatized by that man. At least when we tell her, we can give her the facts."

"We can't let this drag out."

"Agreed again," Luke says, "But right now, we have Ju-Ju to deal with and whatever is going on with Sierra."

We.

Not: *me.*

Not: my problem.

Not: her problem.

This is the part of the Walker clan I hope Sierra is starting to understand downstairs right now. "I need one of the Walker planes."

"When?"

"Sunrise. I want to get there and get back as soon as possible and it's not a short trip."

"What can you tell me?"

"I'm going to Dallas to get the ammunition I need to make Sierra's problem go away. But when I'm there, I'm going to talk Adam into joining us. Does that recruitment bonus still stand?"

"Hell yeah. We need him." He narrows his eyes on me. "Do you need him while you're there?"

"Yes."

He studies me a few beats. "Do you need me?"

"I need you to protect Sierra."

"That would be easier if you told me what was going on."

"She doesn't trust anyone but me and believe me, man, when you find out what this is, you'll understand."

"That's why you brought her here. To get her familiar with everyone and how we operate."

"Yes. It is."

"Give me something here," Luke says. "Give me a scale. On a scale of missions—Cambodia to Syria, how does this rank? How bad is this?"

Sierra steps into the room. "Bad enough for me to go to that safe house you offered me."

I stand up and so does Luke. "You don't need a safe house, Sierra," I say. "You have me."

"And me," Luke says.

"I believe you," she says. "I believe everyone in this house would help me." She looks at me. "I know that's why

231

you brought me here and thank you. It worked. They're great. They're wonderful. They're *all wonderful*."

"Whatever you're running from," Luke says. "We can—"

"I'm not running," she says. "I want to fight. I want to shut him down forever, if that is even possible, but I can't do that while placing other people in the line of fire. I need to go to that safe house, Luke. You have to be the one to take me there. He can't see it because he's—we're—It's just—it's the right move."

"We'll talk about it," Luke says.

"We can talk on the way out of here," she presses.

"Sierra," I say.

"No, Asher," she says. "No to whatever you're going to say."

"Whoever this is," Luke interjects. "Or whatever this is—"

"Devin Marks," Sierra shocks me by saying. "I'm his wife, who he wants dead. Are you ready for me to leave now?" She holds up a hand. "Don't answer. Don't be the hero like Asher right now. I'm going to do the right thing, the thing two SEALs would do. I'm leaving before someone gets hurt." She turns and heads down the stairs.

Chapter Twenty Eight

Sierra

The minute I turn to go down the stairs, I find Blake standing in front of me. "Welcome to your safe house," he says.

My mind explodes with one word: *No. No. No. No.* What part of 'I'm married and Asher is trying to get himself killed does this man not understand'? "Do you even know who Devin Marks is?" I demand.

"I'm ex-ATF, sweetheart. Yes. I know who he is."

"What does the ATF have to do with him? He sells military weapons."

"Some of which ended up in Mexico, in cartel hands, more than once."

Asher's hands come down on my shoulders. "Come sit down, Sierra."

I turn to face him. "I'm married, Asher. To *another man.* What part of that *do you not understand*? And now they, all your people, know that fact."

"Sierra—"

"Why don't you get it?" I demand, curling my fingers around his shirt. "You can't run off to Dallas and plot some attack. You can't do it. I'm married to a man who will kill you all. He's not you. I'm married to another man. I'm—"

He kisses me, and he kisses me like no one is watching, like he'd kissed me in the thrift store. His hands on my face, his lips on my lips and his tongue stroking deep, long, and when his mouth parts mine, he says. "That's how much I care about your marriage to a man who wants to kill you."

"You cannot—"

"I can," he says. "I will."

"They all know. They all know I'm married now."

He lowers his forehead to mine. "Stop, Sierra. I know what you're doing."

"I'm trying to leave."

He pulls back and looks down at me. "You're freaked out about me going to Dallas. I'm going to get the evidence you gathered. I'm going to get him. And I'm not going to let you go. I'm not backing away from this."

My chest knots and I have a rare moment in all of this where I want to cry. "I don't want you to die. I don't want anyone to die because of me."

He cups my face. "Easy, sweetheart. We're okay. I'm okay. No one is going to die. That's the reason we take action. To stop him from killing again. Come sit. We'll figure it out. Yes?"

"You're a stubborn, stubborn man."

"And you're a stubborn, brave woman." He kisses me. "Come." He laces his fingers with mine and I don't pull away. I cave to the moment and let him walk me into the room, but I don't give up on my cause, which is protecting him, because he's not going to give up on me and protecting me. In other words, my only other option is to try to get the Walker brothers on my side and drag him out of this. With that in mind, I let Asher lead me further into the room to a chair, while he claims the one next to me and Blake and Luke sit across from us.

"I'm going to let you tell your story, Sierra," Asher says, and I know this is because he doesn't want to tell more than

I want told. Because this man is pretty much perfect except for his hero complex.

"I married him thinking he was Prince Charming," I tell the Walker brothers. "Turns out he's the Beast under the bridge." I pull the recorder from my pocket and play it for them.

When it's over, Luke looks at Asher. "We should have killed him when we had the chance."

"My exact thought," Asher agrees.

"That was Norman Casey, the Deputy Director of Intelligence of the CIA, on that tape with Marks, wasn't it?" Luke asks.

"Yes," Asher says. "It was, and to make matters even more complicated, Sierra went to a federal agent in Dallas for help. He turned on her."

"What's the name?" Blake asks, pulling his phone from his pocket.

"Dirk Bennett," I say. "He's high up the chain."

He types a text message and then looks at us all. "I just group texted Royce and Kara and asked if either know him."

"Devin Marks has connections in every agency and armed service operation," I say. "People you think you trust are with him, I promise you. Dirk. I liked him. I thought he was a good guy and I don't know why you want me to help with Ju-Ju or why I thought I could. I didn't figure him out."

Blake leans forward, arms on his knees. "When you're studying a killer, you look for the bad you know exists, even if it's in someone who is just a suspect. When you're with someone who is supposed to be in law enforcement, you look for good because that's what the fuck they are supposed to be."

"And everyone in our inner circle knows this," Asher assures me. "We know bad hides inside good all the damn time."

"You can't be sure everyone on your team is clean," I argue. "It's impossible."

"You're right," Luke says. "But all of us have a handful of people we completely trust. When you bring that list together, it's powerful."

"We need to know what we're bringing them together for, though," Asher says, looking at me. "We need in that lock box."

I want to tell him to back away. I want to tell him this is insanity. He knows. He reads me and says, "This isn't just about our lives. Every weapon he sells to an enemy could kill an American solider or one of our allies' soldiers."

"Worse," Luke says. "Innocent women and children, not to mention however many more people end up having the accidents you've accounted for."

Now it's my turn for a reality check. They're right. It's a thought I've had in the past, but staying sane when I had no option but to run meant setting it aside. I look at Asher. "The key is in my money belt in your safe."

He gives me a nod and looks at Blake. "If I leave at sunrise—"

"If *we* leave at sunrise," Luke says. "I'm coming with."

Asher gives him a nod this time. "If we leave at sunrise," he says, "we can watch the box for a day, and grab it and leave Tuesday. That gets me back in plenty of time to be at the bar Wednesday night."

"I thought we weren't due in until Friday?" I say.

"We're on call for Wednesday and Thursday," Asher explains, "and so far, I've been called into work both days."

Blake's phone buzzes and he looks down at his messages. "Kara doesn't know Agent Bennett, but Royce has heard of him." He sets his phone on the round stone coffee table. "I'll contact Royce on a secure line when we're done and find out more," he says to us all before focusing on me. "And we'll look out for you here, Sierra. What you did to get here, what you're doing now: It's all the right choices and brave, very brave."

"Agree one hundred percent," Luke says. "And, Sierra. My wife is one of the top divorce attorneys in the country. She's sought out by movie stars and athletes. And I promise you she will tell you this isn't a marriage you're in. It's a prison with a death sentence that is his, not yours."

This hasn't gone as I thought it would in my mind. I didn't get any sense talked into Asher. I made myself the scorned married bitch who is going to hurt Asher. "Do not underestimate him," I say, standing up. "None of you get to die," I say. "Not one of you. None of you." I turn and start walking.

Asher is behind me an instant and just before we clear the wall, I stop and turn to him. "Please don't stop to talk. I need out of here."

His hands settle on my waist. "They're on your side, just like I am."

"I'm married."

"Stop fucking saying that. It only makes me want to fly to Denver and kill him now."

"You don't listen." I turn and head down the stairs only to find Kara, Julie, and a very pregnant Lauren now standing at the bottom.

I inhale and let it out, starting down the steps, not sure what to expect. When I reach the lower level, Julie steps forward. "If he lives, you have a divorce attorney."

"I'm not letting him live," Asher says.

"Then I'll help you kill him," Kara says.

"And I'll be everyone's criminal attorney," Lauren says.

They're all exaggerating, of course. Or I think they are. "You're all insane."

Asher slides his arm around my shoulders. "Isn't it beautiful?" He doesn't give me time to respond. He eyes the three musketeers in front of us. "We're going home." And with that, he turns us toward the door. *Home*. We're going home, as if his place is my place. This idea burns a hundred emotions in my belly.

"See you tomorrow, Sierra!" Julie shouts out, followed by a similar goodbye from Kara and Lauren, while I grab my tote on the way past the table.

Once we're in the hallway with the door shut, Asher doesn't look at me. He leads me forward and toward the stairs. "Asher," I say, as we start down them.

"Not now. When we're alone."

He's angry. I get it. I sideswiped him. Well, he sideswiped me too, asking Luke for a plane and deciding to go get my lock box open. Anger crackles between us and about twenty other things, some of which are way too early to name. I may never have the luxury of naming some of the things I might feel for this man. That he doesn't get that just burns inside me, like his touch burns up my arm, and across my chest.

We exit Walker Security and cross the street, more silence between us. The elevator is next and when I would retreat to one side as I had before, he doesn't let that happen. He catches my waist from behind and places me between him and the panel. "Key in the code," he orders, and I know he's testing me. Making sure I know what I need to know when he's gone. Damn him, still trying to take care of me. The elevator opens and he takes my hand in his and leads me forward, more of that hard determination in his steps, that anger between us damn near explosive now.

I don't let him continue to take the lead. I'm the one who took action tonight for a good reason. I step ahead of him and key in the code to the door. He walks me inside from behind, his big body up against mine, and the minute we're in the foyer, he shoves the door shut and pulls me to him, his fingers tangling in my hair.

"Asher, damn it—"

He kisses me, a drugging, intense kiss that I don't fight. He tastes of a heady mix of confident male and power that consumes and overwhelms me in all the right ways. I kiss him back, my hands pressing to the strong line of his shoulder blades until too soon, his lips part from mine, those green eyes of his piercing. "You won't be married to him for long. That's a promise." He doesn't give me time to argue. "Don't claim him as your husband again. I don't like it."

LISA RENEE JONES

Chapter Twenty Nine

ASHER

I set Sierra away from me, focused on the list of things I need to get done before I leave her alone for two days. "Come with me and bring your purse." I don't wait for a reply. I start walking with purpose, across the living room and up the stairs, and I don't stop until I'm back in the weapons room, behind the table. I don't sit.

She enters the room, the look on her beautiful, stubborn face as determined as I feel. She crosses to stand in front of me. "Set your bag down," I order.

She does it, clearly aware that right now, I'm all business. "Now," I say. "I want you to put your revolver in your purse, but before you reach for it, tell me everything you've learned."

"Never point it at anyone that I don't want to shoot. Align my index finger for accuracy." She repeats everything I've taught her methodically, to finally add, "Shoot to kill. Anyone I injure could be pissed off enough to kill me instead."

"Grab your new purse and put the revolver inside, positioned to grab and point."

She nods and follows that instruction, appearing focused on what I'm teaching her. "Put the strap across your chest, purse at your hip."

While she does that, I round the table and step behind her, my big body encasing her smaller one, and I push past the fact that I'm rock hard. "That's a loaded weapon," I say, my hands on her shoulders. "Zip the purse and practice unzipping it and pulling the weapon." She struggles and makes a frustrated noise.

"Do you have to stand behind me like that?"

"Is that making you feel performance pressure?"

"Yes," she says. "Among other things."

"Good. Because if you have to pull that gun, you'll be scared shitless." I turn her to face me, hands on her hips. "The idea that carrying a gun is as simple as point and shoot, is false. You need to practice when I'm gone." I release her and grab the semi-automatic, expelling the cartridge.

"Where are the bullets?" I ask.

"Inside the cartridge."

I remove them. "Put them in again."

"Asher can we just—"

"Do it, Sierra." I'm pushing her. I know I am, but one thing sitting with Luke and talking about Devin Marks did for me was remind me that Marks really will kill Sierra if he gets the chance. "This is me helping you protect you."

"Yes. You're right."

She loads the blanks I have her using and then pops the cartridge into place.

"Cock it," I say, and that's where she, and most people, slow down.

She has to focus to get her hand right and get the job done. "Hand it to me," I say, and she manages to point it at me.

"Damn it," she says.

"That's why you practice without real ammunition, but I'm going to see if Jacob can take you to the shooting range.

He's a sharpshooter with a calm, cool disposition. He's also stoic as hell, which means intimidating. Those are all skills you need to have when handling any firearm."

"I'd ask to wait on you, but I get it. I need to learn now."

"Yes. You do." I walk around the table and open a closet, removing a case for the pistol and returning. I show Sierra how it fits in place. "We'll take it with us in the morning. That way if he has time, he can just swing by and get you at Walker Security. Put it in that big, black bag-thing we bought."

"A tote," she says, her full pink lips quirking, her pale skin flushed. "But big black thing works, too."

God, she's beautiful and selfless enough to try to stop me from helping her, when of course, she's human. She wants the help. She even knows she needs it, which is exactly why I'm staying focused on preparing for my trip. "This way," I say, heading out of the gun room, down the hallway and into the bedroom, this time continuing on through the bathroom to the closet and safe. Sierra joins me and I motion her forward. "Open it."

She does as I say, and I'm under no misconception that this means she's going to make a habit of taking orders. She gets it. She's in danger. I'm preparing her for the worst. She unlocks the safe and removes her money belt, unzips it and hands me the key. "It's at a storage facility a few blocks from the DFW airport. It's the only thing in the unit and the building locks." She gives me the address and I text it to Luke and Blake.

"I need to call one of my SEAL brothers in Dallas and yes, I trust him. How about ordering us some food? Anything. Pizza is probably easiest."

"What do you like?"

"Anything and everything." I cup her face and kiss her. "I'll be in my office. It's just past the gun room. Hang your clothes in the closet."

"I hung up some of it."

Her words from our fight back at Luke's place, reply in my mind: *I'm married to another man* and punch me in the damn chest. "Some is not good enough right now. Fuck, Sierra. Convince me you're staying." I let her go and walk out of the closet, hating the idea of leaving her here, but knowing damn well that she gave me that key because she trusts me.

I head down the hallway and walk into my office and cross to the wooden writer's desk with cross legs that I wouldn't have if Kyle's wife, Myla, hadn't decided to use her design skills to decorate every male home in the Walker clan. She'd called the desk a "statement piece" or some shit like that. It's supposed to complement the brick and wood finish of the walls. I told her whatever. Decorating is not my thing, but hell, I'm glad she did it now that Sierra is here.

I bypass the desk and walk up the three steps that lead to a sitting area behind a wooden railing, where two leather chairs and a table sit in front of an arched window. My thinking spot. And for a few minutes, that's all I do. Think. I start to process the people in my mind that can help me end Devin Marks beyond my SEAL team, and there are only a few I trust completely.

I dial Luke. "Are we on the same page?"

"Yes," he says. "The only reason I haven't done it is that I was waiting to talk to you."

"I'll do it."

I disconnect, open the drawer in the table next to me, and pull out a disposable phone. I dial the number that only a small group of ten SEALs know, some active and some not.

Once the line connects, I type in a ten-digit code that identifies me and sends a message: Be ready for war. Over the course of the next twenty-four hours, everyone who is able will check in with a location.

I stick the phone back in the drawer and return to my regular line and call one of those SEALs direct. He answers on the first ring. "No, I don't want a job."

"Well I got one for you anyway," I say. "It's personal. I need you."

"When and where?"

"I'm coming to you and I'm bringing Luke. We'll be on the ground by ten tomorrow."

He pauses and there is movement before he says, "I just got the notification. I'll be waiting when you get here."

We disconnect, and I push to my feet, walking down the hallway and into the bedroom to find Sierra nowhere in sight. I walk through the bathroom and step into the doorway of the closet to find her hanging her things next to my Navy fatigues. Seeing her clothes there, next to mine, should freak me the fuck out considering commitment isn't my thing, but that's not what bothers me. It's how little she has.

I reach into my wallet and remove a credit card. I've just stuck my wallet back into my pocket when she turns around, and lifts her hands to her things. "Does that prove I'm fucking staying?" she challenges.

"It's a start," I say, closing the space between us and offering her the card. "Go shopping online or if Kara can take you, with her. And I mean shop. Shoes. Clothes. Dresses. Whatever you need. The things you need to start over here."

"I'm not taking that card or buying more clothes."

"You have nothing, Sierra," I say, and driving her to a certain response I want her to give me, I add, "If you don't do it, I will. I'll order a shit-ton of stuff and you will have to weed through what you want."

"You're impossible."

"Prove to me you're fucking staying," I say again.

"I'll cash my check and shop."

My lips curve. "Good. Claim the job. That works."

She scowls. "That's what you wanted, wasn't it?"

"We're getting there, but take the credit card anyway."

"No. I'm not taking it."

"If you have to run, use this card. Leave me a trail. I'll use it to track you."

Realization washes over her face and she reaches for it. "Thank you." She sticks it in her purse that's sitting on the bench beside us.

"And it has twenty thousand dollars on it, if you need it for anything."

"I don't need your money, Asher." Her hand comes down on my chest. "But I do need you. So quickly. I don't know how I already need you this much. And I don't want you to be okay with me calling him my husband. I was just trying to protect you. I really need you to be safe. I need—"

I kiss her, tongue licking into her mouth, and when she reaches under my shirt, her palms soft and cool against my hot skin, I'm about ten seconds from snapping. "You cannot leave. You stay here."

"I'm not leaving."

"When I'm gone, Sierra, do not go to the bar. Do not go to the grocery store. Do not go anywhere alone. Do you understand?"

"Yes. I do."

"Say it. You will not—"

"I won't. I promise."

I kiss her again, and lift her, carrying her to the bed. We both go down on the mattress, and when we should be undressed and fucking that's not what happens, compliments of the doorbell. "The pizza," she says.

"The pizza," I repeat, but neither of us move.

Her hand settles on my cheek. "Asher."

"Yeah, sweetheart?"

"I'm really starving."

I laugh and kiss her hand. "Me too." I roll her over and rest on my elbows above her. "You can be dessert."

"*You* can be dessert," she says, and when I roll off of her, I'm smiling.

I head down the stairs, the scent of her perfume clinging to my skin, and that damn sweet floral scent gets to me. It makes me want to lick every part of her body. And I will. Over and over and over again because she's already my fucking woman. I've never called any woman *my woman* but she is. That's just *how* it is. She came. She became. She is. On some level, she already knows it.

On every level, Devin Marks is about to find that out, too.

Chapter Thirty

ASHER

As much as I want to set the pizza on the bed, strip Sierra naked, and just savor every inch of her, I don't. She is more to me than sex. I want to know her inside and out, and right now, with me leaving, and leaving her here, I need her to know that. And so we sit on the bed, eating pizza, and I make sure we talk about everything but monsters and killers. Movies. We both love super heroes. Books. We both love to read. Christmas.

"What do you do for Christmas?" she asks.

"I was overseas for about five years, but since I've been back, the Walker women come over here and put up a tree."

She smiles. "I like them. I like that they do that for you."

"I have to buy a baby shower gift and Christmas gifts. You have to help me with all of the above."

"I'd like that," she says. "The baby shower is soon. If I do go shopping, do you want me to just grab something?"

"Yes. Please grab something."

"What is your budget?"

"Make it good. Spend whatever you want to do that. What about your Christmas, Sierra?"

"My mother and father made the holidays fun. They went big. Decorations. Food. It was fun. After my father died, it was never the same."

"When did he die?"

"The year I met Devin. Some professionals, like myself, might say I was looking for a male figure in my life, and it contributed to why I was susceptible to him." She waves a hand. "I don't want to go there. Your mother? Do you remember her?"

"Yes. I do. I remember her being good and sweet, always working for charity organizations and having me help. I remember my father yelling at her. Talking down to her. And yet she'd get up the next morning and try to make someone in need smile. Unfortunately for you, I'm more like my father than my mother."

"That's not true, Asher. You are nothing like your father."

"I can be. Not to you, Sierra, but when I want to hurt someone, I'm good at it. And I want to hurt Devin Marks. I'm not going to feel regret when I do, either. Which means you might wake up one day and see me as just another version of Devin, but I'm still going to do what I'm going to do on this." I shut the empty pizza box and I stand up. "I need to pack a bag." I turn and walk toward the bathroom. Before I ever get in the door, Sierra is in front of me, her hand on my chest.

"You're nothing like him. You're nothing like your father."

"You don't know that part of me."

"I do," she assures me. "I feel it in you. I know that you can be hard. I know that you can kill, but that's not the same as living for those things."

"What the hell do you think I did in the SEALs, Sierra? I killed. I lived for the next mission that would set me up to kill again."

"You take that part of yourself and choose how you use it and you use it to help people that can't do what you do.

That is not Devin. That is not your father. You are amazing. Harvard. SEALs. Singer. I heard you sing. You are amazing."

"A singer who watched his friend overdose and went to Harvard because I let my father bully me into it."

"You were young and yet you still excelled. You still did your own thing. I saw you with him. You could have his money, but you have all you have because of you. I love that about you." She takes my hand and pulls my arm forward. "I want to know what every single one of these tattoos means to you, Asher."

For the first time in my life, I want someone to know what they mean. For the first time in my life, I wonder if I'm worthy. If I'm wrong. For the first time in my life, rather than saying "fuck you" to my damn father, I want more. I want her. "I'm all yours, Sierra. What are you going to do with me?"

"I can think of a lot of things," she says. "Right now though, there is this." She lowers herself to her knees and just like that, I'm rock hard, adrenaline surging through my body. My good intentions to leave sex out of tonight's equation have gone right out the damn window. She strokes my cock through my jeans. Oh fuck. I need to be honorable here.

"Sierra."

She unzips my pants and looks up at me. "You can say please or you can say stop. Your call."

"Please. If you expect any man to be foolish enough to stay stop, I'm here to tell you that—"

She pulls my cock out of my pants and I breathe out. "Okay. Did I say please?"

She laughs. "Twice now."

"Please again."

This time when she laughs, she does it while closing her lips around my erection, her tongue stroking the underside and then pretty much everywhere she can reach. And then she is sucking me, and sucking me some more, and I really think this might be love. She's the perfect woman. Really damn perfect, as proven by the fact that she won't stop when I try to get her to stop.

She sucks me all the way through the quake of my body, and I do what any good man should do. When it's over, I strip us both naked and lay her on the bed where I thank her. I kiss her nipples, I lick them. Then, I lick and kiss a path all the way down to her belly and beyond until I'm suckling her clit, stroking a finger through the wet, slick core of her body. And I make damn sure that I don't stop licking and stroking her until she quakes just as hard and good as I did.

Then, and only then, do I move up her body and kiss her while settling beside her, my cock hard between her legs. "I'm going to remember you on my lips, every minute I'm gone," I promise, before pressing inside her for what becomes a slow sway of our bodies. I make love to her and I can't say I've ever made love to a woman. I fuck. That's what I do, but that is not what this is.

A long time later, she falls asleep, naked and pressed to my side, while I lay awake, replaying every touch we'd shared, my protectiveness of her, even possessiveness, growing with each passing moment. That damn recording she'd played for us all is now in my mind, my plans for Devin Marks expanding just like my feelings for Sierra. When I finally slip into a light sleep, it's two in the morning. My alarm goes off at three. I ease Sierra off of me, and she snuggles deeper under the covers.

By three-thirty, I've showered, dressed and I sit down on the edge of the bed, and caress her cheek. "Sierra."

She blinks awake and sits up, her hair a wild mess I made right about the time I was kissing her nipples and then her belly. "You're already leaving?"

"Soon."

She throws off the covers, exposing her naked body and appearing comfortable enough not to care. "I want to walk you out." She scoots off the bed and hurries across the room, her naked backside ensuring I'll leave her this morning hard as a rock, and guaranteed to have sweet dreams on the plane.

I pull on the thin black leather jacket I've set on the bed, and then grab the small duffle I've packed. "I'll meet you downstairs, Sierra," I call out, because if I follow her, we'll both end up naked, and Luke will be waiting on me.

Heading out of the bedroom, I walk down the hallway to my office, flipping on the light as I enter. Returning to my thinking spot, I open the drawer inside the table and grab the burner phone there, dialing into the voice system to discover four replies. That makes seven of us on board, counting me, Luke, and Adam. And the seven of us can do a lot to fuck up Devin Marks's world. I stick the phone in the pocket of my jacket, and make my way back to the door. I reach the stairs and start down them to find Sierra already downstairs and standing at the coffee pot.

She turns at my footsteps and abandons her cup, rounding the island to meet me on the other side. I set my bag down on a stool, and we step to each other. "Can we just go back upstairs and back to bed together?" she asks, her hand flattening on my chest. "I don't want you to go. I have a really bad feeling."

I stroke a strand of hair behind her ear. "I'll be back soon. I have Luke with me and our SEAL mate, Adam, is joining us in Dallas." My hands settle on her hips. "Jacob is coming over to stay with you. He'll take you to the Walker offices to work on the Ju-Ju file around ten."

"Do I really need him here? Isn't the building secure?"

"I'm just being cautious," I say. "And Kara wanted to be here, but she needs to be at your apartment early to make a showing in case anyone is watching."

"I thought Jacob was watching Ju-Ju, or Terrance, or both?"

"We have Ju-Ju and Terrance well covered. I trust Jacob and he's going to be in the Ju-Ju meeting today anyway, so this makes sense this morning, but tonight I need you to stay with Julie. She'll be alone and Jacob lives in the building."

"I'd rather stay at home or—I mean—here. At your home." Her gaze drops to my chest.

I cup her face and tilt her gaze to mine. "This is where you live now, Sierra. I want you here. I want you to want to be here. I don't know how many ways I can say that to you."

"For now. I'm staying here for now. Right now, you're riding the high of being a hero. I'm riding the high of you. We don't know where this will land when it's over."

I don't expect the punch to the chest those words deliver, but the line she is drawing is clear. "Right," I say. "I guess we don't. I guess we'll see. I'm going to give you your freedom. Then you can decide where you want to be."

The doorbell rings and I release her. "I need to go." I reach for my bag and head to the door.

"Asher."

I stop in my tracks and when I turn around, she's in front of me, hugging me and pushing to her toes. "I had a moment of panic over how fast we're going and how hard I think I

could fall for you. He can kill me. You can hurt me. I just—
I'm sorry. I don't want to leave, but if you decide you want
me to leave—"

I cup her head. "You belong with me now. You'll see." I
kiss her. "Don't leave. Don't go anywhere alone. Promise
me."

"I promise. Please call me when you can."

"I will and call me if you need me, but don't worry if I
don't answer. It only means that I'll call you the minute I
safely can. You have an army here to protect you."

I release her and walk to the door, opening it and
greeting Jacob, who is stoic and cold, which makes him the
perfect man to place with another man's woman. "Take care
of her," I say, before walking down the hallway and stepping
into the elevator. The doors shut, and I've left Sierra in my
apartment with another man while I go after the man who
is technically her fucking husband.

I head downstairs and Luke's Escalade is pulled up to
the door of the apartment. I climb inside and shut the door,
and my mind replays that recording of Devin Marks plotting
Sierra's killing all over again. I think of Kyle and Myla, and
the way Alvarez will always haunt them, dead or alive. There
was no body, no proof that he's dead and thus they can have
no real peace. No closure. I won't let that happen to me and
Sierra. I will not only end this, and Devin Marks decisively,
but with absolute closure.

LISA RENEE JONES

Chapter Thirty One

Sierra

Suddenly I'm standing in Asher's apartment with a strange man. Jacob enters the apartment and locks up. I walk to the kitchen and grab my coffee cup, which is apparently still empty. I set it back down and turn to find him joining me. He's in a blue T-shirt and dark blue jeans. He's big—a Mr. GI Joe, with short hair and a big muscular body. The kind of guy that once would have been my thing, but he's not now. Asher, and his long blond hair, tattoos, and piercing green eyes is my kind of man.

"Hello, ma'am."

"Hello, Jacob. Sorry you had to come here this early."

"There are those who should pay for my need to be here, but you should never apologize for being in danger."

"You mean Ju-Ju should pay."

"And Devin Marks. Yes. I know. I heard the tape. Luke felt I needed to know the magnitude of the threat. I'm not in his pocket. I'm not in anyone's pocket."

I study him for several beats, and while I have misjudged a few people in the past, I believe Blake was right. I was allowing my expectations to affect what I saw in people. Now, I expect evil and yet I still believe Jacob.

"You should get some rest," he says. "We need to leave here at about nine-thirty for the meeting at the office."

"It's going to be hard to rest. I'm worried about him."

"Asher is smart and dangerous."

"So I'm told."

"He'll be fine. Devin Marks will not be."

He says those words without inflection in his voice, but somehow, they are fierce. "You need to sleep too. I saw a spare bedroom upstairs."

"I'll catch some sleep on the couch."

"I was going to leave," I say. "I would have, to protect Asher, and all of you, but it's too late now. You're too involved."

"We don't need protection. We need information and a plan, which hopefully your documentation will deliver. And for the record, I'm not worried about you going out of the apartment. I'm down here to give a gift to anyone who tries to come in it."

"A sharp-shooter gift?"

He gives a nod of his head. "Yes, ma'am. The best gift you can give an asshole who intends to do you harm. I understand I'm taking you to the range to help you learn how to deliver a little justice yourself."

"Yes. Please." I turn away with the flashback of Asher saying *please*, and my cheeks heat. I lower my lashes and force away my obvious reaction while the warmth spreading through my body is here to stay.

"You okay?" he asks.

Am I okay? Well, I'm falling in love with a man I just met, like a school girl, while the man I'm married to and hate wants to kill me, and soon, Asher too. There's only one way to answer that. I turn and face him. "I will be when I can deliver some of that justice myself."

"We'll make sure that you can," he says, but his expression remains unchanged.

"You're cold. You're calculated. You protect yourself by never letting anyone get close to you."

"Is that your professional opinion?"

"Yes. It is."

"And what is Ju-Ju?"

"Insane, but just as smart and calculating."

"Then we need to catch him. Go. Get some rest."

I nod and start to turn but stop. "Part of me envies you. You can't get hurt if you never let anyone close. It was my strategy on the run."

"Was?"

"And then Asher happened. So, while part of me envies your steely wall, the other part of me hopes your version of Asher comes into your life, and changes that. Goodnight, Jacob."

"Goodnight, ma'am."

I stop and face him. "Don't call me ma'am. I don't plan to leave anytime soon, and friends don't call friends ma'am and sir."

"What would you like me to call you?"

"I should say Kelli. That's the new me, but that also means I accept leaving the real me behind because of Devin Marks. I don't accept it. Call me Sierra."

I walk away then and hurry up the stairs, stepping into the bedroom that I now share with Asher. It smells like him. It feels like him. It's missing *him*. I shut the door and walk to the massive four poster wood bed, staring down at it. Thinking of the way he'd touched me. The way he seemed to savor me. I sit down and lower myself to the mattress. There was a time when I wanted to go back home to Denver, because it was the only home I knew. Now, Asher is the only thing that feels like home, but he's not here and that bad feeling about this trip continues to claw at me.

Chapter Thirty Two

Sierra

I doze off until six in the morning and that's it. I need to get up. I need *to do* something and since that something can't involve Devin Marks right now, I decide that something needs to be catching Ju-Ju. The sooner I start calling people who once knew Ju-Ju or perhaps still do, the better. I quickly shower, and throw on a pair of dark blue jeans, and a red T-shirt with a glittery butterfly on it. I decide red stands out too much, and trade it for a black BeBe logo T-shirt. I do need to shop. I only have a few things that fit. I pull on lace-up flat boots and a waist-length black Burberry quilted jacket. I like the extra pockets and it's getting cooler outside now.

I quickly apply light make-up and with my hair flat ironed, those blonde roots are showing more than ever. My mascara is too dark to cover it, which means I need to get color today. I have so much to do that I need to get this day moving. I grab my purse and tote, the revolver in the purse and the case and gun in the tote. I head down the stairs to find Jacob at the island, a steamy cup of coffee by his side and a computer in front of him.

"You're awake," he says, surprised.

"Yes. Why are you awake?"

"Ju-Ju on the brain," he says. "I'm going through the old bar footage for the third time, trying to find anything that might convict him."

"Any luck?"

"No. No luck at all."

"I'm all for going into the office and digging into investigating him, if you are."

He stands up. "You had me at 'why are you awake?' Let's go."

Just that easily, we head out and waste no time making our way to the Walker offices which are still dark. A few minutes later, we're in the conference room, both of us with coffee cups beside us and we begin looking for a strategy. "Do you have the lists Asher made of the connections to Ju-Ju?"

"I do," he says. He reaches for a MacBook sitting in front of an empty seat. "That's the computer from your apartment. Kara texted me. She left it here in case you wanted it."

A few minutes later, I have the computer fired up with a spreadsheet to match Jacob's to log my calls. We split the list and start making them. Unfortunately, not with much luck. No one is answering our calls. "In hindsight," I say. "Evening might be the better call time. People are at work now."

My cellphone rings and I pull it from my purse to find Asher calling. "Are you there?"

"Yes. We got a hotel near the storage facility. Is Jacob with you?"

"He is," I say. "We're at the office."

"Put me on speaker so he knows what's going on."

I look at Jacob. "Asher wants to talk to both of us." He nods, and I hit the speaker button before setting the phone

PULLED UNDER

down on the table. "Okay," I say to Asher. "You're live with me and Jacob. No one else is here yet."

"Hey man," Jacob says. "What's the word?"

"We're in a room a few blocks from the storage facility," Asher says again.

"Any sign of trouble?" Jacob asks.

"All is quiet here," he replies. "Sierra."

"Yes?"

"Just to be clear," Asher says. "You got this locker before you were on anyone's radar, correct?"

"Oh, yes," I confirm. "I was in Dallas for a few weeks, but I rented the locker the day I got there."

"I checked. They have rental lockers with a monthly fee. It's one of those, correct?"

"Correct," I say. "I've been sending a money order and verbally confirming receipt. And I used one of those google redirect numbers."

"Smart," Asher says. "Good."

"Is there something wrong?" I ask.

"We're just establishing the likelihood anyone might be watching the locker," he says.

"Because," I say, realization hitting me. "If someone was watching it, "then it's already been emptied and you'd be walking into a trap."

"That would be our assessment as well," Asher says. "It would be easy to take the contents, lock it back up, and wait for someone to come for the contents."

He means: wait for me, and kill me. "If it's gone, that was everything I have on him, other than what's in my head."

"We're going to watch the facility today," Asher says, skipping any comfort that might now be justified. "We'll hack the computers and security system, and dive into your

263

FBI agent pal's activities. What month and day did you leave here?"

"July 11ᵗʰ," I say.

"Got it," he says. "Anything happening there with Ju-Ju?"

"Not a damn thing," Jacob says. "We're making calls, but we're not getting people on the line."

"It's still early," he says. "I'll check in later. Pick up, Sierra."

I take the call off speaker, and set the phone against my ear again. "I'm here."

"*Do not* go out alone."

I frown. "Why are you saying that to me again?"

"Just making sure."

"I'm not a fool. I know the risks."

"Good. Keep knowing. I'll call you later."

He ends the call just as Kara and Blake walk into the conference room. "Good morning, you two," Kara says, claiming a seat to my left. "Any luck with anything?"

"Nothing," I say. "What about you guys? Any sign of Ju-Ju?"

"He's still tucked in his house," Blake answers, sitting down next to Kara. "And we see no signs of Terrance or anyone else for that matter. If you're the target, your address is unknown."

"Because Jacob stopped him from following us," I say, "and blew his cover. I should just go to the bar, and fill out the paperwork that I never filled out. If Ju-Ju, or anyone shows up at my apartment after that, then we'll know Ju-Ju and Terrance are working together."

"And that would be a no to you going to the bar," Blake says. "You wait until Asher gets back."

"We need to catch Ju-Ju," I argue. "I can go during the day in broad daylight and—"

"Howdy ho."

That interruption comes from the sandy haired, thirty-something man that enters the room. "I have arrived." He stops short just inside the doorway and eyes me. "Hey. I'm Smith Wesson and don't make a gun joke. I haven't had enough coffee this morning to pretend it doesn't piss me off."

My brow furrows. "Wesson?"

"Smith and Wesson," he says, claiming a seat across from Blake. "My name and the gun. Is playing dumb your joke?"

"Ah no," I say. "I don't know guns or what this is about."

He grimaces. "Right. I forgot. You're not one of us. You're an outsider."

Outsider.

That word might as well be a punch in the face.

I don't belong here.

"Shut up, Smith," Blake snaps while Kara gives him a sharp look.

"Sierra is one of us," she says. "She's the entire reason we have another angle on Ju-Ju." She looks at me. "You work for us now. You're one of us and we need you."

"In other words," Blake says dryly. "Smith and Wesson is badass and Smith Wesson, the dude running his big ass mouth, is just a little bitch."

Smith grimaces. "I worked with Rick Savage all night. He's the little bitch. The only dude on this team I hate and you paired me with him." He looks at me. "Sorry for being an asshole. I hope you never have to deal with Savage, but if you do, you'll get it. Aside from that, I really do want to get this prick Ju-Ju. Where are we on that?"

I inhale and let out a breath, setting aside my uber-sensitivity. He wants to help. We have a killer to catch. "We need to do the same thing we're doing with Ju-Ju, with the victims. We need to look for ways their past connects to his past."

"We have a basic outline done," Jacob answers. "And for the record, that was a little bitch comment but I'll send you the spreadsheet so you can work off it it. I'll work on victim backstories if everyone else can make calls."

And that's what happens. We all dig in and we all hit roadblocks. The few people we talk to just don't remember Ju-Ju. By noon, Kara and Blake leave for my place again, while Julie and Lauren take over making calls. "Let's go to the shooting range," Jacob says. "We need a break."

He's right, I think. We do, and I gladly agree.

A few minutes later, we're on the street, and he stops by the bank. "I've been instructed to make sure you deposit your check. Tell them you lost your bank card. Do you remember your bank code and social?"

"Yes. I memorized them. Are you sure this is safe?"

"Safe is making sure you look like a real person. I'll wait right here by the door."

He means he'll make sure no one has followed us thus far. I exhale, because apparently, I'm holding my breath. I start to walk, and he catches my arm. "Blake is a badass at this stuff. You're good. Be calm. Be confident."

I think back to every fake moment I had with Devin Marks and nod. I can do this. I walk into the bank, and the idea that cameras are watching me, filming me, has me on edge. I cross by a cluster of desks and quickly end up with a customer service rep, who is about sixty and slow. Fifteen minutes into the process that should take ten, I've just presented my ID when I have this sensation of being watched. I don't zip my purse back up, my hand in fact, rests just above the revolver, but I also don't turn around. I don't want to appear obvious if I am being watched, but the sensation only grows stronger.

Finally, I finish up and stand, slowly turning and scanning the customers. Two young girls, a middle-aged man with curly gray hair in profile at another desk, and a fiftyish, black woman with an infectious laugh. I'm all right. There is no trouble here, but as I step outside and join Jacob, I still feel nervous. "Was there anyone suspicious that you saw?"

"No one," he says, glancing at my hand that's inside my purse, on the gun. "Did something happen, Sierra?"

"No. Yes. I felt what I felt in Dallas right before I got attacked."

"What does that mean?" he presses. "What did you feel?"

"Like I'm being watched."

He studies me for a moment, and he must believe me, which I appreciate because his hand comes down on my arm, and he says, "Let's go back to the office."

"No," I say, holding my ground. "I don't want to lead anyone to them and it feels like a good time to shoot a gun."

He considers that a moment. "Yes. Maybe it is." He motions me forward, and we start walking, with him carefully placing me between him and the wall, while he stays streetside.

"Should we call the office and warn them?"

"After we're off the street," he says. "The firing range is only two blocks down."

Two blocks that feels like ten but finally we're inside and Jacob calls the office. "Smith is going to shadow us."

I nod and a few minutes later, I'm in safety goggles and I'm in charge of a loaded weapon. I thought the idea of holding a gun capable of taking a life would bother me. It doesn't. It feels necessary.

———————————— ⟡ ————————————

At nine o'clock, I still haven't heard from Asher and I'm still in the Walker offices, long after everyone but Jacob and Smith have left. "Where are you sleeping tonight?" Jacob asks.

"Kara, Julie, and Lauren, all offered me a bed," I say, thinking of the conversations I'd had with them all in between calls. "Asher suggested Julie since she's alone, but I forgot to bring something to wear."

"I can stay with you again, if you want," he says.

"That would be great. Yes. Thank you."

"I live in this building. I'll let everyone know, and grab an overnight bag."

"I'll stay with Sierra while you get your bag," Smith offers.

Jacob nods, obviously trusting Smith, which means Asher trusts Smith, who turns out to be a nice guy with a fetish for crossword puzzles. A personal habit that he's put to use to help build a wall of notecards that are all about Ju-Ju and the different paths of his life. I stand up and stare at it, and he does the same. "Somewhere on this wall is an answer," I say. "There has to be."

We've debated that point to death. Neither of us have words. We just stare at it until Smith seems to give up and looks over at me with another topic in mind. "Put my number in your phone," he says. "In case you need me."

"Yes. Thanks." I walk to the desk and grab my phone, only to discover it's already in my directory, which means that Asher added him at some point. "I already have it," I say, as my cellphone rings in my hand. I glance at the caller ID and then at Smith. "It's Asher. I'm going into the lobby to take it." I answer the line. "Asher?"

"Yeah, sweetheart. How are you?"

"Good," I say, heading to the door.

"Don't leave the lobby," Smith calls after me.

"I won't," I promise over my shoulder.

"I see you met Smith," he says as I walk down the hallway.

"Yes. He's been here helping on the Ju-Ju investigation all day."

"He's a good guy that I should have mentioned," he says. "Did you find out anything about Ju-Ju?"

"Nothing and we've been beating this to death. Did you get into the locker?"

"We're not going to grab it until tomorrow night. Or possibly even Wednesday morning depending on how a few things shake down. We'll sweep in, take the files, and then head straight to the airport before we hit any trouble."

"Wednesday? Really?"

"Maybe. We'll see but I'll be back Wednesday no matter what. Where are you sleeping tonight?"

"Jacob just volunteered to stay with me." It hits me that I invited another man to stay with me. "That is okay, right?"

"Yeah. That's okay. But are you okay?"

I hesitate, and he knows. "What happened?" he asks.

"It's probably nothing, but I went to the bank today and I just had this weird feeling of being watched. I'm sure it was paranoia, but I really don't want to stay here and make anyone anymore of a target than I already have."

He's silent a moment. "Stay close to Jacob."

"I will. Of course, I will."

"I have to go, sweetheart. But Sierra?"

"Yes?"

"I miss the fuck out of you, woman. And that's another first for me."

"I miss the fuck out of you, too."

"Good. Keep missing me. Goodnight, Sierra."

"Goodnight, Asher."

We disconnect and Jacob appears in the lobby. "You ready?"

"I just need to grab my stuff and tell Smith we're leaving."

He gives an incline of his head, and I hurry to the conference room. "See you tomorrow, Smith," I say, once I'm packed up.

He gives me a salute, and I head back to the lobby to join Jacob. From there, it's not long before we're outside, that feeling of being watched I'd felt earlier, noticeably gone. I comfort myself with the fact that if this was Dallas all over again, it wouldn't be gone. I'd probably be dead. Still, I'm relieved when we enter the building, and even more relieved when we are inside the elevator.

"Thanks for this," I say, glancing at Jacob, who is standing tall and ramrod straight beside me. "I'm used to being alone. It's a little overwhelming to be with so many people."

He cuts me a look. "Funny how alone can feel safer, isn't it?"

"Yes," I say, curious about how much understanding I feel like he has for that statement, but he's not going to tell me. Because I am certain that alone, which means private, does feel safer to him.

The elevator stops and we quickly head down the hallway. We've just entered the apartment when Jacob's phone rings. "Smith," he announces, before taking the call.

He listens a minute that turns into a few clipped replies, and while Jacob's expression and tone are impenetrable, his voice monotone, by the time we are both standing at the island across from each other I know something is wrong.

He hangs up. "He talked to Ju-Ju's high school principal."

"And?"

"She said that she knew Ju-Ju's father well. Ju-Ju was in the marching band. His father took all the photos for the school football games and events."

My throat goes dry. "And now Ju-Ju is taking pictures of his victims," I say. "Which means there's a chance his father killed his mother or maybe he was a killer himself. Or a serial dater. Something is there."

"Put that aside. He took your picture, Sierra."

"I know." I think back to the file. "I read that Ju-Ju's mother died of a heart attack. Could it have been drug-induced? Did his father kill his mother? Is that what Ju-Ju is duplicating?"

"That will be hell to prove, and pulling that body from the dirt will alert him that we're onto him. It needs to be saved for court."

"Right. Good point. I need to go to bed. I'm exhausted."

"Sierra—"

"I'm fine. If he's targeting me, he's not targeting someone else."

I turn and walk up the stairs, then into the bedroom. I shut the door and I wait to feel something I don't feel. I'm numb. I knew he took my photo. I knew he was targeting me. Okay, I'm not numb. I have a cold spot in my chest. I lean on the door and shut my eyes, flashing back to one killer I sat across from and how cold he'd been. Just like that spot in my chest. I pant out a breath and I can't seem to make myself get undressed. I need to be dressed and ready for something, whatever it is. I walk to the bed and I don't lay down until I have my semi-automatic on the nightstand. I set the revolver on the mattress and I don't even think about turning off the lights.

Chapter Thirty Three

Sierra

I drift in and out of sleep, and at some point I know I'm having a nightmare. I know The Beast is in that nightmare. I try to pull myself out of it, but I just can't seem to escape my own mind. I'm back in my life with him. We're at a dinner party. I'm in an emerald green gown that we'd fought over but I'd finally agreed to wear. I flash back to the moment I'd caved and agreed to just wear it. I'm sitting on the vanity in our bathroom in a robe.

"I put the dress I want you to wear on the bed."

I look up to find Devin standing in the doorway, already in one of his six-thousand-dollar suits, Mr. Tall, Dark, and Good Looking to most, but no longer to me. "I saw it," I say. "I'm not wearing that."

"Why aren't you wearing that?"

"My breasts will barely be covered."

"Wear the dress."

"I'm not wearing that."

"I pay for everything and what do you do?" he snaps in that cutting tone that tells me the nastiness is about to flow like a river. "You go to school. And you can't even wear a fucking dress for me?"

I rotate in my chair. "The neckline plunges to my belly button!" I shout.

"This is a fifty-million-dollar night. I need this deal to go down. Wear the damn dress."

"My breasts are not going to make or break you."

"Your tits work miracles on men, darlin'." He walks over to me and pulls me to my feet, yanking open the front of the robe, his gaze raking over my nipples. "Should I suck them now or are you going to put the damn dress on?"

Anger burns through me and I start to tremble. I want to leave him right now. I hate him. "I'll wear the dress."

"Good girl," he says, and damn it, he reaches down and pinches my nipple, and then twists it. "Make it fast." He releases me and leaves.

The nightmare is over. It's darkness now until it's not. I fight it off again, but I'm back at the party.

We sit at the long, elegant table, with powerful people from around the world, all men. The women are all arm candy. China. Saudi Arabia. Mexico. Cuba. "You look beautiful," Devin says, leaning over to whisper in my ear.

He means my breasts look beautiful, since my cleavage is on display and every man at the table keeps looking at my chest. "I hate that you made me wear this."

"I wanted to show you off. I'm the envy of everyone here."

I stab at some kind of potatoes and endure another hour at that table. Finally, we move to the den, which smells of old books, cigars, and cedar, perhaps from the bookshelves inset in the walls left and right. The guests work the room, all mingling, and I manage to detach myself from Devin to cross the thick cream-colored rug to stand by the fireplace and chat with several of the wives. A mistake, considering they too stare at my breasts, disdain in their eyes. Awkwardly, I ease away from them and scan for Devin only to find him missing, which allows me the excuse to exit to the gardens.

I step outside and weave down one of several paths, walking toward a gazebo, when Devin's voice lifts in the air. "Make him go away," he says.

"That's a tall order," the other man says. "It's going to cost you."

"How much?"

"A hundred grand and I get to fuck your wife."

"Seventy-five, and if you do this right, you can fuck her ten ways to Sunday for all I care."

"I can live with that deal. Can she?"

"She'll do whatever the fuck I want. Make it look like an accident, or you'll have an accident."

"Carter Grant is as good as dead," he says. "Get me my cash."

I turn and start walking, all but running. I have to get away. I have to get away.

I open my eyes and sunlight beams into the room, while my cellphone buzzes against my belly. A cold spot forms in my chest. Oh God. How did I end up back in that memory? That was one month before Carter Grant died of a heart attack. I glance at the caller ID and quickly answer Asher's call. "Hello."

"Sierra," he breathes out.

"You heard?"

"I just heard. He takes fucking pictures of his victims. You were right."

"We think I'm right," I say. "I'm pretty sure I'm right, which means the photos of the other victims are somewhere we're missing."

"Other victims. You're convinced you're the next."

I think of Carter Grant, that cold spot in my chest all about guilt. "Asher, I knew what Devin was long before I left. On some level, I knew, and I have blood on my hands for it. People died. He killed them."

"You are not to blame. He is and we're going to get him."

"Just like we have to get Ju-Ju."

"Yes. And we will."

"*We*, Asher. *We*. Please don't tell me that I can't help catch him. I can't let anyone else die."

"We means you and me. *We* happen when I get back. Do you understand?"

"I do and I'm not stupid. I need you to do this, whatever this ends up being, but I do think I need to go fill out my paperwork at the bar. Then Terrance has my address, and if Ju-Ju shows up there, Kara has a chance to catch him."

"You wait until I get back."

"I'll go during the day and only with your people with me, and Ju-Ju nowhere near the bar."

"I'm coming home tonight. You can go with me tomorrow. We, Sierra. You go with me. Do you understand me because I swear—"

"Whatever barbaric thing you're about to say, don't say it."

"Sierra—"

"I'll be waiting on you when you get here."

"Tonight," he says.

"Good."

We disconnect and I can hear Devin's voice in my head: *She'll do whatever the fuck I want.*

No, I didn't. But I did too little, too slow, in collecting data that may or may not destroy him. I can't do too little again.

Chapter Thirty-Four

Sierra

Forty-five minutes later, I'm dressed in black jeans and a black shirt, with my lace-up boots and I still haven't colored my roots. I grab my purse and tote and place my guns inside, and this time the semi-automatic is not in the case. I head downstairs and to my surprise the house is full. Jacob, Kara, Blake, and Smith are present. "I brought donuts," Smith says as I join them all at the island.

"And I," Kara says, "brought you some hair color tools." She indicates a bag on the bar. "That has a couple color kits, several root-only kits, and hair mascara that you can use to cover up now."

"Thank you very much," I say. "But that isn't why all of you are here. What's going on?"

"We were impatient to work this new angle on Ju-Ju," Blake says. "And we wanted Jacob involved."

"What new angle?" I ask.

"We're working on where to find Ju-Ju's photos," Kara says.

"We were already doing that," I say.

Blake chimes in from where he sits on the other side of the table, with a computer in front of him. "I'm working through a history of his father, and people who knew him. So you know, there is no police record at all, but he had two co-workers over five years that mysteriously died at a young age."

"How?" I ask.

"Insulin overdose for one," Kara says. "Stroke for the other. Both under thirty."

Jacob grimaces. "We need a way to get this asshole arrested and off the streets."

"They have to be on his person," Smith says.

"I thought that too," I say, "But right now, processing where we have gone wrong, I go back to this rich man who inherited that money from the father that probably killed his mother. Now he's a drug dealer which perhaps means he feels like he's better than his father."

"Better?" Smith asks. "By dealing drugs?"

"Yes," I say. "Because he can do something that is in the cops' faces and not get caught killing."

"Fuck," Smith breathes out. "That's some fucked up shit."

"It hits the right nail on the head in my mind," Kara says, eying me. "In light of all we know, do you still think he's working with someone else?"

"Yes. I do. He's too clean, too hard to catch, to not have back-up. Maybe, just maybe, it's someone who helped his father."

"Rick Savage took a team into Terrance's house last night while he was off banging some chick," Blake says. "He found nothing there and then went on to the club at six this morning, and just finished up. Nothing. They checked everything, but they also uploaded databases to me. I'm going to go in and sweep the records this morning."

"Asher is coming back tonight," I say. "We're going to go to the club tomorrow and bait Terrance with my address. If Ju-Ju shows up at my place, we know it's Terrance, but I'm doubtful now. I really think if he has a partner, that partner is more sophisticated than Terrance."

"Maybe he's watching me be you, and we just don't see him," Kara says.

"Let's get to the office," Blake says, shutting his computer. "We need to have the work we did yesterday in front of us."

We all pack up and I grab the hair mascara on the way out. Fifteen minutes later, I'm in the conference room, working alongside the Walker clan. I have a moment, where I sit at the table, listening to them argue in the best of ways— to get to a solution, and I feel like I belong. This is where I'm supposed to be. Fate, Asher has said. It is fate, and just as these amazing people are going to help me stop Devin from hurting anyone else, in my heart I believe I'm here to stop Ju-Ju from killing again. Why else would I walk into that bar, meet Asher, and attract the attention of the very killer he was hunting?

I didn't come here to die. I came here to make sure no one else does.

———— ∞ ————

ASHER

The sun is down and the storage facility is closed for the day. Luke and I sit in the SUV we rented in the parking lot across from the storage facility with him in the driver's seat, and a laptop in my lap, the security camera feed live on the screen. Adam is dressed like a damn homeless person, his normally wild dark curls, wilder than usual, his clothes ratty. The backpack on his shoulder is filled with junk and just as ratty.

We have the cameras set up for our viewing and no one else's, not that it would matter. The place has a shoddy system and crap employees. Adam climbs the fence, despite the hack that gave us the code to enter, trying to look like a dude searching for a place to sleep. He heads toward the building that is sealed by a locking door, and tries to open it, failing by design. That's our plan. He moves to the next building and continues on four times. He finally reaches the building that is our target, which is unlocked thanks to my tech skills, and pauses to scratch his ass. "Did he really just scratch his damn ass?" Luke says. "And we trust this man with our lives?"

I chuckle. "If your ass itches, man, you gotta scratch it. What's wrong with you?"

We laugh, but there is tension in the air as we watch Adam slide open the door and it shuts behind him. I pull up the view inside the unit, keeping the exterior view open in a smaller window. Adam turns on his flashlight and then walks down the hallway. He unlocks the storage unit and we wait. And wait. "Fuck, anytime," I say. "We should have made him wear a microphone."

"That's dangerous if he gets cornered," Luke says. "Give him another three minutes." He hits the timer on his watch.

At two minutes exactly, Adam exits and shuts the door, and then does this staggering, fucked up walk here and there that takes forever. "If I didn't know better," Luke murmurs. "I'd believe he was really drunk."

Adam reaches the fence and falls three times before he gets over this time. Finally, finally, he starts walking, continuing to stumble here and there until he goes into the McDonalds, three blocks away where a matching backpack is waiting on him, as well as a phone. Luke thrums his fingers on the steering wheel while we wait. My phone rings and I answer on speaker. "I have the package and it is intact. Call me when you get it."

"Copy that," I say, and Luke has already started the SUV.

We make the drive to McDonald's and I shut my laptop, slip the empty leather briefcase we bought at Walmart over my shoulder, and get out of the car. I walk inside the restaurant as Adam walks out and neither of us look at each other. I scan the restaurant, spot a line, and act disgusted, before walking to the bathroom. I shut the door, lock it, and quickly pull open the cabinet under the sink where the backpack waits. I pull the paperwork out of the backpack and stick it in my briefcase and then toss the backpack back under the sink.

I exit the restaurant and give the line another grimace before walking back to the SUV. I climb inside. "I have it," I say, and Luke places us in reverse and backs up.

I dial Adam. "Package on board."

"I'm in my car. I got your ass."

We disconnect. "He's got our rear," I announce.

Luke nods and I dial Blake. "Package on board. Prepare to receive it."

"I'm ready," he says. "And I've already wiped any record of Adam being at the unit clean."

I hang up and pull out a small camera, snapping rapid-shot photos of the documents as back-up. That's the mistake Sierra made. You never keep one copy of the only evidence you have, especially when that evidence can be used as protection. By the time Luke makes the turn toward the private landing strip we're flying out of, I've connected the camera to my laptop and uploaded what I have to Blake. He calls me sixty seconds later. "Got it. All secure. Downloading, and records will be secured, and transitions wiped. We'll wait on you with Sierra at your place."

He hangs up and Luke and I park, leaving the rental for Adam to handle. The plane is flown by a pilot we employ and know well, who is waiting at the open door. We hurry up the ramp and we're inside, secure and taxiing in ten minutes flat. Luke and I sit down at a booth in the back of the jet, and I set the file on the table. We both start reading, studying, and holy shit, Sierra is right. The corruption runs deep and wide. I glance at Luke. "I can't connect Sierra to this. She can't be the one who takes these people down."

"None of us can," Luke says. "If we go at this directly, we all die."

We both sit there a minute and then suddenly turn to each other, slow smiles curving our mouths. Both of us know what the other is thinking. There are ten ways to skin a snake and we're going to use all ten.

My relief that Asher and Luke have my files, is short-lived when Blake and Kara seem to grow more and more tense as they read through them. By eight, Jacob leads me out of the offices and takes me to shoot, which I suspect is to give Kara and Blake space to have a meltdown over the trouble I've got them into. Jacob is quiet too, but that isn't new. That's why they chose him to take me. He's silent. He's impenetrable.

We're an hour into my practice when he gets a text. "Kara and Blake want us to meet them at your place. They'll stay with you until Asher gets back."

"Is anything wrong?"

"Nothing I've been told," Jacob says.

I stare at him. "Are you lying?"

"No." He holds up his fingers. "Scout's honor and I really was a Scout."

"Then you'd better be acting like a Scout."

"I am," he assures me. "Asher and Luke will be here. They're safe. They've confirmed that they are on the plane and the pilot has called in."

"Okay." But it doesn't feel okay.

A few minutes later, we exit to the street, and I don't think I'd know if we were being followed. I know nothing but the knot in my belly. The walk is short and we enter the apartment, to have Blake meet us at the door. "We ordered pizza," he says, motioning Jacob to the hallway.

I grimace at the secrets and march to the kitchen table where Kara is sitting, setting my tote down on a seat. "What is going on?"

"Nothing yet," she says. "We're just processing."

"Right. Trying to figure out how to get me the hell out of your life. I get it. Send me to a safe house. I'll go right now."

"We are not sending you away," she says. "Not now or ever."

Blake re-enters the apartment. "Jacob is bringing Julie over to wait with us for Asher and Luke." He stops at the table.

"Send me to a safe house," I say.

"I told you," he says. "We are your safe house."

"I can sense the change in all of you," I say.

"We're focused on keeping everyone alive," Blake says. "And we will keep everyone alive."

Right.

Alive.

Focus they need because I'm here.

I grab my tote and move to the living room to sit down, dreading the moment Asher walks in the door to tell me whatever they are not, as surely as I hunger for that moment to be now. I really need it to be now.

Thirty minutes later, Julie arrives and Jacob leaves. She sits down next to me, gorgeous and blonde, and I have a flashback of me as a blonde. But I don't want to be blonde. I just want to be alive and with Asher. "How are you?" she asks.

"Worried. Nervous. I want them to be here already."

"It gets easier, I promise."

"Maybe, but this time is all about the hell I'm bringing to your family."

"You didn't do this. A monster did this."

"The Beast," I say. "That's what I call him."

"I'll help you divorce him."

"I can't divorce him. He'll kill me."

"Not from jail."

"His reach is wide," I remind her. "I keep saying that. No one listens. Or—maybe they do now. They know. I see it in everyone's faces."

"Our men will make it non-existent. One day, you'll have the faith in them that I do."

I glance at her watch. "Midnight. Shouldn't they be here by now?"

As if answering my question, the door opens. Julie and I are on our feet as Asher walks in the door, followed by Luke. I forget about bad news. I'm across the room, my arms around Asher in ten seconds flat, and Julie is right there with me, with Luke. "Asher, I—"

His hands are in my hair and he is kissing me before I ever get the rest of my sentence out. I kiss him right back, molding my hands to his back, breathing him in, and when he pulls back, I say, "I was so worried."

"Yeah?" he asks.

"Yes. So much."

His eyes warm. "I've never had anyone worry about me. I think I like it."

"I worry about you all the damn time," Luke assures him, his arm around Julie.

Asher waves him off. "Fuck you, Luke."

Luke laughs. "I love you too, man."

Asher drags me under his arm and our sides meld together. "Let's talk to Blake and Kara, and then hit the bed. I'm exhausted."

I have a million questions for him, but I just want to get him alone. Together we walk to the table and collectively all of us gather there. "Why don't we talk alone," Blake says, his eyes meeting mine.

"Sierra can handle this," Asher replies.

"I'm sorry," I say. "I tried to warn you all."

"Don't be sorry," Asher says.

"No," Luke says. "Don't be sorry. We have a plan."

"We cut the legs off the spider," Asher says. "Devin being the spider."

"The legs being his loyal subjects," Blake says.

"Exactly." Asher says. "We hit each person involved with Devin with a criminal scandal, and eventually we connect Devin to one of them."

"But we don't go slow," Luke say. "We make sure Devin will get nervous. We make sure he acts guilty and we document it, so when it turns on him, he can't run."

"We don't use the real crimes to take these people down," Asher says. "Which means, we all mobilize our closest allies. We divide up the bad guys, and formulate a plan for each."

"Asher and I have already put our SEAL team on standby," Luke says. "We all have insiders."

Blake rubs his hands together. "Damn, I love my job. I'm up on this in a big way. I can make a lot of things happen. Securities fraud or how about child pornography? That's the kind of fun you wish on these kinds of assholes."

"He'll still come for me," I warn.

"He'll be in jail," Luke says, "and everyone in his resource pool will be dead in the water."

"And everyone who tries to help him will go down, too," Blake says. "Until he's the plague no one wants to touch. And no one wants to touch a rich dude who looks at naked pictures of kids. Hell. When I dig in, it might even be true. He's the kind of dude you see doing that shit."

I want to believe them, but I can feel the panic rising in me. They're all in. They're all wonderful. Too wonderful to die. Asher must sense what I feel, because he says, "Go home, everyone."

"You don't have to tell me twice," Luke says, eyeing Asher and giving him a salute.

Julie walks to me and hugs me. "They're good. They'll make this go away." She doesn't wait for a reply. She hurries away with Luke.

Kara rounds the table and hugs me. "We got this and you," she says by my ear.

She moves away, and Asher kisses me. "I'll lock up," he says, releasing me and walking to the door. I watch him, the graceful, yet lethal way he moves, but there is exhaustion in his face, worry, strain. The minute he's back in front of me,

286

he laces his fingers with mine. "Come," he orders, and in silence we walk up the stairs, every part of me aware of this man. Every part of me is falling in love with this man.

The minute we are in the bedroom, I turn to him. I step in front of him, hands on his chest. "I told you, you would regret me—us."

"The only thing I regret, sweetheart, is that he's still alive."

"Asher, damn it, don't be a hero. Talk to me. I sensed how stressed everyone was when they saw those files."

"You did good, Sierra. You painted a picture that might seem daunting at first, but in the end, it becomes a map for their destruction, not ours." He links our fingers again. "I need a shower. Come take it with me." I don't even think about saying no. Maybe I should leave. Maybe I should let go of him, but I'm selfish. I don't want to leave him. I don't want to let go.

And so, I let him lead me into the bathroom and I savor every moment of us both undressing. Those gorgeous tattoos of his shift with every flex of his muscle. He turns on the shower, and we step beneath with him backing me into the corner, his hand gently stroking a lock of hair from my face. "Devin Marks will die before I will ever let him hurt you again."

The passion, the fierce emotion in his voice, steals my breath, but I push past it, I focus on him. "How do I make sure he can't hurt you, though, Asher?"

"That's easy, sweetheart. You belong with me. You stay with me."

His mouth closes down on mine, his kiss, both wicked and sweet, demanding and somehow a question. I don't know what that question is. I only know that anything with Asher is a yes for me. And so, with every stroke of my tongue, every touch of my hand, I tell him yes. He presses inside me as he holds me up with his hands on my backside, and I am certain in these intense moments in this shower that he's telling me he's holding me. He's not letting me go. Well, I'm not letting him go either, and much later, as I lay next to Asher, my head on his chest, his heart thrumming beneath my ear, I know that this man will fight and even die for me.

And I silently vow that I will kill Devin Marks before I let him take Asher from me.

Chapter Thirty-Five

Sierra

I wake the next morning naked and on my belly with Asher's hand on my ass. I have about two seconds to appreciate how that feels before he turns me on my side to face him. Another second to appreciate his long, naked leg between mine, his hand between my shoulder blades, my breasts to his chest before he's kissing me. Somewhere in my mind I compare him to Devin, when I do not want to compare them. Only the thing is that Devin made me feel used. Asher makes me feel savored. He kisses me like he's afraid he will never kiss me again. He touches me like he's the lucky one to be with me, when most of the female population would want this man pressed close to them, like he's pressed close to me.

A long time later, we're both dressed, me in that red T-shirt I'd rejected the other day, and a pair of pale thrift store jeans because they are clean and they fit. Asher in distressed jeans, a tan AC/DC T-shirt and brown boots, that makes him look all kinds of rocker hotness. So does the two-day stubble on his jaw that he insists on shaving. He lathers up and I decide to put my foot down. I push between him and the sink and use my hands to wipe it off. "I don't want you to shave."

We both look at my hands and start laughing. He leans in to kiss me and his cellphone rings. "I'll bet you anything that is Blake." He kisses me and foams up my face before grabbing his phone from his pocket. "Oh fuck," he grumbles.

"What?" I ask urgently. "What's wrong?"

"Just Royce, the cranky father-to-be." He answers the call. "What's up, oh great one?" he says, wiping his face and tossing the towel in the sink before heading out of the room.

The part where he heads out of the room, like he doesn't want me to hear the call, does a perfect job of bursting my happy bubble. Royce is now involved in my situation. He might even be the one who decides that I need to be in that safe house. Maybe I should. Maybe Royce is the one about to bring us all back to the reality I've lost. The one where I'm married to a crazy billionaire.

I grab my purse with the revolver inside and head downstairs to find Asher with his back to me, inspecting the empty fridge. He shuts the door and we each claim the opposite side of the island. "In my professional, ex-SEAL opinion," he says, in good humor, seemingly unaffected by his call with Royce. "Based on the current state of our refrigerator, we would starve to death in an apocalypse. We need to grab groceries and get you some clothes," he says.

"I'm waiting on my bank card for clothes."

"My casa, your casa, sweetheart. My money, your money. You need stuff. Let's go get you stuff."

There's a trigger in the back of my mind I try to shut down, echoes of captivity with Devin I just can't escape. "I have money. I want us to be equal."

Understanding fills his gaze. "I'm not him. I'm not my father. Money is not leverage or ammunition to me. I've lived that. I won't ever make you live that."

"I know that," I breathe out. "I do. I really do. I don't want you to think that I think you're like either of them."

"Then don't keep tabs on what's equal. I'm not. I mean, hell. I do have a greedy side, Sierra. If I want to eat the entire bag of Funyuns, I'm going to eat them. If you want to eat the entire bag of Funyuns, then eat them. We'll just buy extra."

He delivers that with such seriousness that I laugh. "That comment was crazy and I'm pretty sure out of context with the conversation."

"It made you laugh."

"Yes," I say. "It did. You do. And for the record. I might eat the whole bag. I really like Funyuns."

He winks. "Good. Then we can make Funyuns bets, while naked, of course."

I laugh again. "I don't even know what that means."

"No?"

"No," I assure him.

"I'll show you tonight." He glances at his watch. "Right now, we have just enough time to catch a brunch joint up the road before they stop serving and as a plus, they're right next to the firing range." He motions to the door. "Yes?"

"Actually," I say, coming down from his sweet talk about Funyuns. "What happened with Royce?"

"He's back. He wants to meet you this afternoon."

"He's worried," I say, simplifying all he might be thinking or feeling considering everything that was in those files Asher recovered.

"He's Royce, sweetheart." Asher says. "He's always worried. He's also always overbearing, intense, cranky, smart, and honorable. Once you get past his initial gruffness, you'll like him."

"But he's worried," I press.

"He's always worried," he repeats. "You're overthinking this."

"I do that."

"I know."

"You do?"

"Yes," he says. "I do." He rounds the island, snagging my fingers, and walks backward toward the door. "Me, man. You, woman. Oh hell. Whatever brilliant joke I was going to make is gone. I'm fucking starving."

I laugh again, and let him guide me into the hallway: So we can eat. And practice shooting. Right before I go in front of a one man firing squad named Royce Walker.

After lunch, and an hour at the firing range, Asher and I manage a bit of shopping. The grocery portion of that outing, is perhaps the most expensive, as at one point, I think Asher might order the entire store. Nevertheless, groceries are set up for delivery, as are a few personal items for me, and a baby shower gift for Lauren and Royce. By two o'clock, Asher has confirmed Royce is in his office, and we head to the Walker offices to meet him and then work with the rest of the crew to catch Ju-Ju.

We're just about to enter the offices, when Asher pauses at the door. "Give Royce a chance. He's a good man."

"I'm pretty good with challenging personalities," I promise him, my nerves eased a bit now. "I interviewed serial killers."

He laughs. "Let's not tell Royce you said that."

"Yeah," I say, crinkling my nose. "Let's not."

We head inside, and Asher locks up because apparently, Walker takes visitors by appointment only. Asher indicates a corner office, and we cross the lobby to reach the open door. Stepping inside, I find a tall, broad man standing at a window, with his back to us, with dark hair tied at his nape.

"Hey baby daddy," Asher says, motioning me to one of the two leather visitor's chairs. "Feeling any more morning sickness?" Asher and I sit down and he looks at me. "Royce had sympathetic morning sickness, or something like that. What was it called, Royce?"

Royce turns around, a scowl on his handsome face, and while he favors Luke and Blake, his features are harder, sharper. "You're an asshole," he replies to Asher. "That's what you're called," he looks at me, "I'm called Royce, Sierra" He walks to the desk and offers me his hand. "Nice to meet you."

I lean forward and shake his hand. It's a quick but firm grip that is nothing but friendly, but I can feel him sizing me up. He doesn't even sit. He leans on the credenza behind his desk and stares at me. "I need to let you know that I've worked with your mentor."

My throat goes dry with this unexpected, potentially dangerous turn of events. "You and—you worked with Glen Masters?"

"Why don't I know this?" Asher demands, protectiveness in his tone.

"I didn't see it in the files until about an hour ago," he says. "It unfortunately has to color the tone of a meeting I'd meant to take in another direction."

"What direction?" I ask.

"To welcome and assure you that you have our support."

"But you worked with Glen Masters," I say flatly, not sure where this is leading. "Aren't you a former hostage negotiator?"

"Yes," he confirms. "But a serial killer who took hostages led to myself and Masters working a situation together."

"And?" I prod.

"And Master's is an arrogant prick, but he's good at his job."

My defenses prickle hard and fast. "Have you read the documents on Masters in my files?"

"I damn sure have," Asher chimes in. "Masters took detailed notes on the deaths of four people that Sierra clearly tied back to Devin Marks."

"And he wrote those notes before the people actually died," I add.

"I saw the files as well," Royce confirms. "And I have no problem taking down a killer, especially one masquerading as a hero. My problem here, is how this affects you, and really all of us."

"What does that mean?" I ask, looking between them.

"He's connected to you," Royce says. "You had a direct link to his work. That means you could become a focus of an investigation depending on what we expose. That brings all of us into that focus."

I reject that idea immediately. "I don't want that. Is there no way to take him down that won't bring attention to me?"

"The obvious answer to me," Asher says, "Is simply discrediting him."

"In what way?" I ask.

"I'm sure you've figured out how creative Blake can be," Royce says. "Masters is an expert witness. He'd likely create evidence of false testimonies, among other damning activity."

"The problem with that," Asher says, "Is that you worked with Masters to gain your credentials. He becomes the damaged mentor, and you could become the damaged protégé."

"In other words," Royce says. "Are you ready for that to happen?"

"This is a man who I heard plot my murder, before I knew he was plotting a murder," I say. "He told Devin that he'd need a replacement when I was gone. I thought he meant when I graduated. Of course, I now know that he meant when I died. So, am I ready? Yes. And as for my credentials I still interviewed high profile killers. I still learned things from him and processed those things my way. He doesn't define me."

Asher's phone rings and he pulls it from his pocket. "Terrance," he informs us and obviously he expects Royce to know that name.

"Yes," he answers. "What can I do for you, boss?" He listens a minute. "I thought you'd like me all submissive and willing to work your bar all night long?"

Terrance yells so loudly I can hear him through the phone, and much to my surprise, Royce fights off a laugh, giving me a glimpse of a lighter side of the Walker patriarch. "We'll both be at work tonight," Asher continues, "but only if Kelli fills out her paperwork for a paycheck first." He doesn't wait for a reply. He ends the connection and looks at me. "If you didn't need that paperwork on file, to take attention off yourself, you wouldn't be going tonight."

"Yes, I would," I say. "Because you're a hero and you want to catch a killer and that means doing things we both don't want to do."

"Sierra," Royce says. "Can Asher and I have a few moments? The rest of the Ju-Ju team is in the conference room."

"Of course," I say, standing up and quickly heading to the door.

"Sierra," Royce says, just before I exit.

I pause and glance around at him. "Yes?"

"What you've done is brave and strong. You're as much a hero as Asher."

"No," I say, my eyes meeting Asher's. "But I'm lucky enough to have him to inspire me." I slip away then, and I make it to the hallway just outside the conference room when Asher catches me, pulls me to him and kisses me until I can't think straight.

"I just needed to do that," he says, his voice low and gravelly. And then he walks away. I lean on the wall, the scent of his spicy cologne lingering in the air and on my skin. The taste of his passion still on my lips, a smile with it. That man is too perfect for my own good.

Voices lift in the conference room, and I push off the wall and walk into the room to discover Smith and Blake heatedly debating the attitude of someone named Rick Savage. Kara and Jacob greet me as Blake and Smith pipe down to do the same. I'm about to sit down when Blake stands up and motions me to the wall opposite the one pinned with a roadmap of Ju-Ju data on notecards. I join him there and study the collage of notecards with him, most of which include names of people my files added to. "It's begun," Blake explains. "Underneath each notecard with a name, you will eventually see the date we wipe that person off the map, in one way, shape or form." He taps the one that features the Dallas FBI agent who betrayed me. "He's first. He and his minions, which we now know stretch beyond Texas, will soon be implicated in a criminal drug operation, by my creation, of course. Everyone else on this wall will fall as well, and soon. Including him." He points to the largest piece of paper, the one in the center of the wall that reads: *Devin Marks.*

The Beast.

Asher chooses that very moment to enter the room. "Sierra and I are going to the bar tonight," he announces. "If I win the fight, that I'm sure I'll soon have with Sierra, this will be Sierra's last night at the bar, so let's make it count. Let's catch a killer tonight."

Hours later, Asher and I exit the subway tunnel to start the short walk to the bar when he stops and turns me to look at him. "You stay close to me. If you so much as have to go to the bathroom, you make sure I know it and you text Luke, who will be in the surveillance van."

"You already told me this before we left the office."

"When the club closes, I'll walk you to your old apartment. We will pretend to fight and I will leave without going up with you. When you get there, Kara will be waiting on you, and fuck. I have to leave you there with her and I don't like it. Tomorrow morning she'll leave, and you will wear a disguise and leave after her."

He's told me all of this several times. "What's wrong with you tonight?"

"A gut feeling that says tonight is trouble and if you'd let me, I'd take you back home, right now."

"We have to catch him and I have an army protecting me, remember?" I ask, sounding full of bravado, when I'm not. A gut feeling saved me in Dallas. Gut feelings matter.

"Yeah," he says. "I fucking remember." His phone buzzes with a text and he looks at it. "There will be a Bigfoot-looking bouncer with a scar down his face. His name is Rick Savage. I don't like him, but he's one of us and according to Luke, Savage just got called into work by Terrance as a new hire. Savage will text you so you know how to reach him. If you can't get to me, go to him. And keep your purse at your hip with your gun inside. Let's get this over with." He takes my hand and holds onto it a little tighter than usual. He doesn't say another word, and I have this sense that he is on alert, listening for any little sound.

We enter the back of the bar and Terrance is on top of us instantly, like he's watching some camera and knew we were there. "No paperwork," Asher says. "No workie."

Terrance shoots me an irritated look. "On the break room table and good to have you on board, Sierra." He turns and walks away.

"Kelli," I call out. "Can you remember my name, already?"

He doesn't turn. He laughs a roaring laugh.

Asher and I look at each other. "I don't like that," I say. "He called me Sierra like a taunt."

"He knows you dodged a documented paycheck. We can't get around that. Just fill out the application."

I do it quickly and we walk to Terrance's office to find him behind his junky, scraped desk. I walk inside and set it in front of him. "When do I work next?"

"Depends on how well you work. Go work now."

Asher takes my hand and pulls me out of there. "Like I said," he murmurs near my ear. "Let's get this over with." He leads me into the club, through the hustle and bustle of a budding crowd, and soon we are behind the bar. For two hours, we serve drinks and there is no sign of Ju-Ju, no word he's even left his house. At the three-hour mark, I have to go the bathroom and I tell Asher. He sends word to the team and I'm cleared, but Asher leans in close. "If there really is a partner to Ju-Ju in this, that partner could be here. Be careful."

He waits for my promise and then helps me onto the bar. I jump down on the other side, feeling the nerves in my belly with every step. I move quickly through the bar and down the hall leading to the bathroom. There is a line. I text Asher and Blake: *There's a line. Three before me.*

Blake messages back: We have eyes on you now and Ju-Ju hasn't left his house.

I should be comforted but Asher's reminder about a potential partner to Ju-Ju has me watching the hallway for anyone approaching, until finally it's my turn. I walk into the bathroom, lock up, and quickly do my thing. I text again: *Leaving the bathroom.*

I exit and there is no line. Why is there no line? There is a loud speaker announcement and I realize that open mic is starting in the concert area. Everyone is there. I take two more steps and suddenly Ju-Ju is in front of me. "Gorgeous," he says, snapping my photo with a phone again.

"Stop," I order firmly. "Stop now."

My hand goes to my purse, but I have no right to shoot him now, and if I do, I'll get police attention, I'll get The Beast's attention. I remind myself that I'm being watched. Help is coming. I try to step around Ju-Ju and he shoves me against the wall, pinning my legs with his legs. I shove against him and he snaps my photo. I knee him rather ineffectively and grab the phone in his hand. He snatches it right back, opens the bathroom door and shoves me inside. I stumble and fall backward and now, I reach for my gun. I remember my lesson, even as I unzip my purse. *Never shoot unless you intend to kill your target.* I'm shooting to kill. I reach inside my purse, my hand on the grip of my firearm and that's when Ju-Ju opens a baggy and waves it in my direction. White powder floats in the air and right into my face.

299

Chapter Thirty Six

ASHER

The code red for Sierra hits my phone, and in all the code reds I've gotten in my life, this is the only one that made my entire body clench. I'm over the bar and shoving a drunk asshole out of my path in all of ten seconds. Savage is by my side by the time I land, and linebacker that he is, he charges forward ahead of me into the thinning crowd thanks to the open mic, and clears a path. We reach the hallway leading to the bathroom and something smacks into Savage. "Got him," Savage growls. "Get Sierra!"

Savage backs up, and holy shit, he's dragging Ju-Ju who isn't even fighting him. Like he just got his version of having his fucking cock blown and he's satisfied. Which freaks me the fuck out, and has me running full speed down the hallway. How the fuck is he even here? Where the fuck is Sierra? Please let her be alive. I round the corner and Sierra steps into the doorway of the bathroom, covered in some kind of white residue. "Don't touch me," she warns, holding up her hands. "I don't know what he threw on me. You can't touch me."

"Like hell," I say, scooping her up, carrying her through the bar, shoving people out of the way as needed. Our quickest exit is down the employee hall and that is where I go. And my team damn sure better be waiting. I get to the back door and Luke opens it.

Exiting to the alleyway, the surveillance van is not only waiting, but the doors are open and I immediately help Sierra inside and sit her down on a chair built into the wall. I follow her and go down on a knee in front of her. "Are you okay?"

"How is she?" Luke asks, climbing inside and shutting the doors.

"Hospital?" Smith calls back from the driver's seat.

"No," Sierra says. "I feel nothing. I'm not hurt. I'm not sick." She touches my face. "Stubborn man. It's all over you. How do *you* feel?"

"Same as you. I feel nothing." The powder bleeds into my mouth and it's familiar. I lick my lip. "It's fucking baby powder. That little prick."

Sierra smells her fingers. "It is. It's baby powder. He was scaring me. Or us. He was setting us up."

"Holy hell," I murmur, eying Luke. "Where is Ju-Ju now?"

"Savage has him at the front, giving him hell for mistreating one of the bartenders. There's no way he's seen us back here."

"I should go back inside," Sierra says. "He can't think that—"

"No," I say. "That is not happening. You're done here and I will tie you to the damn bed and keep you there if that is what is necessary. Or drug you and put us both on a plane. Tell us what happened."

"He cornered me, and I didn't want to shoot him until I had real cause. But then he shoved me onto the bathroom floor and I was going to shoot him. I had my purse unzipped. I was reaching and then came the powder. And he took my picture again. Can Savage get the phone?"

"If he can, he will," Luke says. "Savage is an asshole, but he's good under pressure."

"He was under pressure because Ju-Ju was in the building and Sierra and I didn't know," I say. "How the fuck did that happen?"

"It has to be a decoy," Luke says. "Like Kara is for Sierra, which is probably why he saw through our attempt at the same."

"That means he knows he's being watched," Sierra says.

"Agreed," I say. "And I'd bet money that he has a spotter watching us right now."

The sound of the back door of the bar opening has Luke eyeing the monitor. "Savage."

I rotate to face the doors as they open, and Savage leans in to talk to us. "How is she?" He eyes the powder on me. "How the hell are you?"

"It's baby powder," I say. "Where is Ju-Ju now?"

"I had to let him go or they were going to call the police," he says, "and I didn't think my cover would hold if that happened. And I didn't think you'd want Sierra to talk to the cops. Tell me someone has eyes on him."

"Jacob," Luke interjects. "He just sent me a text confirmation."

"I have to get back," Savage says, "but I grabbed this." He holds up a phone. "The only photos on that phone are Sierra's. No calls. It's clean. He had his day-to-day phone but there were no photos." He hands it to me. "I'll update the team when I can." He pulls back and shuts us inside.

"I have to go to the apartment," Sierra says. "Stay the course." She focuses on me. "We can fight over what just happened. Kara is there waiting on me, but we have to finish the night."

"No," I say. "You won't go back in that bar. You won't go to the apartment. He knows we're watching him."

I look at Luke. "Tell Blake and Kara to be careful, but Sierra is out. I'm taking her home."

"I don't blame you, man," Luke says. "I'll have Smith shadow you."

"No," I say. "Ju-Ju is outsmarting us. I have Sierra. Just stay on Ju-Ju."

"This could have been a distraction for another kill," Sierra warns.

And with that grim note, I take Sierra's hand. "Let's get out of here."

She doesn't argue, and when we step onto the street, I don't speak. We don't have back-up. I need to focus and her silence says that she understands. The walk is short, but feels like forever before we are safely inside a subway car with four other people.

We can't talk, but the realization that she could be dead right now is punching all kinds of holes in me for the entire ride. I grab the pole and pull her to me, and she sinks against me, trembling, as if it's just hit her that she battled with a serial killer. Incredible, she not only battled, she survived and wanted to keep fighting. I look down and her purse is unzipped, her weapon a reach from being pulled. I leave it that way and just hold her until we arrive at our stop.

Once we're street-side, the walk is short to the apartment. The walk through the lobby to the elevator even shorter. Inside the elevator, I punch our floor and pull her to me, tangling fingers in her hair. "You scared the shit out of me, woman," I say, and I kiss her, a deep, drink-her-in, I-almost-fucking-lost-her kiss that I don't end until the ping of our arrival. Then and only then do I part our lips, take her hand and lead her to the apartment.

The instant we are inside and locked up, we walk side-by-side up the stairs to the bedroom, and straight to the bathroom and the shower. Before we ever undress to wash off all this powder, Luke calls. I answer on speaker. "Sierra and I are here," I tell him.

"He went straight to his house," Luke announces.

"Are you sure it's him?" I ask.

"We're sure. I talked to Blake. He hacked the security system at Ju-Ju's apartment and upon inspection, found a loop."

"A what?" Sierra asks.

"A disruption that makes you think you're looking at present time footage, but you're not," I explain. "Which means he hired a hacker or he has skills we didn't know he had."

"Whatever the case," Luke says. "We know now. We have eyes on him. You two can have some peace with that."

"He's done with me," Sierra says. "He'll go underground now. He won't kill anytime soon. He'll wait until you give up."

"We never give up," Luke says. "Not on something like this, even if our client does. You two try to get some much-earned rest." He disconnects, and I set the phone on the counter, and step into Sierra, cupping her face. "He made you. You can't go back. You know that, right?"

"Yes. Now that I'm coming down from the high of it all, I know that." Her fingers curl on my chest. "I was scared and that seems to be my trigger to do that overthinking thing. I could have killed him. I *should* have killed him. If I get the chance again, I will kill him."

LISA RENEE JONES

Chapter Thirty Seven

Sierra

I wake the next morning to no change in the news on Ju-Ju, and needing an outlet. Asher and I go running, and then spend two hours at the firing range. When we finally shower and head to the office, we enter the lobby to come face-to-face with a massive man with a scar down his face.

"What are you doing here, Savage?" Asher growls.

"Trying to catch an asshole," he says. "But I need sleep. I'm leaving." He looks at me. "I'll kill him if I get the chance, don't you worry."

"For the record, Savage," Asher says. "I still don't like you, but I no longer hate you. Badass assist last night."

"I still hate you, motherfucker," he says, "but I got your back." He looks at me. "Your back before his." He steps around us and starts walking and I turn to call after him.

"Thank you for last night!"

He lifts a hand and exits the office. "What's the story between you two?" I ask, glancing at Asher.

"He's an asshole. I hate assholes."

Royce heads out of his office and toward us. "The baby shower is delayed. Lauren wants to have it after the baby is born in February."

"Isn't it this weekend?" I ask. "Aren't there guests coming over?"

"Yes," Royce says, "But Myla is in Europe with Kyle, and pretty upset that she can't be here. The only way I could keep her off the plane yesterday was to tell her and Kyle the truth. The bottom line here is that Kyle has time to chase this Alvarez rumor and we don't." He looks at me. "We're going to keep you, Savage, and a field team on Ju-Ju right now. You'll earn a bonus for taking on more responsibility. The rest of us are powering through the Devin Marks situation." He looks at Asher. "I assume you'll work both cases, but as of now, unless either of you have an objection, I'm on board with your plan to move this Marks plan forward quickly and I'll throw the resources at it we need."

"We have six total targets, and any spawn they lead us to," Asher says. "If we take one down a week, at least disrupt their world, we can force Marks into a corner by Christmas. Merry fucking Christmas from Walker Security."

"I'm on board," Royce says. "Let's make it happen."

My heart is now racing at the idea of this particular Christmas gift, but I'm nervous, too. We're dealing with Devin Marks and no one knows his variety of evil more than me.

I spend the afternoon at one end of the conference table, researching any detail to nab Ju-Ju while listening to the rest of the team work on the battle with The Beast. I offer random tips and thoughts to help them while making calls related to Ju-Ju's father. Looking for anything to take him down before he's so dormant that we may never link him to any of the murders. By early evening, Savage is the only insider we have at the bar, while his field team runs surveillance. Ju-Ju doesn't show up, which is no surprise to me. Asher and I stay at the office until two in the morning, and then head home.

Friday morning, Asher and I repeat Thursday, jogging, grabbing breakfast, and then hitting the firing range, where I am showing improvements. Savage and I have no luck digging up dirt on Ju-Ju or his father, but the Devin Marks team, is pleased with their progress.

Friday evening, Ju-Ju not only stays away from the bar, he goes out to dinner by himself, and then to a movie. By Monday, Royce pulls Savage's undercover role, and he's about to scale the Ju-Ju case back to field surveillance, which Savage and I fight. Out of options, ten days pass, and Ju-Ju seems to fade into the background, while Asher becomes my world. I wake up in his arms and fall asleep the same way. And as we all focus on Devin Marks, the arrests and scandals begin to post on our wall. Each step we take, each move we make, makes the fall of The Beast feel a little more possible.

But on day eleven since the baby powder incident, I wake up with a gasp that has Asher jerking to a sitting position, because apparently, I'm sitting up. "Nightmare?" he asks.

"Yes," I say, my mind flashing back again to that dinner party, and then the garden, where I'd heard The Beast plan to kill a man, and use me as payment. "Very much a nightmare."

Asher lowers me to the bed, and rolls us both to our sides, facing each other. "About The Beast?"

"Yes and no. Yes, it was about him but it's really about me not doing enough fast enough to save lives. I want to work on the Ju-Ju case again today."

"Tell me about the nightmare, Sierra."

"You don't want to hear this."

"Yes. I do."

And so I tell him and he just listens, his jaw hard and getting harder. When I'm done, he inhales and gets out of bed and, still naked from the night before, walks into the bathroom. I blink, confused, and sit up. The shower comes on and I don't know what to think. Is he turned off by what I've told him? By the fact that I stayed after that? Or that I wore that dress? I don't know but I have to know. I climb out of the bed and rush into the bathroom. He's in the shower and I stop beside it.

"Do you think less of me now?"

The door immediately opens and he pulls me inside, his lips coming down on mine in a kiss that is angry and almost brutally passionate. And then he presses me into the corner, his hands on the wall above my head. "Did that taste or feel like I think less of you?"

"You said nothing. You walked in here and said nothing."

"I'm in love with you. *I love you, Sierra.* Don't tell me it's too damn soon because that won't change two things. I love you. And I'm going to kill him."

"You will go to jail."

"You still underestimate me. It will look like an accident, which considering he kills just that way, is poetic justice."

I press my hands to his chest. "I don't want to be the woman who made you kill."

"You aren't. He's simply the man who deserves to die. Tell me you love me, Sierra. I really need to hear it."

"Oh God, yes," I say, despite the fact that I haven't let myself think it until now. But I do. So much. "You know I do," I add.

"Say it," he orders.

"I love you, Asher. I love you more than I thought possible and I—"

He slides his hand under my neck and drags his lips to mine. "Show me."

I smile against his lips and then he kisses me again and we are wild and crazy and perfect. But there is anger under his surface, so much anger that I have to control because killing to save a life is different than murder. Murder will change him. Murder will always be between us and because of me.

I can't let that happen, and the only way I know to stop it right now is to kiss him deeper, touch him everywhere, and just hold onto him.

Hours later, at the office, Asher is driving everyone to push the timeline forward on the takedown of Devin Marks' minions. He's intense and I sense that I just have to let him ride this out for now, work through the anger and come down a bit before we can talk this out. Besides, I'm feeling pretty intense over the news we were met with today on Ju-Ju. Apparently, he's taken a job at his father's old stockbroker firm, a killer hiding in clear sight just like Devin, and that idea fires me up. I start watching the hours of surveillance footage on him, of him, looking for what we have missed. By evening, I'm focused on the many reels of diner footage, when my eyes go wide and my heart skips a beat.

"I think I know this man," I say, pausing the footage on the fiftyish man with gray, wavy hair. "This man who was in the diner with Ju-Ju. He's familiar."

Asher, Luke, Kara, Blake and Savage are instantly behind me. "He bought from Ju-Ju several times," Blake says. "I remember him."

"I know him, too," Savage says, "and not from the bar or the diner. I saw his picture."

He walks back to his seat, sits down and begins punching keys on his computer. "Grant Miller," he says, glancing at us. "He was the tech guy at the brokerage firm Ju-Ju's father worked for. He retired two years ago."

Asher kneels beside me and turns the computer in his direction while Blake walks back to his seat and focuses on his keyboard as well. "He lives in Westbury, Long Island," Asher says. "It's a rental house. And there is no credit card activity in a week."

"His light bill is a month past due," Blake adds.

"No bank account activity," Asher says. "Fuck. It was drained two weeks ago, like he was planning to run."

"I got the address," Blake says, standing up. "Let's go."

Asher faces me, his hand on my leg. "Stay here. Don't leave the office, but go tell Royce what's happening." He eyes Savage.

"Nothing would please me more than to stay with your woman."

"Don't push your luck, Savage," Asher says, kissing my hand. "I'll call you soon."

He stands and exits the room, and Savage and I look at each other one beat before we both turn back to our computers. "Look for anything that might help them," he says.

I pull the video footage back up and I watch the interaction Grant has with Ju-Ju in slow motion. "Oh wow," I breathe out.

Savage's gaze jerks to me. "What do you have?"

"Ju-Ju doesn't sell him drugs. He hands him a small, bulky envelope."

"Like it has a phone with a picture on it inside," Savage says, following my thoughts exactly. "Call Asher. They need to look for those phones."

ASHER

It's me, Luke, Blake, Kara, and Smith, crowding into the Escalade in the Walker parking garage, with Blake and his control-freak ass behind the wheel. We're barely out of the drive when Sierra calls me with the news about the envelope exchange. "I think he's the keeper of the souvenirs."

"Got it," I say. "We'll find them if they're there." I end the call. "Sierra thinks Ju-Ju handed off his picture phones to Miller."

"Fuck," Blake growls. "We spooked the jerk-offs. We know where this is going and it's nowhere."

We all fall into silence, focused on the mission ahead, aware that when a man is cornered, he does insane things, even kills himself and tries to take others with him. Forty-five minutes later, we pull to a stop a few houses down from Miller's. "I don't know about the rest of you," I say. "But I don't plan on knocking."

"I do," Blake says. "As in knock the fucking door down."

"Sometimes I think I love you," I say as I pop the back door open.

"Don't feed his attitude," Luke grumbles. "We'll all pay the price."

On that note, we all exit the vehicle and I take the lead, motioning Blake and Luke to the left while myself and Smith

LISA RENEE JONES

go right, just before we split up to ensure we don't scare the neighbors. Once we're at the house, Smith and I draw our weapons and scan the windows, only to find the drapes are too thick to offer a visual inside the property. We round the corner to the back yard, going slow. "Watch for booby traps," Smith says. "I'll go first. This is my thing."

When an ex-Green Beret, who specialized in setting booby traps wants to go first, you let him. I wave him forward. He motions for me to wait. I scan while he clears our path and finally, he motions me forward. There is no back porch and we both flatten on the wall by the door. I give him a nod and kick the door open. He steps to the entrance and checks for wires, then slowly enters the house. I follow to find it empty, but the danger of a bomb or trap still exists.

Luke enters through the front door, Blake at his heels. Smith motions for us all to wait. For ten minutes we stand there while he clears the top level, then gives us an all-clear sign. He motions to a stairwell leading to the basement and I follow him, patiently waiting as he does his thing, and clears our path. Finally, we reach the bottom of the stairs. "Holy fuck," I murmur as I find a wall of pictures, all familiar since they are the victims killed by our serial killer.

I stand my ground until Smith says, "All clear and what the fuck?"

"Down here!" I shout, and Blake and Luke hurry down the steps, both cursing to various degrees.

The five of us stand there, staring at the photos and I try to take comfort in the fact that Sierra's isn't there. Either she's now taken off the list, or she's not on it yet because she's not dead. "He left this as a taunt," I say. "A message."

"Agreed," Luke says. "But what's the message?"

"It could be a kiss my ass goodbye," Blake says.

314

"Or a promise that he'll kill again," Kara says, "and we didn't catch him now and we won't then." She turns to face me. "The FBI will get involved. Ju-Ju will be interviewed and Sierra might come up, at which time I'll claim that is me."

"But there are pictures he took of her that could show up," I say.

"He has money," Kara says. "His attorney will keep his mouth shut."

"Our six-week plan to take down Marks just turned into four," I say, looking at Blake and Luke. "I need Devin Marks ended and ended now."

"We'll come up with a plan in the morning," Blake says, tossing me the keys. "Get your woman. Tell her she did good and keep her away from the offices until the FBI storm passes."

I nod and head for the door, and I don't stop until I'm in the Escalade. Once I'm on the road I dial Sierra. "What's happening?" she asks, sounding nervous.

"He's cleared the house but left the photos behind."

"Oh," she breathes out. "Were there...photos of me?"

"No. Not of you. Just the victims. We called the police. Ju-Ju and even Terrance will be questioned. If anyone brings you up, we'll play dumb and point to Kara. And you need to know that the FBI will be called in, probably tonight. You're going to want to keep a low profile until the storm passes."

"I'm fine with that. Just get them. Stop them from killing again."

"We're closer thanks to you. This might even lock Ju-Ju up and keep him behind bars. We'll know more in the morning."

"What do you think of Miller leaving those photos for us to find means?"

"He has a God complex, much like The Beast. He thinks that he's untouchable. He's mocking everyone who thinks they can catch him."

"That's good news," I say.

"How is that good news?"

"Because men like Devin Marks, who believe they're untouchable, get too confident and make mistakes. And then they crash and burn, or in Miller's case get arrested."

"And in Devin Marks case?" she asks.

"You know how he ends. I'll be there in forty-five minutes."

I disconnect the call, and just thinking about the moment I get to kill that man makes me ten shades of happy.

Chapter Thirty Eight

Sierra

Asher and I wake up the next morning to pounding on the door. Both of us throw on sweats and T-shirts to find Royce is our visitor. "Ju-Ju confessed," he announces.

Asher and I gape.

Royce crowds us and enters the apartment. "I need coffee. Kara and I were at the station all night. I haven't slept."

We back up and he heads into the kitchen, where he pops a pod in the pot and turns to face us.

"Did they find evidence to use to get the confession?" Asher asks as he and I sit down at the island across from Royce.

"None." Royce grabs his cup and takes a sip. "He just buckled under the pressure of six hours in the interrogation room. Apparently, his father used to lock him in the closet."

"Oh no," I say, having seen this kind of thing before. "Let's hope they don't claim emotional distress to throw out the confession."

"Even if they do," Royce says, "he gave up details that will take him down. And get this. He says Miller is dumb as a rock, and nothing more than a retiree on his payroll, who believed he was a photographer."

"Tech guys are not dumb as rocks," Asher argues.

"He had a stroke five years back. Ju-Ju claims it affected him. They have an APB out on him but Ju-Ju says he's on a cruise."

Alarm radiates though me at the idea that cruises are common ways to escape. I suddenly really want Asher to check on my mother. Royce's phone buzzes and while he reaches for it Asher leans in and whispers, "I tried to find her and couldn't," he says, clearly reading my mind and noticing my reaction. "We'll have Blake try, too. If we both come up dry, then that's good news. That means no one else can find her, either."

I let out a relieved breath and look at him. "Thank you."

"The wife wants me," Royce says. "I need to go, but I still have more good news. I heard from my buddy in the FBI that I've had helping us with the Marks case. We're about ten minutes and a week from cornering Devin Marks. Arrests are imminent."

"What does that mean?" I ask, looking between them.

Royce answers, "Your mentor and your beast have been fingered for insider trading and child pornography. Marks will also be nabbed for knowingly hiding engine flaws in military jets that killed men fighting for this country. And that's true. Bastard really did that." He eyes Asher. "Adam was a good find."

"Adam?" I ask. "Your SEAL buddy?"

"Exactly," Asher confirms. "His mother is a CIA agent who believes Devin Marks has to be stopped and took action to help us."

My head is spinning. "What happens next? I stay underground until he's so buried in jail on these new charges that I'm not at risk any longer?"

"I'm taking extra precautions," Asher says. "Once he's arrested, I'll make a copy of the data you collected. An anonymous source will mail it to his attorney with a promise that if anything happens to you or anyone close to you, that file will be distributed to authorities and sent to all the major publications, thus ending any hope he has of staying out of jail."

"It's a good plan," Royce says, downing the rest of his coffee. "You should talk to Julie, Sierra. The minute that happens, she can file your divorce and take that bastard to the cleaners."

"I don't want his money," I say.

He looks between us. "You two need to learn that it's better to put the money in the good guy's hands. Do good with it, but take the damn money."

There's a knock on the door, followed by the bell. Royce sets his cup in the sink. Asher frowns and heads for the door. "I need to go," Royce says, "but," he reaches in his pocket and sets an envelope in front of me. "Your offer for full-time employment. Two hundred thousand a year plus a bonus."

I blanch. "What? That is incredibly generous."

"It's New York City," he says. "It's starting pay in this city, but the bonuses make up for it."

I laugh. "You're joking, right?"

"You got the wrong brother on that one. Do you accept?"

"Yes. Yes, I accept."

He winks. "Good. We're lucky to have you."

He heads to the door and I walk that way with him to find Asher has stepped into the hallway. Now I'm frowning and when Royce exits, I follow him to find Asher speaking with his father in the hallway. Royce pats Asher on the back as he passes and suddenly I have Asher's father staring at me. "Do you have that dress, Kelli? The party is only two weeks away."

"Goodbye, Father," Asher says, offering him his back and walking toward me. Without another word he urges me inside and shuts the door.

"You okay?" I ask, as he locks up.

He turns to me and says, "Not yet but I will be." He picks me up and starts carrying me toward the bedroom. Once we're there, he settles me on the mattress and comes down on top of me. "Sierra, not Kelli. And your last name will not be Marks for long." He kisses me and that anger I'd tasted before in him is back, a dark, jagged edge that two people seem to bring out in him: his father and Devin Marks.

———————— ∞ ————————

The next morning, Asher's stormy mood has passed, and I celebrate the demise of a serial killer and the future demise of The Beast with donuts, but only after we jog to earn the junk food. We run by the firing range again and I'm pretty darn happy with how well I've progressed. We arrive at the apartment to shower and change to find several packages at our door. Asher grabs the card and reads it out loud, "*For: Kelli, From: Asher's beloved father.*" He crumples the note.

"It's going to be dresses," he says. "Do you want them?"

"No," I say. "Of course not, but make sure that's what it is."

He lifts his face skyward and huffs out a breath before opening the door and then picking the boxes up. He enters the apartment and sets them on the island before walking to the living area where he sits on the ottoman of a chair. I open the first box, and Asher is right. It's a dress. I shut it and open the second box. And of course, it's another dress, but inside is also a copy of the invitation which features former

Navy SEAL Asher Montgomery, who will be honoring the wounded warriors of the armed services.

I pick up the invitation and join Asher, sitting next to him. "There was this inside." I hand him the invitation.

"That bastard. No. He's a little bitch."

His phone rings and he pulls it from his pocket. "Royce." He answers the line and almost immediately hangs up, to reach for the remote. The television comes to life where it hangs in the center of the wall and I gasp to find The Beast on the screen. Not just on the screen. He's cuffed and being walked to a police car. I hold my hands to my face and laugh, though I think I might cry. I'm a ball of emotions. "I can't believe it's real."

Asher goes down on one knee in front of me. "Are you happy?"

"Yes. So happy." I cup his face. "You did this. You. All of you, but it's because of you."

"Now you can go to this damn party with me as Sierra, not Kelli, but I'm buying your damn dress."

"I will go anywhere with you. I will—" He kisses me and then pulls me to my feet. "Let's go see Julie and get a damn divorce."

"Don't we need to wait until you mail the documents to his attorney?"

"Call me impatient," he says. "But I want you to talk to Julie today." He molds me close, his hands on my lower back. "You're mine now."

"And you're mine?"

"Why did that sound like a question? I've been yours since the first time you called me an asshole." He laces his fingers with mine. "Let's go see Julie."

"What about the FBI and me avoiding the offices?"

"We'll go in through the garage, but you're starting that divorce today."

I don't argue. He'd once told me he'd give me my freedom to choose. And I want him to know that I choose him, and nothing, and no one, is going to change that, now or ever.

Chapter Thirty Nine

Sierra

The Friday of the party, two weeks after Devin's arrest, Asher is at the office, and I'm panicking over a dress. I hate everything I bought, which was four dresses I now need to take back. I'm standing in the closet about to try them on again when the doorbell rings. I hurry downstairs and look through the peephole to find Julie.

I open the door and she holds up clothing bags. "I understand you have a dress crisis. I brought you a couple of my favorites."

"Luke told you," I say, backing up so she can enter.

"Yes. Luke told me." She walks to the island and sets the garment bag over the back of a stool. "Hopefully one of those work."

"Thank you. I'm going to go try them."

"Wait. Divorce talk first."

"Now?"

"Yes, now. I was in conversations with your ex's attorney this afternoon." Conversations that were cleared after we determined he is being held with no bail. Also, Asher mailed my files to Devin's criminal attorney, and he included a note: *Tell Devin Marks to remember* Mali, which was an obvious threat to kill him.

"Is there a problem? Of course there is. It's Devin Marks."

"He offered you five million to settle. I told him that's not enough."

"I don't want his money," I say. "Just make the divorce happen."

"You're taking the money," she says. "Donate it to starving children if you want, but don't leave it with that monster. And furthermore, he's a billionaire and you didn't sign a prenup. Considering who he is and how he behaves, you'll get more than five million. Go try on the dresses and if they don't work, I can go raid my closet again."

The door opens, and Asher walks in with a garment bag in his hand. Julie glances my direction. "That's my cue to leave. Have fun tonight. We'll work out the money stuff next week." She heads to the door, and Asher stops in front of me, giving me a quick kiss. "What did she mean? The money stuff?"

"She wants Devin to pay me. I said no. She ignored me."

"Do you want the money?"

"No, but she told me donate it to a charity, and I could do that." I wave it off. "Is that your suit for tonight?"

"No. This is a dress I picked out for you. You may hate it, but I was walking by a window and it just looked like you to me."

I wait to feel uncomfortable, the way I had with Devin, but I don't. "I'm eager to see it." I indicate the other bags on the stool. "Those are from Julie."

"Surely you can find one you like between all of these," he says, grabbing all of the bags. "Right?"

I laugh as we start walking upstairs. "Right. Surely."

"No 'surely,'" he says.

"A dress is not an easy choice."

"Holy fuck, I'm glad I'm a man."

He sets the bags on the bed and kisses me. "I'm going to shower."

He walks away, and I open the only bag that matters. The one from him. The minute I bring it into view, I smile. It's a rich navy blue that is velvet with a hint of shine and figure-hugging, but in a classy way. And the neckline: Turtleneck with open shoulders to contrast. I try it on and I love it so very much. I take it back off and walk into the bathroom, where Asher is getting out of the shower and walking into the closet. I quickly touch-up my make-up and hair, and then put on the dress, which I've paired with black closed-toe heels with ribbon ties around the ankles.

Asher walks out of the bathroom in a dark gray suit, with a gray silk tie, just a hint of his colorful tats showing above his watch, and my jaw drops. "Wow. You look stunning."

"You like me better like this?" he asks.

"No. I like you better the other way, the real way, but it's hot. You're always hot."

He saunters toward me and stops, his hands on my waist. "You look beautiful. Just like I knew you would."

"I know why you picked this neckline."

"I don't think you do."

"The story, Asher."

He links our fingers and walks me back into the bathroom and has me face the sink. "Close your eyes," he says, stepping behind me.

I do as he orders, and he slips a necklace around me, which sets off butterflies in my belly.

"Open your eyes," he says now.

I blink and bring the most stunning platinum marquis necklace into view with three tiers of flowers. It glistens in the lights, catching different colors, a perfect complement to the dress and neckline.

"That's why I picked the neckline." His eyes meet mine in the mirror. "Because I don't want to tell people you're available. I want to tell them you're taken." He lowers his lips to my ear. "I love you."

My heart squeezes and I rotate to face him. "I love you, too."

"Good. Because I'm going to need a lot of love to get through this shit tonight."

"And sex?" I tease, since he'd once made a similar joke to me.

"Oh yeah. Lots of sex. Creative sex. Tie you up and have my way with you sex." He turns me to the door, hands on my shoulders from behind. "Let's go to the party so we can get back and do those things."

I start walking and once I hit the stairs, he follows. "Adding to the list," he says from behind me. "I might have to spank you for making me look at your ass in that dress all night, because it's perfect."

"Don't look," I say, stopping at the bottom of the steps as he joins me.

He stops in front of me. "You can't look this beautiful and expect me not to look." He kisses my hand and settles it at his elbow, before facing forward. "Shall we, my beautiful woman?" he asks all proper and debonair.

"Yes, we shall, my arrogant, alpha hero."

He gives me a devastatingly sexy smile and we are on our way, but as we're about to step into the elevator, I tug Asher to a halt. "Am I Sierra tonight?"

He catches the elevator doors. "Yes, and every night."

"How do we explain Kelli?"

"An undercover operation we weren't willing to pierce for him."

"Are we good?" he asks.

"Yes. We're very good."

He smiles and we enter the car.

We arrive at the hotel by way of a driver and present our invitation. We're directed to a bank of elevators and we head upstairs, along with a cluster of people and an elf. Asher and I end up crushed against the wall and he smiles. "Why are you smiling?" I mouth.

He leans down and whispers, "Aside from the fact that you're pressed against me, this is not the way my father would want his event to go down."

The elevator dings and we exit as a hoard of people try to enter. Once we're out of the car there is another cluster of too many people all along our upcoming path, including a half dozen elves. Asher laughs again. "I love this."

"You're evil," I say as we walk toward our event location.

"Is that a problem?"

"Maybe."

His cellphone rings and he pulls it from his pocket to frown. "Royce. He knows we're here. I need to take this." He punches the Answer button. "What? When? Are you sure? Right... Yeah... Get me back up." He ends the call.

"What just happened?"

He snags my hand and walks me toward a wall, out of the hustle of people and elves. "Everything is fine."

"No. No it's not because I know you. What is going on?"

"They let The Beast out."

"What?" My heart starts to race. "When?"

"Yesterday and it was kept under wraps, but the good news is that we have confirmation that he fled the country.

Even his attorney says that he's in Switzerland, where they're unlikely to extradite."

"I don't believe his attorney or anyone who works with him or for him. And you don't either, or you wouldn't have asked for back-up."

"He would be a fool to come after you, Sierra."

"Or arrogant enough to think he can get away with it. And he is *that* arrogant."

"Let me rephrase. If he's that stupid, he'll die. End of story. It's my end game for him anyway. I'm armed. You're armed. He will regret it. He will die."

"I'm armed." I pat the sparkly purse at my hip. "I chose it to fit my weapon."

"Good. And you know how to handle it now. Remember—"

"Shoot to kill."

"Asher!"

He grimaces. "That would be my father." He offers me his arm.

I inhale and accept it before forcing a smile. His father steps in front of us, and in a dark blue suit and his graying hair, he looks elegant and arrogant, much like The Beast. He proves the similarities by looking Asher up and down and saying, "If you'd cut that hair, you'd clean up nicely, despite those tattoos."

"Then someone might think I'm like you, Father. And I'm actually not the nice one. You don't realize that and I promise you, you hope you never do."

His father arches a brow. "Is that some sort of threat?"

"An observation," Asher says.

His father beats him up with a stare and then looks at me. "Twenty thousand in jewels," he says, looking at Asher.

"At least you know how to decorate. The ceremony is in an hour. Mingle until then."

He walks away.

"You know how to decorate?!" I whisper. "He is—"

"A prick," Asher says. "Now you see why I said I'd ruin him if I worked for him?"

"Yes. I do. Maybe we should leave?"

"Wounded Warriors, sweetheart. We're here for them. Let's go mingle and make some people feel the love."

He guides me into a giant room that is dimly lit and crowded. A stage sits at the opposite side of a dance floor, while soft music fills the air played by an orchestra in the right corner, and various food stands tempt visitors. A stage is at the very front and Asher is immediately cornered by a soldier in uniform with only one leg and he gives the man his full attention, as do I. There is another soldier without an arm that is next and I end up dancing with him, as Asher dances with a female veteran. We both become completely absorbed, and the respect they have for Asher as SEAL Team Six, is overwhelming.

"I should have invited Luke," Asher says, as we steal a spot on the dance floor. "He would have been honored to be here."

"So your father did a good thing?"

"For the wrong reasons, but yes. They charged for the event and wrote off the costs while asking for donations tonight. But don't let him fool you. He's—"

"A prick. I know."

"I will never take his money. You need to know that. He'll pull stunts like this tonight, but it will never change anything."

I touch his face. "I love this necklace and this dress, Asher, but I had money before you. I was miserable. I just want you."

There is an announcement and Asher is called to the stage. He leads me that direction and finds me a seat at a table close to the front. He then leans in and kisses me. "Don't go far."

"I'm watching you," I promise. "I'll be right here." He hesitates, like he doesn't want to leave me, and really, I don't want him to, but this is an important event. He turns away and heads up the nearby steps leading to the stage and I clap with the audience as his father announces him. There are wounded warriors across the stage and each tells a short story, all heart-touching, and a singer who performs a patriotic song, which really energizes the crowd. Soon people are on their feet, crowding the stage, and I do the same. Finally, Asher is called to speak and the warrior in him radiates from beneath that suit. It's in his eyes, his grace, his power.

He begins to speak when someone nudges me from behind and grabs my arm. I turn and my heart sinks. I know him. This middle-aged graying man is Ju-Ju's partner. He lifts his coat and shows me a gun. My heart races and I can barely breathe as he yanks me toward him, pressing his lips to my ear. "I will kill them all if you don't come with me."

And he will. He's that volatile. I ease through the crowd and start walking, and he is behind me, watching me, ready to shoot. The minute we clear the room, he directs me left and we start walking. Almost immediately we turn left again and there is a stairwell door. Part of me wants to bolt, but I know others could die. The other part knows entering that stairwell makes this me against him, and that means one dies, not two. He opens the door and my hand goes to my purse. I step through the doorway and I unzip my purse.

He's right behind me though, shoving me and I stumble forward. "Get up! Walk."

I do it, one reach from my gun, but he's behind me. If I move wrong, he could drop me before I can kill him. And so I charge up the stairs, but I try to keep him distracted. "It was never Ju-Ju, was it?"

"Of course not. He's a fool. A tool. My bitch slave. He really is. He protected me. He went to jail."

"How many have you killed?" I ask.

"Dozens. Ju-Ju, like his father, favored poison, so I humored him. Just like I humor all my seconds, but tonight it's my way. Tonight, you're my pick."

"You were sloppy," I dare, realization hitting me. "I saw you at the bank."

"I wanted you to see me," he says. "That's the fun. You see it coming, but you can't stop it."

"It?"

"Death."

We are now at the exit to the roof and I know that I have to act or I am dead. I push open the door and the minute I do, I pull my gun and turn, my finger on the trigger. He enters the rooftop and I shoot him in the chest. He falls to the ground and I lower my gun, just about to finally breathe. That's when Devin appears, and he too is holding a gun, but his is pointed at me, while that moment that I lowered mine could prove fatal. The door slams behind him and now we're alone, the lights dim, the sky dark.

"Good to see you, beautiful," he says, and he's actually come to kill me in an Armani suit.

"What happened to escaping to paradise?"

"Drop your gun or I will make sure you lose the hand holding it."

He will. I know he will, and I drop my weapon, praying that Asher finds me in time. Before it hits the ground, Devin is charging me and I am knocked to my back, the breath forced from my chest. He comes down on top of me. "Maybe I should fuck you one last time right here. Maybe. After you talk. Who did you share that file you gave my attorney with?"

"Just me. Just—"

He slaps my face and it hurts. God, it hurts. "Who?" he demands. "Next time it will be my fist."

"No one. I told no one."

He rears back to punch me and suddenly he is gone. I scramble to my knees to find Asher holding him, a gun pointed between his eyes. "Asher!"

"Yeah, sweetheart. Sorry about being a little late. But I'm here now."

"Remember me?" he asks Devin. "Remember my promise?"

"You're a SEAL. You couldn't kill me then and you won't now."

"Ex-SEAL. I got tired of saving lowlifes like you." Asher grabs his shirt and shoves him backward until he's by the ledge. "Get up on it."

"No."

Asher smashes him in the nose and he howls in pain while Asher sets him on the ledge. "Stand or die," he says before releasing him.

Devin wobbles but stands, and he's still holding his gun at his side. "Asher! He has a gun."

"Yes, he does," Asher says, lowering his. "Now we're even. Let's do it Old West style. Let's count down. One. Two. Three." Devin raises his gun and fires, but it's too late.

Asher's bullet is in his head and he stumbles, falling face first onto the pavement.

I scream and Asher is in front of me, pulling me to him, and I punch at his chest. "You asshole arrogant man with a hero complex. You dropped your weapon. You showboated."

"I made sure that it wasn't murder." He cups my face. "I made sure he can never hurt you again. I made sure your mine. Marry me."

"Are you serious? You're asking me now?"

"Yeah. Death and near death has a way of making you never want to lose another moment. Marry me."

"Yes. Yes, I will. When can we go home?"

"Not soon enough, but when we do it's over. It's really over. All of it. And then there is just you and me, sweetheart. Forever."

Epilogue

ASHER

Thanksgiving...

Since leaving the SEALs, Thanksgiving has been about food, football, and friends but this Thanksgiving is really about thanks, as it should be. Almost losing Sierra made me understand that. She's made me understand that. A week of her going through a million interviews and the emotional stress of killing someone made me understand that. All these things will take time to heal, but I want to heal her and what I can't heal, I want to mend and mend again, as many times as she needs me. And sometimes when she thinks she doesn't.

So, come this Thanksgiving morning, with Devin, Ju-Ju, and Miller behind us, I aim to make this day special. So we have our friends, football, and food, and watching Sierra joke and interact like family with everyone only makes it more clear to me how much she belongs here, and with me.

By early evening, she wants to pick out a tree and for the first time in my adult life, I find myself in my living room, willingly putting up a tree, while she fawns over ornaments we've picked, and smiles. I love her smile. How the hell did I live without that smile?

Apparently, I need roasted chestnuts too, because her mother said so, and now she says so, and while she fires up the oven and puts them in to cook, I set the blue box I bought when I bought her necklace under the tree. She returns and points at her turkey shirt. "Can you believe I have a turkey on my shirt?"

"No. I cannot."

"Never make a bet with Savage over cookie baking. Lesson learned." She joins me by the tree. "He can really bake."

"His cookies were good but—"

"He's an asshole," she finishes for me. "I know."

I lean in and kiss her. "There's a present under the tree."

"Already?"

"I want you to open it now, Sierra."

"Oh no. We have to wait. That's the fun of it. You'll see."

I go down on one knee and grab the box. She sucks in air. "I'm going to do this right this time. Sierra. I cannot think of a way I could live without you. Will you marry me?"

She starts crying. "I don't know why I'm crying. I just—I never thought I'd feel this happy and—"

"Say yes, sweetheart."

"I already said yes and yes. A million times yes."

I open the box and slide the heart-shaped platinum diamond ring on her finger. "Julie found your size for me." I kiss her hand. "Do you like it."

She holds it up between us. "How can I not love this ring? It's stunning and perfect."

"I have one more gift."

"That gift has to wait until Christmas."

"Actually, it does," I say. "I found your mother. She's engaged. She wants to know if we want to have a double wedding on Christmas Day here in New York City."

She wraps her arms around me and hugs me until I can't breathe and yet that hug and this woman is the only reason I can breathe.

Sierra

Christmas...

I stand in front of a Christmas tree in Rockefeller Center in a pink silk dress while my soon-to-be husband is in a tuxedo, his tattoos peeking from his sleeve, the perfect touch. My mother, on the other hand, wears red, because her new man has made her daring and happy. Her soon-to-be husband who is twenty years younger than her, wears a tropical shirt. A preacher takes us through our vows, while our friends who are now family to me, watch. I think of the money I may inherit, and it means nothing. I've seen how it corrupts and hurts people. I want to donate it. I want to help those in need. This, Asher, is what happy is. I have never been so happy in my life.

When it's done and Asher kisses me, it's like coming home. He is home and when we dance, the past fades away and there is only this. Him. Us. And when he leans in and starts singing to me, I think I fall in love all over again. But then, I'm pretty sure that's what happens when you marry an arrogant asshole who doesn't just think he's a hero. He is a hero. My hero.

THE END

FALLING UNDER—JACOB'S BOOK, COMING JANUARY 23, 2018—AVAILABLE FOR PRE-ORDER EVERYWHERE!

LISA RENEE JONES

Want more Walker Brothers? Turn the page for an excerpt for DIRTY RICH ONE NIGHT STAND, a sexy standalone featuring fun cameos from the alpha men of WALKER SECURITY!

Hi readers!

Thank you so much for picking up PULLED UNDER, Walker Security book two! Have you read Kyle and Myla's story yet—it's available now! And are you excited for Jacob's story—it's available for pre-order and coming January 23, 2018!

Check them both out here:
http://lisareneejones.com/walker

And don't forget to check out the original series: Tall, Dark and Deadly (all standalones and available now):
- Hot Secrets (Royce's Story)
- Dangerous Secrets (Luke's Story)
- Beneath the Secrets (Blake's Story)

For more information on the available titles visit here:
http://lisareneejones.com/TDD

If you're looking for more WALKER BROTHERS check out the following excerpt which is chapter one of my standalone title, DIRTY RICH ONE NIGHT STAND! It's available now, and has a lot of fun Walker Brother moments in it!

xoxo,
Lisa Renee Jones

LISA RENEE JONES

Chapter One

Cat

Day 1: The Trial of the Century

Coffee is life, love, and happiness. Actually, it's just alertness, and on a day that I'll be covering the trial of the century along with a horde of additional reporters, I need to be sharp. That need is exactly why I've dressed in my sharpest navy-blue suit dress and paired it with knee-high boots before enjoying a fall walk to the coffee shop three blocks from my New York City loft. Only two blocks from the courthouse, it's bustling with people, but the white mocha is so worth the line, and I've allowed myself ample time to caffeinate. In fact, I have a full two hours before I have to be inside the courtroom, and I plan to sit at a corner table and draft the beginning of my daily segment *Cat Does Crime* before heading to the courthouse.

I step into a line ten deep that slowly moves, and google the name of the defendant, looking for any hot new tidbit that might not have been live before bed last night. I tab through several articles, and I've made it to a spot near the front of the line when some odd blog linked to the defendant's name called "Mr. Hotness Gets Illegally Hot" pops up in my search. Considering the defendant is a good-looking billionaire accused of killing his pregnant mistress,

I buy into the headline and click. The line moves up one spot, and I move with it and then start reading:

I need help. I've done something bad. So very bad. I was told he would take care of me. Protect me. That was three months ago. I remember that day like it was yesterday. But now, it's today, a world behind me and in front of us. I enter his office and shut the door. We stare at each other, the air thickening, crackling. And then it happens. That thing that always happens between us. One minute I'm across the room, and the next I'm sitting in his chair, behind his desk, with him on his knees in front of me. Those blue eyes of his are smoldering hot. His hands settle on my legs just under my skirt, and I want to run my hands through his thick, dark hair, but I know better. I don't touch him until he tells me I can touch him.

I grip the arms of the chair, and his hands start a slow slide upward...

"Next!"

I blink out of that hot little number of a read and pant out a breath, feeling really dirty and gross, and with good reason. I'm hot and bothered over what I think is a fantasy piece about a man who is accused of pushing his pregnant girlfriend down the stairs and killing her. Correction, his pregnant mistress. Only the baby wasn't really his, and he says he wasn't her lover, and he was stilled charged over fingerprints on a doorknob.

"Cat!"

I jolt at my name as Jeffrey, who works the register as regularly as I visit, shouts at me from behind the counter. I take a step forward, only to have a man in a dark gray suit step in front of me. Frowning, I instinctively move forward and touch his arm. "Excuse me." He doesn't respond, and I am certain he's aware I'm now standing right next to him. "*Excuse me*," I repeat.

He doesn't turn around, and now I'm irritated. I tug on the sleeve of what I am certain is his ridiculously expensive jacket and achieve my intended goal: He rotates to look at me, the look of controlled irritation etched in his ridiculously handsome face telling me I've achieved my goal. He now feels what I feel, and as a bonus: He now knows that despite my being barely five foot two, blonde, and female, I will not be ignored. "I was next," I say.

"I'm in too much of a rush to wait for you to finish playing games on your phone."

"Games? Are you serious?" I open my mouth to say more and snap it shut, holding up a hand to stop him from doing or saying something that might land me in a courtroom today for the wrong reason. "Wait your turn, like the gentleman you should be."

His eyes, which I now know to be a wicked crystal blue, narrow ever so slightly before he turns to the counter. "A venti double espresso and whatever she's having." Mr. Arrogant Asshole looks at me. "What do you want? I'll buy your drink."

"Is that an apology?"

"It's a concession made in the interest of time. Not an apology. You were the one on your phone playing—"

"I was not playing games. I was working, while you were plotting the best way to push around the woman who was ahead of you."

"That's the best you've got? I'm pushing around women?"

"No, you're not pushing around women today," I say. "You tried and failed. I can buy my own coffee." I face the counter. "My usual."

"Already wrote up your cup," Jeffrey says. "It should be ready any minute."

"Thank you," I say, and while I should just move along, I find myself turning to Mr. Arrogant Asshole because apparently, I can't help myself. "I'll leave you with a helpful tip," I say, "since you've been so exceedingly helpful to me today. The phrases 'thank you' and 'I'm sorry' are not only Manners 101, but failure to use them will either keep a man single, or make a man single." And on that note, I move on down the bar, which has a cluster of people waiting on drinks, but thankfully, I spot the corner table I favor opening up. Hurrying that way, I wait for the woman who is leaving to clear her space, and then murmur the "thank you" that Mr. Arrogant Asshole back at the counter doesn't understand before claiming her seat and placing my bag on the table. Settling into my seat, I have no idea why, but my gaze lifts and seeks out Mr. Arrogant Asshole, who now stands at the counter, talking on his cell phone and oozing that kind of rich, powerful presence that sucks up all the air in the room and makes every woman around look at him. Me included, apparently, which irritates me. *He* irritates me, and the only way you deal with a man like him is naked for one night, which you end with a pretty little orgasmic goodbye, and that *is all*. Anything else is a mistake, which I know because I've been there, done that.

Once.

Never again.

It's in that moment, with that thought, that Mr. Arrogant Asshole decides to turn around and somehow find the exact spot where I'm sitting, those piercing blue eyes locked on me. And now he's watching me watching him, which means I'm busted and probably appear more interested in him than I want to appear. I cut my stare and pull out my MacBook, keying it to life, and just when it's connected, I hear, "Order for Cat!"

At the sound of my name, I eye one of the regulars, a twenty-something encroaching on thirty, who got fired from his job and started some consulting business. "Kevin," I say, and when he doesn't look up, I raise my voice. "Kevin!"

His head jerks up. "Cat," he says, blinking me into view.

I point to my table and the coffee bar. He nods. I push to my feet and, not about to cower over Mr. Arrogant Asshole, who is now standing at the bar with his back to me, I charge forward. I'm just about to step to his side and grab my drink when he faces me, holding two drinks, one of which he offers to me. "Your drink," he says.

I purse my lips, refusing to be charmed. "Thank you." I pause for effect and add, "But you're still an asshole."

His lips, which I notice when I shouldn't, because *he really is an arrogant asshole*, curve. "You have such good manners," he comments.

"My mother taught me right. Manners and honesty."

"I won't argue the accuracy of your statement, considering the fact that I *was* an asshole."

"Well, good," I say, curious about this turn of events. "We agree on something."

His eyes light with amusement. "I'd apologize, but then this would be over."

I frown. "What does that mean?"

"Meet me here in the morning and we'll negotiate the terms of my apology." He steps around me, and I whirl around to face his back.

"You're an attorney, aren't you?" I say, because I know the lingo, the style, everything about this man. And I am, in fact, a Harvard gradate attorney myself, as are two of my

345

three brothers and my father. Them by choice, me by pressure that I stopped caving into two years ago next week.

He stops walking and rotates to face me now. "Yes, Cat. I am. Which means that you can handle Manners 101 and I'll handle Negotiation 101." He smiles—and it's one hell of a smile—before he turns and walks away.

I watch him disappear in the crowd, knowing I have two options: Forget him or show back up. This is crazy. Men like that one are trouble, and I don't like trouble, so why the heck am I staring after Mr. Arrogant Asshole? I'm not meeting him. End of story.

Shaking off any other thought, I walk back to my table and glance at the computer screen, where I've typed "Mr. Hotness," and decide that hot little blog post is half the reason that Mr. Arrogant Asshole was able to get to me. I'm not meeting him. Of course, if I did, I'd do so with the understanding that trouble can be managed, and in this case, in his case, that would be with a *dirty, rich one night stand.*

Or by simply not meeting him again, but this is my coffee shop and I won't be run out of it.

An hour later, I've written my intro for today's courtroom activity, detailing what I know of the crime in question and the accused killer himself, before heading to the courthouse. I arrive forty-five minutes before the start of the trial, and it's a good thing I do. The outside of the courthouse is crowed with picketers and press. Inside the courtroom, cameras and people have hoarded ninety-nine percent of the space. I squeeze into the back row and remove my brand-new leather-bound notebook, open to the first page, where I write: *Murder: Guilty or Innocent?* I follow with random questions I hope to answer today and during the trial, as I did in the prior two major trials I sat in witness to prior to this one.

I've just finished my list when the courtroom activity begins. The jury enters. The defendant and his counsel enter, but the stupid cameras block my view. The judge enters next, and we all stand, which means I have an even worse view. Finally, we all take our seats and the lead counsels for both sides approach the bench. They are only there for a minute at most before they turn back to the courtroom. It's then, as Reese Summer, lead counsel for the defense, takes center stage for opening statements, that my lips part in shock, and with good reason. Reese Summer is Mr. Arrogant Asshole. I sit there, staring at him, dumbfounded for the first five minutes of his opening before I even remember that I need to take notes. I start writing, studying him as he walks, talks, and presents not just his case, but himself, to the jury, audience, and cameras.

"Nelson Ward met Jennifer Wright when she was scared of her boyfriend and he didn't look away like most people would. He looked at her. He saw her instead of seeing through her or past her. He told his wife about her. And together he and his wife, helped her seek shelter and a job. Nelson did not have an affair with Jennifer Wright. The DNA has proven that the child Jennifer Wright was carrying was not his, but rather her boyfriend's, who was abusing her. The prosecution wanted to make the public happy and they needed a victim to convict. And that's what my client is: A victim. The prosecution will present fingerprints on the doorknob of Ms. Wright's house as evidence. That was the bombshell that landed Nelson Ward in this courtroom. My fingerprints are all over this courtroom. Did I commit a crime here? No. I did not. Has a crime been committed here? Yes. In fact, there have been three murders on this very property. According to the prosecution's handling of this case, you all must now need lawyers. Why? Because that is the only evidence they have against my client, fingerprints on a door. I don't know about you, folks, but I'm terrified at the idea that we can be convicted of a crime off nothing but our fingerprints on a door. Not on a weapon. On a doorknob used over and over by many people.

He continues, and there are quips, and murmured laughter, and intense scowls. He takes everyone on an emotional journey. When he's done, I sit back to assess his skill, and I judge him as a man that can seduce a courtroom as easily as he seduced me.

He's trouble.

Big trouble.

And it's now my job to make him my obsession for the remainder of this trial. Which means a dirty, rich (naked) one night stand can't happen until there can be that pretty little orgasmic goodbye. Anything else would be a mistake I've already made. Once. Never again.

DIRTY RICH ONE NIGHT STAND IS AVAILABLE NOW!

Also by Lisa Renee Jones

THE INSIDE OUT SERIES
If I Were You
Being Me
Revealing Us
His Secrets*
Rebecca's Lost Journals
The Master Undone*
My Hunger*
No In Between
My Control*
I Belong to You
All of Me*

THE SECRET LIFE OF AMY BENSEN
Escaping Reality
Infinite Possibilities
Forsaken
Unbroken*

CARELESS WHISPERS
Denial
Demand
Surrender

DIRTY MONEY

Hard Rules
Damage Control
Bad Deeds
End Game (January 2018)

WHITE LIES

Provocative
Shameless

TALL, DARK & DEADLY

Hot Secrets
Dangerous Secrets
One Dangerous Night
Beneath the Secrets

WALKER SECURITY

Deep Under
Pulled Under
Falling Under (January 2018)

ebook only

About the Author

New York Times and USA Today bestselling author Lisa Renee Jones is the author of the highly acclaimed INSIDE OUT series.

In addition to the success of Lisa's INSIDE OUT series, she has published many successful titles. The TALL, DARK AND DEADLY series and THE SECRET LIFE OF AMY BENSEN series, both spent several months on a combination of the New York Times and USA Today bestselling lists. Lisa is also the author of the bestselling the bestselling DIRTY MONEY and WHITE LIES series. And will be publishing the first book in her Lilah Love suspense series with Amazon Publishing in March 2018.

Prior to publishing Lisa owned multi-state staffing agency that was recognized many times by The Austin Business Journal and also praised by the Dallas Women's Magazine. In 1998 Lisa was listed as the #7 growing women owned business in Entrepreneur Magazine.

Lisa loves to hear from her readers. You can reach her at www.lisareneejones.com and she is active on Twitter and Facebook daily.

CPSIA information can be obtained
at www.ICGtesting.com
Printed in the USA
BVOW08s1508090118
504835BV00001BA/1/P